ROARING RIVER RANGE

ROARING RIVER RANGE

Arthur Henry Gooden

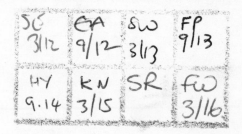

GUNSMOKE

First published 1946 in the UK by Harrap

This hardback edition 2012
by AudioGO Ltd
by arrangement with
Golden West Literary Agency

ISBN 978 1 445 88150 8

British Library Cataloguing in Publication Data available.

Printed and bound in Great Britain by
MPG Books Group Limited

1

THERE was good reason for Poco Gato's happy mood as his roan horse jogged him along through the shimmering midday heat towards the town of Roaring River. The pleasant jingle of numerous gold pieces in his pockets gave him a comfortable feeling of virtue. He had not always earned good money so honestly. Conchita Mendota would have a warm smile for him and many words of commendation for his upright conduct.

Poco winced as he thought of those months of honest toil. Not for many times the gold that made such merry music would he have his friends know the source of his wealth. He would be jeered at for one whose wits had approached the state of a very ancient egg. No longer would he wear the amusing sobriquet given him because of his huge stature and girth by those droll *Americanos*. He would become Pedro Loco—the very mad one.

Poco Gato shrugged away the brief misgivings. Truly he was astride the world, the future large and rosy before him; and always there was the delectable Conchita so gloriously in the background of his ambitions. She had given him the sting of her tongue the last time he had ridden into Roaring River, called him a good-for-nothing.

The big Mexican laughed loudly as he complacently envisaged his next meeting with the fair Conchita. No bite to that tongue of hers this time, but honey-sweet words from her rosy lips, and a vast admiration in her languishing doe eyes as she listened to the tale he had for her pretty ears. Those gold pieces he would pour into her lap made only a small part of the beginning. Soon he would be the owner of many thousands of sheep that would graze over countless leagues of range. Men would no longer lightly speak of him as Poco Gato. He would be El Señor Pedro Gato, the rich one. Even those ribald *Americanos* would lift their hats when he passed.

A harsh voice broke rudely into Poco Gato's happy musings. He jerked the roan horse to a standstill and gazed with shocked eyes at the riders grouped in the bend of the trail.

"Our slippery little friend himself," grinned one of the men. His eyes were cold, unsmiling.

"El Gatito!" rasped another voice. "Our little pet kitten, all fat an' slick as can be."

Despite their pretended amusement, Poco Gato could read hostile intentions in the faces of these half-score horsemen. There were reasons why he feared the worst.

"*Buenas dias*, señores." The Mexican spoke huskily. "You wan' somet'ing?"

"You bet we want somethin', Poco." The first speaker, a lanky, droopy-moustached man, climbed from his saddle and slouched closer, hand on holstered gun. "We always want a low-down cow-thief like you."

Poco recognized him now for the foreman of the Double Star ranch. His fears grew apace.

"Señor—I hones' man——" The huge Mexican's voice quavered. "I no steal the cows——"

"Climb down from your saddle," was the foreman's curt rejoinder. "Choctaw—you take his gun."

Poco obeyed in silence, stood on legs that felt as if the massive bone in them had turned to rubber. Seen thus, he towered inches above the tall foreman of the Double Star. His vast bulk seemed to amuse one of the riders.

"Won't no single rope dangle a feller big as him, Luce," he commented, with a thin laugh.

"We can use a *couple* o' ropes if one won't hold him," Luce Henders said curtly.

"Take *some* tree to swing him," chortled another rider. "A bullet would do the work, Luce—an' save plenty time."

"We *hang* cow-thieves, Selmo," reproved the Double Star foreman.

Choctaw removed the gun from Poco's belt, and in a few moments the Mexican's hands were tightly lashed behind his back. The other men were down from their horses now and staring at him with callous curiosity. There was no pity in their hard eyes, no hint of mercy.

Poco Gato came out of his temporary paralysis. His time was growing very short, he realized. Soon, too dreadfully soon, he would be speechless indeed.

"Señores——" His words came in broken, painful gasps. "I no steal the cows. . . . I hones' . . . work hard . . . make my *dinero* hones'——"

"No use talkin', Poco," Luce Henders said in his uncompromising voice. "You've been ridin' with Rengo's gang, Poco. You can't have rode with Rengo an' not be a rustler. We got to swing you, Poco."

Poco Gato clung despairingly to his lie. He swore he was no friend of the notorious Rengo, and that if he had been seen in the rustler's company it was because of some foul mischance wrought on him by the devil. Poco also, in sheer desperation, resorted to the truth, gasped out the shameful secret he would have kept locked away in his bosom.

"Herdin' sheep, you say!" exclaimed the Double Star foreman sceptically. "Fellers, our little kitten claims to be a sheep-herder!" He gave his companions a look of mock horror.

"All the more reason we should hang him," waggishly observed one of the cowboys.

"Get your rope on him, Choctaw," curtly ordered Luce Henders. "No sense foolin' with him."

The dark-browed Choctaw stepped up and dropped the noose of his rawhide rope over the shocked Poco's head.

"Señores," implored the luckless Mexican, his voice lifting to a scream, "eet ees true w'at I say. I have mooch gold I make for 'erd the sheep. Forty dollar a month I get from Señor Moore for 'erd hees sheep in Loma Paloma. You take eet . . . you no 'ang me."

"We're not thieves, Poco," virtuously reproved the Double Star foreman. He hesitated. "Search him, Selmo," he added.

Selmo's search produced the gold pieces that had jingled so pleasantly while Poco Gato rode and dreamed his dreams.

The cowboy muttered a startled oath. "More'n a hunderd dollars," he exclaimed. "Wonder how many cows he stole for Rengo to git so much?"

"I make heem *dinero* hones'!" babbled poor Poco. "I make heem for 'erd the sheep!"

The Double Star men regarded him in grim silence, an ominous silence that Poco understood. He ceased his frantic protestations, stood there, gazing at them with pleading, terrified eyes.

"We ain't low-down thieves, Poco," finally repeated Luce Henders. "We've got no use for this money of yours, honest-earned or not. Who do you want to have it, Poco?" The cowman's tone sharpened. "Make up your mind quick. Ain't wastin' no more time on you."

Confronted now by the doom he knew he was powerless to avert, the giant Mexican suddenly took on a calm dignity that obviously amazed his callous, self-imposed executioners. They gazed at him wonderingly, something like grudging admiration in their looks, a hint of shame for what they were about to do.

"Señores——" Poco's great frame straightened to its full height. "I am a man . . . I can die like a man. You say you 'ang me . . . eet ees murder. . . ."

"The money," interrupted Henders harshly. "Who do you want to have your money?"

"You please to geeve the *dinero* to the Señora Conchita Mendota," directed Poco in his newfound calm voice. "Tell her eet from Pedro Gato and ees hones' *dinero*."

Luce Henders nodded. He knew Conchita Mendota, owner of the *cantina* in Roaring River's Mexican quarter.

"I'll see that she gets it," he promised. His voice hardened. "All right, boys."

A tree was speedily selected, a scraggly limbed oak on the slope below the trail. Poco was roughly helped back to his saddle and the roan horse brought to a halt under the gallows-tree. Choctaw made the rope fast to the limb and drew it tight. Beads of sweat broke out on the Mexican's broad-featured face as he felt the hard clutch of the rawhide noose. Luce Henders lifted his quirt.

"I wouldn't do that," drawled a voice, a quiet voice, chill as cold steel. "You'll die faster than he will if you jump that horse from under him."

Henders seemed turned to stone for a brief moment, the hand holding the quirt tensely rigid. Slowly he twisted his head to look at the speaker. The faces of his companions swung round in the same stunned, slow motion, like the faces of puppets pulled on the same string.

The young man on the rangy buckskin horse stared back at them from the trail some twenty feet above. There was rage in his eyes, a furious anger that reached out like forks of lightning to the cow-boys clustered near the man they planned to hang.

"Cut that rope." The gun in his hand menaced them. "Cut that rope," he repeated. "I'll start shooting if you don't cut that rope *now*."

Luce Henders and his hard-bitten riders made no attempt to argue at that moment. There was the rising menace of instant death in the stranger's quiet voice, the gun so steady in his hand.

The Double Star foreman spoke hoarsely. "Cut him loose, Selmo," he said. His gaze swept across the faces of the other men in a sly, meaning look. They gave him back equally sly, scarcely perceptible nods.

Selmo slashed the rawhide rope, and, obeying the young stranger's further command, he cut the thongs that bound Poco's wrists. The Mexican came down clumsily from the saddle, stood there, a support-ing hand clutching the pommel, a vast wonder in his eyes, and some-thing like mingled awe and reverence, as he gazed up at the tall shape of his unknown deliverer silhouetted against the rugged slope that lifted steeply above the trail. It was plain that Poco regarded the affair as the miraculous intervention of his patron saint. He crossed himself, muttered pious words in his native tongue.

Luce Henders lowered his quirt and spoke in a complaining voice. "You're actin' some hasty, feller. This here Mex is a cow-thief. Reckon I don't need to say more. You have the looks of a cowman. You got no more use for a cow-thief than we have."

"I'm a cowman," acknowledged the stranger. "I don't like cow-thieves, but there's a law that takes care of such things, and "—his voice hardened—"there's a law against murder."

"Swingin' a rustler ain't murder," demurred the Double Star fore-man peevishly. "Your talk don't make good sense." His glance again covered the intent faces of his men. "You're knowin' this Mex feller, I take it," he went on; "you're knowin' Poco Gato."

"Never saw him before," replied the man. His eyes roved alertly down at the upturned faces, then flashed a look at Poco. Despite his coolness, the Double Star foreman sensed a certain perturbation. The stranger was one against ten armed and experienced riders of the range. Luce's moustache twitched. The hand was not played out yet. Again his covert look flashed slyly at his men, read in their tense faces a fierce readiness for the chance to explode into action.

Poco's deliverer broke the brief, pregnant silence.

"Come on up, Poco," he directed, "bring your horse." His gun continued to menace the Double Star men. "I'm giving you a chance to hit the trail away from here."

Poco's hand went to bridle rein, he started cautiously past his late captors. Luce Henders spoke softly, a friendly, resigned note in his voice.

"You'll be wantin' your gun, Poco. Reckon you might as well have your gun back."

Too late to heed the sharp cry of warning from the man on the trail, the unsuspecting Mexican paused to reach for the proffered weapon. In the same fleeting instant the dark-browed Choctaw was crouching behind the Mexican's broad back, the gun Poco had reached for belching bullets up at his would-be rescuer. The latter dropped behind a jagged slab of rock, a shot exploding from his own gun as he sought cover.

Choctaw spun round, Poco's gun flying from his hand. The half-breed swore as he stared at his bloody fingers. His companions gave him no heed. Each man of them was prone behind a boulder, guns spurting flame and lead up at the big slab of rock that covered the man who had dared so rashly to intervene for the life of a worthless Mexican cow-thief.

"We're holdin' the aces, feller," triumphantly yelled Luce Henders. "Don't keep on playin' the dumb fool."

There was a long silence. The trapped man was obviously considering the matter. The lanky Double Star foreman exchanged grins with his men.

"We can get up on the slope back of you," he pointed out. "Better act sensible."

Apparently the young man realized the hopelessness of his predicament and was disposed to parley.

"How about Poco? You'll turn him loose?"

"He's a rustler," reminded Henders curtly.

"Well—why not turn him over to your sheriff?"

"Listen, mister—you ain't in no shape to tell us nothin'. I'm givin' you ten seconds to come out from that boulder."

Another tense silence, and then he was suddenly standing in the trail, hands up in token of surrender.

"Come on down here," ordered Luce Henders brusquely. His eyes signalled Selmo, who promptly loosed the dangling rope from the tree.

The stranger came scrambling down the slope.

"Tie 'em up," ordered Henders. The look he bent on the tall, would-be Good Samaritan was ominous.

Selmo cut the rawhide rope into the needed lengths and bound the two prisoners' wrists.

"Stranger in these parts, ain't you?" Luce Henders stared curiously at the newest captive.

"What's it matter?" The young man's cool gaze swept the circle of hard, intent faces. "Nice, friendly country you've got here."

"Your talk sounds like Texas," guessed the Double Star foreman.

"Suit yourself," responded the prisoner, with a careless shrug of powerful shoulders.

"Was hearin' talk the Pecos Kid was down this way," Henders said slowly. "Reckon you've heard of the Pecos Kid."

"I've heard of him," admitted the young man.

"Mebbe you've heard of a rustler name of Rengo," Henders went on. "Rengo's kind of well known down this way."

"I've heard of him too," again admitted the prisoner. "I told you I was a cowman," he added. "Most of us have heard of Rengo and the Pecos Kid."

Henders exchanged significant looks with his deeply interested riders.

"I ain't talkin' just to air my voice," he said grimly. "I've been hearin' things—I've been hearin' the Pecos Kid is down from Texas to join up with the Rengo gang."

"It's possible," agreed the young man, with a thin smile. "The Pecos got too hot for the Kid."

"I'm thinkin' you're the Pecos Kid," Henders said harshly. "Why else would you come bustin' into our necktie party on account of Poco Gato? He's one of the Rengo gang."

"You're crazy," declared Poco's would-be rescuer. His tone was amused. "If I'm the Pecos Kid you're Rengo."

"The Kid is a big, tall young feller like you," observed the Double

Star foreman. "He's got dark reddish hair like you wear, and the same blue-grey eyes, and from the talk I've heard he's as cool as ice —don't scare easy—same as you."

"Thanks for the compliment," grinned the prisoner. "Just the same, you're crazy as a loon."

The lanky Double Star foreman stared round at his men. "What you think, boys? Ain't I right, claimin' he's the Pecos Kid?"

There was a moment's silence, then an oath from Choctaw, who had been binding his bullet-torn fingers with a bandage improvised from a gaudy bandana. Choctaw was in an ugly, vengeful mood.

"I'm for swingin' him here an' now," he announced. "Ain't carin' who he is, the Pecos Kid or just plain dumb fool. I vote we dangle him an' the Mex on the same limb." He spat a vicious oath at the tall Texan.

"I'm votin' with Choctaw," put in the bow-legged Selmo. His thin, beak-nosed face creased in a mirthless grin. "Even if he ain't the Kid, we had ought to swing him. Serve him right for hornin' in like he done."

There was an assenting rumble from Selmo's fellow-riders. Luce Henders turned a wicked smile on the young man.

"Seems like the boys has called the play," he commented heavily. "Might as well tell us straight, young feller. Are you the Kid?"

"You're not fooling me," retorted the prisoner contemptuously. "You know I'm not the Pecos Kid. . . . I savvy what's in your head —an excuse to put me out of the way, so I won't talk. You daren't turn me loose."

"Mebbe you're not so wrong at that," remarked the Double Star man dryly. A startled oath drew his attention to Selmo. The cowboy was staring up at the trail.

"Cole Bannock an' his Triple R bunch," Selmo muttered.

Luce Henders swore softly as his gaze raked up at the approaching horsemen. "Sheriff Harker along with 'em," he said disgustedly. "Take things slow, boys. No sense startin' a ruckus."

The riders drew rein, stared silently down at the group under the gallows tree. A big, grey-bearded man on a powerful bay gelding spoke brusquely.

"What's goin' on here, Henders?" There was a note of displeasure in his bull's voice, an angry gleam in the deep-set eyes under their heavy thatch of frosted black brows.

"Reckon it ain't hard for you to guess." The Double Star man's tone was surly. "You was never slow in givin' a rustler his due, Bannock."

"Just when did I ask you Double Star fellers to come huntin' rustlers over on my range?" asked Cole Bannock icily. "Turn those men loose, Henders. You're not pulling off any lynch law on Roaring River Ranch."

The sheriff broke into the argument. He was a small, wiry, greyish man, with an enormous grizzled walrus moustache and shrewd, sun-wrinkled eyes.

"If you think there's no law in this county, Luce Henders, you're kind of guessin' wrong," he observed tartly. "So long as I'm sheriff, even a rustler's got his day in court." One closely observing the sheriff might have noticed an odd momentary gleam in his keen eyes as he flicked a glance at the tall young Texan. "Cut 'em loose, like Cole said," he added. "I'm takin' 'em off your hands, Henders."

"Turn the coyotes loose, Selmo," grunted the Double Star man. He flung Sheriff Harker an infuriated look. "If we was across the line over in *my* county, your word wouldn't make any hay with me, Ed Harker. They'd swing spite of your say-so."

"I ain't caring a hoot what you do over in your own bailiwick, Luce," rumbled big Cole Bannock. "All I'm asking is for you and your Double Star outfit not to think you can run things over in the Roaring River country. The Triple R don't need your help."

Henders gave him a surly look for answer and turned to his horse.

"Never did like that long-jawed galoot," grumbled the bearded owner of Roaring River Ranch. "I'll sure be lockin' horns with him some day if he don't watch his step."

Cole Bannock's bold, domineering gaze went to the man whose gallant attempt to save Poco Gato from a miserable fate had come so close to failure. "Henders claims you're a rustler," he said. "You don't look it."

"Your guess is good," smiled the young Texan. "Mr Henders had different ideas—in fact, insisted I was the Pecos Kid."

There was an amused chuckle from the wiry little sheriff. "I could have told Henders he was barkin' up the wrong tree," he said. "The Kid is safe in gaol, where I put him my own self."

"You should be more careful of your company," reproved Cole Bannock. "Can hardly blame Henders for getting wrong notions when he finds you with Poco Gato." The big cowman bent a grim look on the Mexican. "There's talk that Poco is too friendly with the Rengo gang."

"Señor"—Poco spoke vehemently—"he no ride weet me. I no see the brave *caballero* until he come and stop them from 'ang me. He pull hees gun, tell them not to 'ang me."

Bannock and Harker looked curiously at the stranger, and the former said slowly, admiringly, "Held 'em up single-handed, huh? You've got nerve, young man." He wagged his head. "That Double Star bunch is plenty hard. I'd say the Mex wasn't worth the risk you took."

"I don't like murder," the young man told him simply. "Lynching is murder."

"Stealing cows is bad business," declared the owner of the Triple R. "There's time when honest cowmen get awful provoked."

"I no steal the cow," protested Poco. "I hones'——"

"Since when?" scoffed Bannock. He gave the sheriff a look. "Best throw him in your gaol, Ed . . . if you've got a cell big enough to hold him." He chuckled.

Sheriff Harker shook his head. "I don't want him," he said tersely. "I happen to know Poco's telling the truth. You're not interested in cows now, are you, Poco?" There was dry humour in the smile he gave the giant Mexican. The latter's answering look was grateful, mixed with embarrassment.

"*Si*, Señor Harker," he muttered humbly, "eet ees the truth, w'at you speak."

"Well——" Cole Bannock shrugged wide shoulders. "Don't care a hoot what you do, Ed. Suit yourself. Poco ain't ever stole from my range that I know of." He stared with speculative eyes at Poco's unknown saviour as the latter went to his buckskin horse. "I kind of like your nerve, young man," he went on. "I can use your sort on the ranch. I'm Cole Bannock," he added, "and this gent with the bar-handle moustache is Sheriff Harker." He grinned at the law-officer.

The stranger settled himself easily in his saddle and produced cigarette-papers and tobacco. He was from parts a long way from Roaring River, he affably informed them, but he had heard of Cole Bannock and he'd heard of Sheriff Ed Harker, of Roaring River County. He was down from the Pecos country and not on the dodge from the law, and was using his own name, which was Allan Rand.

"I like your style of talk," declared Bannock heartily. "You don't waste your breath nor a man's time with words. I'm sayin' again, there's a job for you on my ranch."

"I'll think it over," young Rand said, looking at the sheriff. The latter's face was expressionless. "I'd like to have a look at your town, size up the country. Not sure but what I'll push on up north after a few days." His friendly smile softened the half-refusal.

Cole Bannock waved a hand. "No rush," he said, "take your time, Rand. Come on out to the ranch any time you feel like going on the Triple R pay-roll." With a parting gesture he started his big bay gelding up the trail. The sheriff lingered, ostensibly to borrow a light from the Texan.

"Any notion where you'll be stayin' in town?" he queried in a low voice as he cupped match to cigarette.

"Some hotel if there is one," answered Rand.

"Only one hotel—the Cattleman's," Ed Harker said. He hesitated, threw a cautious glance at Poco Gato. The Mexican was absorbedly counting his gold pieces. "Got some business out at Bannock's place," the sheriff went on in the same low, hurried voice. "I figure to be back in town about sundown."

"I'll be at the Cattleman's Hotel," Rand said.

The sheriff nodded. "We'll run into each other kind of accidental, maybe in the bar," he arranged, "long about eight or nine in the evenin'."

"I'll be round," agreed Rand briefly.

The sheriff swung his bald-faced horse, keen eyes wrinkling in an amused look at Poco Gato.

"Good money in the sheep business—huh, Poco?" His tone was kindly, a bit sympathetic.

"You know, señor?" The Mexican grinned. "You know I 'erd the sheep?"

"Sure I know," chuckled Harker, "I asked Moore to hire you. Nothin' like a good job to keep a man out of mischief, Poco, and you was sure headin' for trouble, flirtin' with the Rengo gang like you was doin'."

"I was fool, beeg fool," acknowledged the Mexican contritely.

"Watch yourself close," warned the sheriff sternly. "I'm giving you a chance to make good, Poco. You've had a taste of the sort o' medicine a rustler gets sooner or later."

"*Si*, señor," murmured Poco Gato humbly. "I no forget——"

"And don't go gamblin' your gold away," advised the sheriff in a more kindly tone; "hand it over to Conchita. She'll take good care of it for you." He chuckled, spurred away to overtake Bannock a good hundred yards up the trail.

The Mexican climbed into his saddle. "I weel ride weet you, señor?" His tone was hesitant, almost pleading, as if asking too great a favour.

"Why not?" assented Allan Rand good-naturedly. "You can tell me things about Roaring River, Poco."

"Señor "—the big Mexican spoke earnestly—"you save my life . . . eet ees belong you." He touched his heart and added in quick Spanish, "On my heart, I swear to serve you always."

"*Gracias*," smiled Allan. "We will be good friends, Poco." He made the statement in fluent Spanish. Poco beamed, delighted that his new friend could speak his own native tongue.

"The good God sent you," he declared simply; "your coming was a miracle, señor."

Allan nodded soberly. He was thinking the same good God had sent Cole Bannock and the sheriff riding up the trail just when they did.

They swung their horses, pushed on down the hill towards the huddle of buildings that was the town of Roaring River. Allan Rand did not realize at that moment how much he was to owe to his newly won friendship with the simple-hearted Mexican who rode by his side

2

"THE mare's dropped a shoe," Agee Hand said; "was limpin' some as you drove up."

The girl gave him a rueful smile as she climbed out of the buckboard. "I noticed Bess was going lame, Agee. She must have lost it somewhere on the road."

"I'll have Diego take her over to the blacksmith's for you," promised the old livery man. "Won't take Pat Riley no time to fix her up."

"I'll be in town for an hour or two," Kay Bannock told him. "Lots of shopping to do, Agee." She shook out the wrinkles from her short linen skirt. "I'm making a new dress if I can find the material I want at Rankin's," she confided happily.

"If Jim Rankin ain't got what you want, he'll get it," chuckled Agee Hand. "Jim figgers to give his customers what they want, if it's a paper o' pins or a grand pianny."

Kay gave him a bright smile and, with a "Hello, Diego" to the elderly Mexican emerging from the shadowy depths of the stable, she went briskly up the board walk.

A lone horseman rode up the wide, dusty street and halted in front of the Cattleman's Hotel directly opposite Rankin's General Merchandise Store. A stranger, Kay Bannock's quick glance told her as she turned into the cool dimness of Rankin's. She was fleetingly conscious of his frank, sun-browned face turned her way as he swung from saddle.

Allan Rand leisurely made his buckskin horse fast to the gnawed hitch-rail and, after another interested glance across the street, he mounted wide, creaky steps to the hotel porch, where a long-framed man sprawled indolently in a big home-made rocking-chair. A wide-brimmed hat was tipped low over his eyes, and he had a sun-wrinkled, leathery face and a white moustache that drooped under a big, bony nose. He gave the newcomer a sleepy nod, ejected a stream of tobacco juice over the porch railing.

"That was Cole Bannock's girl," he said. "Seen you look at her."

He nodded, jaws moving meditatively over tobacco cud. "Worth
lookin' at, I don't need to tell you, and purty as a pitcher." The old
man sent another brown stream over the porch railing. "Plenty high
sperrited, too, Kay Bannock is," he added. "Smart as the crack of
a whip. Ain't no man can get fresh with *her*."

"Sounds like a warning," Allan said good-naturedly.

"You can take it any ways you care to." There was a probing
sharpness in the look the old man gave Allan that made the latter
suspect those apparently sleepy eyes were keener than they seemed.
"I've knowed Kay sence she was a toddler," he added. "Reckon
I'm her best friend. Kay always knows she can depend on Shawnee
Jones any time she's in a fix."

Allan was mildly amused, a bit puzzled. The old-timer was eccen-
tric, to say the least. It was obvious that he regarded himself as the
Bannock girl's self-appointed guardian.

"Well, glad to have met you, Mr Jones." Allan turned to the
hotel door. Shawnee's head lifted quickly in an inquiring look.

"You wantin' a room?"

"If I can get one," admitted Allan, hand on the latch of the screen-
door.

"Sure you can get a room." The old man came spryly to his feet.
"Dollar a day," he said, suddenly brisk, "two bits extry for usin' the
bath, an' you can eat where you please, in the dinin'-room or over to
Quong Lee's chop-house. The Chinaman sets you a real good meal
for two bits, but I got to charge thirty-five cents."

"Reasonable enough," observed young Rand solemnly.

"Conchita Mendota fixes up mighty good food over at her *cantina*
if you've got a taste for Mex cookin'," Shawnee added as he led the
way into the hotel lobby.

Allan said he was sure the food problem was going to be easy.
He liked a varied diet, and it was evident there was ample choice in
Roaring River and, anyway, he was not finicky about his food.

The old hotel man scrutinized the name that he had scrawled on the
register.

"Allan Rand, huh, an' hailin' from the Pecos country?"
Shawnee wagged his head. "Know the Pecos country like I
know the nose on my face. Boy, I can tell you tales 'bout them days
when the longhorns was rompin' up the cattle trails to Kansas."

Shawnee was suddenly silent, a far-away look on his rugged, weathered old face. Allan guessed that memories were boiling within him, memories of the stirring, history-building days of a lusty youth; memories of turbulent frontier towns, Dodge, Abilene, Tascosa—memories of old friends long since gone. Allan had heard the epic from his father, the epic of countless herds on the march from Texas to distant northern markets—the Red River, the Canadian, the Cimarron; treacherous quicksands, Indians—the dread stampede.

"You've seen a lot," he said sympathetically.

Shawnee came out of his momentary trance, fixed a shrewd look on him.

"You'll be a cowman, too," he declared. "You've got the mark o' the breed stamped on you plain."

"All my life," admitted Allan. He grinned. "Was born that way."

"Got too old for the saddle myself," mourned Shawnee. "Could ha' stayed on with Cole Bannock till I kicked the bucket, but wasn't the sort to lay round bein' useless. Had some savin's an' set up in the hotel bus'ness. Ain't in it for the money—just like to set there in my porch chair an' see things. All the boys from the ranches stop here at the Cattleman's, an' I treat 'em good—an' they treat me fine . . . keep me posted 'bout what's goin' on." Shawnee's voice lifted. "Mrs Riley—I'm wantin' you on the run!"

Mrs Riley appeared, wiping hands on her apron. She was middle-aged, plump, and pleasant-faced.

"Show the young feller up to Bar 7," Shawnee said to her. "He wants the bath, too, he says."

"You'll be taking supper here?" asked Mrs Riley, smiling at the young man.

"I think I'll be eating at the *cantina* to-night," Allan replied, remembering a promise he'd made Poco Gato who had begged the honour of being his host for the evening meal.

"That's all right," Mrs Riley assured him. "I just like to know, although there's always plenty for an extra plate or two." She turned towards the hall with a beckoning smile.

"The Bar 7's the best room in the house," Shawnee Jones told Allan, following him into the hall. "Don't use numbers in the

Cattleman's," he explained. "All my room doors wear brands— 'stead o' numbers. Bar 7 was the first outfit I rode for. Keep it kind o' special for folks I take a likin' to. No extry charge," he added.

Allan declared he felt highly complimented, and added it was not necessary for Mrs Riley to show him the room. He was sure that Bar 7 would suit him down to the ground.

"I'll go on up to that livery stable," he said.

"Agee Hand'll take good care of your horse," Shawnee assured him. "All the boys put up with him." He followed Allan out to the wide porch and resumed his seat in the big rocker.

"Aimin' to get you a job?" he queried, as Allan paused to make a cigarette. "I can put a word in for you with Cole Bannock of the Triple R."

"Met Bannock on the way in," Allan let him know. "He offered me a job with his outfit."

Shawnee's head lifted in a surprised look. "Wasn't knowin' you was friends with Cole."

"Wouldn't say we're friends exactly," demurred Allan. "Never saw him before, until we met back on the trail."

"Don't seem like Cole to act so quick," mused Shawnee. "Cole's kind of choosy 'bout the men he hires." He rocked gently in his chair, big hat tipped low on his face, eyes shrewdly bright under sleepy lids. "Must ha' somethin' happened back there up the trail," he guessed.

Allan gave him an enigmatic smile. "About time I got Buck over to Agee Hand's livery barn," he said, and went on down the creaky steps.

The weather-worn sign above the doors of the big barn drew his attention as he rode up.

PREMIER LIVERY AND FEED STABLES

HORSES AND MULES FOR SALE OR TRADE

A. G. HAND, *Prop.*

The proprietor in person greeted the prospective patron. He stood in the doorway of his little office, unshaven, grizzly jaws moving meditatively on a cud of tobacco.

"Howdy, stranger."

"Howdy," returned young Rand. He swung down from his saddle.

"Seen you sort o' studyin' my sign," the livery man said. "Mebbe you was wonderin' some what them A. and G. 'nitials stand for."

Allan grinned good-naturedly. "Must be some dark secret you're hiding from the world," he chuckled.

The livery man's eyes twinkled. "Ain't nobody knows what them 'nitials stand for. Could never live it down if folks was to learn the truth."

"Sounds mysterious," declared young Rand gravely. "You're getting me awful curious, mister."

"I aim to keep you curious, you an' all the folks," asserted Mr Hand. "Bet you couldn't guess in a hunderd years what them 'nitials stand for."

"*Algernon*," hazarded Allan.

"Hell's bells," muttered the livery man. His eyes bulged.

"*Galahad*," went on Allan, taking another long shot at Mr Hand's mystery. The combination seemed too absurd to be true, but one look at the crestfallen livery man was enough.

"Goldurn it," mourned Mr Hand. "Don't you never tell on me, young feller. I'm boardin' that buck horse of yours free." He gave Allan a wry smile. "Folks call me Agee. Reckon they'd die laughin' if they knowed my name was Algernon Galahad."

"Mum's the word," promised Allan. "Your dark secret is safe with me, Agee."

The old man led the way into the stable, watched approvingly while Allan stripped off saddle gear.

"Cowman from your boots up, from the way you handle your horse an' saddle gear," he commented.

"It pays a man to look out for things," Allan said. He chatted for a few minutes while Diego forked a feed of hay into the manger.

"We'll give him his grain come sundown," promised Agee, following his patron out to the sunlight. And then came the same question asked by Shawnee Jones. "Lookin' for a job?"

"Maybe . . ." Allan's tone was non-committal. "Thought I'd look over the town—size things up."

"Seen you when you rode into town," Agee Hand said. "If you come in from the north, you must have run into Cole Bannock.

He headed out that way, back to his ranch. Ed Harker was with him," he added. "Ed's our sheriff an' a hard-fightin' gent."

"I met them," admitted Rand cautiously. "At least, I met two riders—one of them a big, bearded man on a bay horse."

"Cole Bannock," confirmed the livery man; "owns the Roaring River Ranch, an' about owns the town o' Roaring River to boot. If you're lookin' for a job, he's the man to tie to."

"Much obliged for the tip," thanked Allan. His attention was distracted by the sight of a trim, slim young person approaching up the board walk from the general merchandise store.

"Cole Bannock's girl," Agee told him. "Kay stables her team here when she comes to town." He went back to the big, bearded owner of the Triple R. "Was a killin' out there," he said. "Ed Harker's got the feller that done the shootin' . . . over in the gaol now." The livery man's eyes narrowed in a questioning look at Allan. "Mebbe you'll have heard of a rustler name of the Pecos Kid. He's the feller Ed's got in the lock-up."

He'd heard of the Kid, Allan told Agee. Most men in the cattle business had heard of him. The sheriff had done a good job landing the Kid behind the bars.

"Ed Harker's the best sheriff in the south-west," asserted Agee. "There's some as figgers he's too old for the job, yell their fool heads off 'cause of the Rengo gang."

"They're crazy," Allan said, purposely prolonging the discussion. If he took his time about it he'd have a chance to meet the girl who was as "purty as a pitcher and smart as the crack of a whip."

"Ed'll land Rengo yet," prophesied Agee Hand confidently. "Plenty killin's charged 'gainst that low-down rustler." His gaze went inquiringly to the girl who was hastening up with a pretty air of one who has important matters on her mind.

"You said an hour or two," he complained. "Diego's just goin' over to Riley's for the mare now. She'll want a feed, too, afore you head back home."

"Don't get excited, Agee," smiled the girl. "I've lost the list Moon Quan gave me . . . some things he wanted for the kitchen." She began to rummage in the buckboard seat. "Here it is . . . must have slipped out of my pocket." She held it up, a piece of torn, brown wrapping-paper. "Moon Quan ran out with it just as I was starting away from the yard, and I didn't stop to put it in my bag."

"Mighty lucky you found it," chuckled Agee. "That old Chinaman would have roared somethin' awful."

"Moon Quan is getting simply terrible," laughed the girl. "Dad says he thinks he owns the ranch and everybody on it." She turned away with a brief, cool, little glance at the tall young stranger.

"He's stoppin' at the Cattleman's," Agee said. "He knows who you are, 'cause I told him when we seen you headin' this way from the store. You ain't told me your name yet," he added, with an inquiring look at Allan.

"Allan Rand," obliged the young man. His eyes twinkled at the girl. "I knew who you were before Agee told me, Miss Bannock. You were going into the store, and Shawnee Jones thought I should know without any loss of time that you were Cole Bannock's girl."

She coloured, gave him a demure look from clear, hazel eyes that perfectly matched her gold-brown hair. They were well-shaped eyes, touched with glints of the same bright gold.

"I'm afraid Shawnee talks too much." Kay's demure smile broke into a low, amused laugh.

"Shawnee's old," grunted Agee Hand jealously.

"He's a dear," declared Kay Bannock, with a look of mingled reproval and affection; "so are you, Agee, and you're both the best friends in the world to me."

"Shawnee's a good scout," the mollified Agee generously conceded. "Gets me some on the prod at times the way he figgers he's got to look out for you—like I didn't count."

Kay said she must get back to Rankin's and finish her shopping. Agee held her back for a moment.

"Was tellin' young Rand he might get him a job with the Triple R," he went on leisurely.

"Oh——" Kay's tone was doubtful. "I—I wouldn't know, Agee. You—you might ask Dad," she suggested, looking soberly at Allan.

"I'm in no hurry," Rand answered. "Was thinking I'd loaf a bit —look things over."

The girl nodded, turned away. Allan hesitated. "I'm going back to the hotel," he said, at which she smiled, seemed pleased.

Agee watched them from his office door, a hand rubbing his

bristly, unshaven chin meditatively. A fine-looking pair they made, he was thinking—the girl so trim and lissome, the man so tall and strongly made. Agee frowned, a bit disturbed by the picture. Maybe his suggestion that young Rand get a job riding for the girl's dad was not so good. He'd have a talk with Shawnee Jones about it, see what Shawnee thought of the young stranger. Shawnee was some sharp in sizing up a man.

Unaware of Agee's troublesome thoughts, Allan and Kay made their way slowly up the board walk. Horsemen drifted past, there were grins of recognition for the girl, curious looks for her companion. A man and a woman drove by in a buckboard. The woman had a baby in her lap. Kay waved a hand, blew a kiss at the baby.

"The Stacys," she told Allan. "Jim Stacy used to work for Dad . . . has a ranch of his own now on Roaring River Mesa—just a small outfit." Her eyes danced. "Jim was crazy to marry Nora Riley, and now he has another little Nora . . . just the *sweetest* baby."

"Any relation to Pat Riley?" queried Allan. "Shawnee Jones told me his Mrs Riley was Pat's wife."

"Nora's their daughter," Kay informed him. "You'll probably meet her and Jim and little Nora at supper to-night."

"I'm not eating at the hotel to-night," Allan said half apologetically. "Thought I'd try the *cantina*. Shawnee said the food was good there."

"I've never been to the *cantina*," confessed the girl. "I know Conchita Mendota, though. She's a widow, very pretty in her Mexican way—and good as gold. She cooked for us at the ranch one time, when Moon Quan went on a visit to San Francisco." Kay laughed softly. "Conchita has an ardent admirer, a quite no-good scamp named Pedro Gato. Pedro is so huge he's almost a giant. The boys call him Poco—Poco Gato, and sometimes *El Gatito*. Means the little cat," she added, with another amused laugh.

"Perhaps Poco will mend his ways," commented Allan solemnly. He was thinking that Kay Bannock would be startled if she could have known the details of his meeting with Conchita's admirer, that he'd already met him.

"He's not really bad," Kay conceded, "just weak and easy-going and a little afraid of work."

They were within a few steps of the store now. Kay came to an abrupt standstill and Allan saw that she was suddenly pale. He followed her look, glimpsed a man disappearing through the swing doors of a saloon a few doors below the hotel. He had the impression of a young, reckless face, a tall, burly figure. A second man followed him through the swing doors, a thinnish-faced man in the middle thirties.

The girl spoke, her voice hard, flat. "Well, good-bye, Mr Rand. Perhaps you'll be out at the ranch some day soon." With a tight-lipped little smile she turned into the store.

The puzzled young man made his way across the street and mounted the creaky steps. Old Shawnee greeted him from his big chair.

"Young Bannock," he said, "that was Rod Bannock, the girl's brother, an' the foxy-lookin' feller with him was Steve Starr, owner of the Double Star outfit acrost the river." He gave Rand a contemplative look. "Seems like you got 'quainted with Kay awful quick," he said in an annoyed voice.

"She came up while I was talking to Agee Hand," explained Allan. He had the uneasy feeling of having committed a crime.

"Well—guess it's all right." Shawnee grinned. "Would have been some peeved at you makin' friends so quick if I hadn't kind o' took a fancy to you. Guess Agee figured you was all right, too, else he wouldn't have made you 'quainted." He went back to the brother. "Rod's sure headin' for hell if he don't pull up some o' that slack rein," he grumbled.

Allan forbore the impulse to ask the old man what he meant.

"I'm going up to my room," he said, "to wash some of this dust off me."

"A man picks up plenty dust out in the brush," commented Shawnee, staring up at him critically. " You can use the bath free this once, son, providin' you don't want hot water."

"Thanks." Allan chuckled, went on up the stairs and down the long, narrow hall until he came to the door that bore the iron of the Bar 7.

The window overlooked the street, gave him a good view of Rankin's store. He stood gazing for a few moments, half hoping for a glimpse of Kay Bannock. The pavement opposite was showing

more activity with the approach of evening. Women were suddenly in evidence, most of them vanishing into the cool depths of
the general merchandise emporium. It was apparent that Rankin's
was a popular meeting-place for the feminine population of Roaring
River. A bevy of cowboys clattered up the board walk from the
livery stable. Allan heard Shawnee's drawling voice lifted in greeting. Good-natured laughter floated up from the hotel porch and
loud voices in boisterous repartee. It was plain that old Shawnee
Jones was regarded as a popular institution.

The young Texan's attention suddenly froze on the wide entrance
to Rankin's. The girl hesitating there was Kay Bannock. Allan
could see her face plainly, see the disdain in the look she gave the
man who came across the street and spoke to her. Steve Starr, owner
of the Double Star ranch.

The sight of the man swaggering up to the girl curiously affected
Allan Rand. He was profoundly aware of a surging dislike of Steve
Starr. If he had been a dog he would have bristled, made ugly,
savage noises in his throat. As it was, his eyes took on a hard look,
and he was rather startled to find his hand squeezing down fiercely
on the butt of the gun in his holster.

The exchange between the two was brief. With a quick shake
of her head the girl swung on her heel and was lost again in the store.
It was obvious she had no liking for her brother's friend. The latter
seemed about to follow her; then suddenly he was swaggering down
the street.

Allan turned away from the window and leisurely opened his
small war bag and made preparations for his cold bath. His curiosity
was piqued by what he had witnessed. He recalled those brief,
hectic minutes when the timely arrival of Cole Bannock and the
sheriff had saved him from a miserable fate at the hands of Double
Star men. Cole Bannock had expressed in unmistakable words his
dislike of Steve Starr's outfit, a dislike obviously shared by his pretty
daughter, but not shared by her brother. Old Shawnee had spoken
darkly of the latter, intimated he was going to the bad and that
Steve Starr was the cause.

The sunlight was yellow in the street when he returned from his
bath and got into his clothes. He stood at the window, buckling on
gun-belt, speculative gaze on Rankin's opposite. Kay Bannock

would have left by now, was probably on her way back to the ranch. It was not likely that she would want to be on the road after dark.

A sudden commotion down in the street brought an end to his idle conjecturing. He could hear booted feet clattering on the board walks, and people came suddenly crowding from doorways across the street. A tall, angular, greying man whose serene features astonishingly resembled Abraham Lincoln's, pushed through the women fluttering like wind-driven leaves from the wide doorway of Rankin's big store. Allan guessed he was Rankin. Sunlight struck flashes from the long-barrelled gun in the storekeeper's hands as he ran up the street.

Allan reached for his hat and made for the hall stairs. Something was wrong down there in the street. He was conscious of a curious foreboding as he clattered down the stairs and ran through the dingy lobby to the wide porch.

Old Shawnee Jones stood there by his chair, leaning on his manzanita cane, deep-set eyes snapping with excitement. He gave Allan a brief look, ejected a stream of tobacco juice expertly over the porch rail.

"The Pecos Kid's broke gaol," he said shrilly; "got him a gun some way, an' locked Billy Hall an' Steve Starr up in his cell."

Allan threw him a curt nod and ran up the street. The distraught look of him drew Shawnee's wondering gaze.

"Acts like somethin's scared him 'most to death," muttered the old man.

A crowd was milling in front of the gaol—a squat brick and adobe structure at the end of the street beyond the livery stable. Allan glimpsed Steve Starr in excited conversation with Jim Rankin and a bow-legged man whom he guessed was the gaoler, Billy Hall. He saw Agee Hand push through the throng. The old livery man came up with a quick, choppy stride, met him in front of the long barn. Allan jerked him a nod, hurried on, wordless, vanished into the dim, sweet-smelling stable. Agee's eyes widened. With a startled grunt he followed Allan to the stall where the buckskin horse was munching hay and nosing the emptied grain box.

"You act like you're in one big hurry," Agee commented curiously.

"You bet I'm in a hurry——" Allan pulled his saddle from its peg and slapped it on the buckskin's back. The horse swung its head in a startled look at him.

"Hell's bust loose," Agee Hand said; "the Kid's broke gaol——"

"That's why I'm in a hurry," Allan told him curtly, hands busy with latigo and cinch.

"Don't savvy you a-tall," complained Agee. He was spilling over with the story of the outlaw's escape. "Steve Starr went over to the gaol for a look at the Kid, told Billy Hall he figured he could make the Kid tell him where Rengo holes up with his gang." Agee paused, shook his head. "Your horse sure don't like you takin' him off—an' him not finished his hay," he observed.

"Open up," grunted Allan. The buckskin tossed head, accepted the bit sulkily.

"I was tellin' you about the Kid," Agee went on. "Billy left Steve Starr talkin' with him and went back to his office. Seems like the Kid reached through the bars and grabbed Steve's gun . . . made Steve call for Billy to come. Billy come up, didn't see the Kid was holdin' the gun poked agin' Steve's belly. The Kid told him to unlock the cell or he'd blow Steve's guts all over the place. Nothin' for Billy to do but let him out of the cell. The Kid took his gun away from him an' locked him an' Steve up in the cell." Agee spat into the straw under the buckskin's feet. "That's all Billy and Steve know about it. The Kid got clean away . . . sure one nervy, bad man."

Allan led the buckskin out to the fast-fading sunlight and swung into the saddle.

"How long ago did it happen, Agee?"

"Not so long," answered the livery man, "maybe half an hour, from what Billy says."

"Went off on foot?"

"Ain't nobody claims to have lost a horse," Agee said. "Guess the Kid hoofed it away from here, far as I know." A startled look sprang from the livery man's eyes as he stared up at the grim-faced young man tensely erect in the saddle. "Say—that'll be about the time Kay Bannock come an' got her team!" Agee's tone was aghast.

"I was wondering about her," Allan said quietly. "What would a man like the Pecos Kid do if he saw a lone girl driving through the chaparral, Agee?"

The old livery man stifled a groan. "He'd grab her quick, son—grab her team—use her for a getaway from these parts."

"I'm following the trail," Allan said. "I want a short-cut into the road for Roaring River Ranch, Agee."

The livery man jerked a horny thumb towards a deep gully that made a dead end of the short side-street below the long barn.

"Up the barranca, son," he said simply. "Keep goin' a quarter of a mile an' you'll hit the road where it heads up El Toro Canyon. . . ." His voice trailed away to an agonized groan, and he stood there, staring with fear-filled eyes until horse and man vanished into the rugged wash of the gully that twisted tortuously up to the hills. Suddenly Agee came out of his paralysis, voice lifting in shrill yells for Diego to throw a saddle on the grey horse. As the startled Mexican hurried to obey, Agee went loping up the dusty street towards the crowd still milling in front of the gaol. Dust spurted from his clattering boot-heels as he ran, lifted in a pale golden haze in the yellowing sunlight, and he waved his arms wildly, uttering loud, incoherent cries.

3

KAY kept the team moving at a lively pace. She was later than she cared to be, and it was Rod's fault. She was furious with her brother. He was too friendly with Steve Starr. Kay had no use for the owner of the Double Star ranch. She resented the man's obvious desire to pay court to her. She detested him and the friendship that was ruining her brother. Rod was drinking more than was good for him. He was a changed man since he had taken up with Steve Starr. Kay wondered if their father had noticed the change in Rod. She knew that Cole Bannock heartily disliked the Double Star man. Her father was not given to expressions of tenderness, but Kay knew that Rod meant the world and all to him. Cole Bannock was a rough and violent man, kindly and generous enough when he wanted to be, but terrible in his wrath. Despite his deep affection for his son, there was danger of an explosion that threatened to wreck for ever the peace and happiness of the ranch. Not that there was overmuch peace at any time on Roaring River Ranch, not these days, when continued depredations of rustlers kept Cole Bannock in a turmoil of worried anger.

The high wheels of the buckboard ground noisily across a stretch of gravelly wash that slowed the tough little mustangs to a walk. The narrow road pitched sharply down a steep hill. Kay let the team make a run of it, her lithe young body bouncing to the pitch and rock of the stout little vehicle. She was used to the bumps, gave them no heed, and she was strong and hard-muscled, for all her look of delicate slimness.

She was anxious to make El Toro Creek crossing before darkness overtook her. The old bridge had gone with the last flood, and the ford was treacherous with its shifting quicksands. Her resentment against Steve Starr grew. But for his effrontery in attempting to speak to her she would have beaten the darkness home. She had purposely lingered in Rankin's, wishing to avoid another encounter with the man. And she had hoped for a chance to speak to her brother. Rod had chosen to keep out of sight, no doubt planning to go on another of his disgusting sprees.

Kay's thoughts went to the tall young stranger she had encountered at Agee Hand's livery barn. She was conscious of a little glow as she recalled him. Allan Rand was his name, he had told her, and he was looking for a job—perhaps would ask her father for one. Kay wondered if he would, wondered if she would ever see him again. She hoped so. He was nice, she liked him. Her cheeks warmed a bit as she recalled her abrupt good-bye to him. He wouldn't understand—wouldn't know that his seemingly curt dismissal was caused by the sight of her brother in the company of Steve Starr.

The road levelled out, took a twisting course across the flats through the willow brakes. Another quarter of a mile would bring her to the creek. She would be able to make the ford with the last remaining glimmers of the fading daylight. Once across the creek the road turned up El Toro Canyon for the long ascent to the mesa. On horseback she could have reached the ford in a few minutes by way of the short-cut from town. The wagon road was forced to detour in a wide loop round the lower flats because of the marsh and the almost impenetrable willow brakes. By way of the road it was some three miles to the ford, which actually was scarcely a mile from town by the short-cut.

A man emerged from behind a dense growth of willows as Kay drove down the slope to the creek. The girl gave him a quick, startled glance and reached for her whip. There was nothing she could do but keep on moving. It was not possible to swerve out of the road, which cut like a tunnel through the willow brakes. Her one chance was to send the team into a dead run, force the man to step aside. To her horror she caught the flash of something in his uplifted hand—a gun.

He stood there in the road, a dark and sinister shape silhouetted against the red glare of the setting sun. Kay drew the snorting mustangs to a standstill, gave him a frightened look. He returned her a mirthless grin in which his cold eyes took no part.

"I'm riding a piece with you," he said. "Lucky you come along in time to give me a lift across the creek."

She felt the buckboard springs tilt as he climbed swiftly up and settled down in the seat behind her. Her face turned in a look over her shoulder, and she heard her own voice, husky with rage and fear.

"Get out," she said, "get out . . . I'm not taking you across the creek—or any place."

"I've no time for words." The man's tone was deadly. "I'm in a hurry." The red glow of the sunset made tiny pin-points of fire in the black pupils of his eyes. "Get your team moving."

The hard barrel of the gun suddenly pressed against her back. She dared not disobey. Without further protest Kay started the team, and in another moment the buckboard wheels were churning through the shallows. A desperate thought came to her: she would swerve off the road into the quicksands, force the man to flounder for his life through the treacherous bogs. She was sure she could escape him, make her way back to the willow brakes and elude pursuit.

He seemed to divine her thoughts, ground the hard gun-barrel fiercely into her spine.

"Don't get foolish notions," he warned. "Don't want to pull this trigger, but I sure will if you ain't mindin' me."

She kept her gaze alertly on the cottonwood stump looming darkly on the opposite bank, her desperate plan abandoned now. She sensed the man would not hesitate to kill her if she attempted to thwart his purpose. The old cottonwood stump was a guiding landmark for those who would keep to the narrow strip of firm gravel that made the ford possible. It was why she had been in haste to reach the crossing before the darkness blotted out all view of the tree.

Five minutes brought them to the steep rise of the opposite bank.

"Keep going," ordered the man as Kay drew hesitatingly on the lines. He leaned over, snatched the whip from its socket, and slashed at the team. The horses broke into a run up the long El Toro grade.

"You're Cole Bannock's girl, ain't you?" It was a statement rather than a question.

"What of it?" The girl's tone was resentful. "He'll kill you for this," she added.

"I've got it in for Cole Bannock," the man said. The hot breath of his mirthless laugh on her neck made her cringe. "Your dad figured to have the law swing me. I've got him fooled—him and that old sidewinder he's got for sheriff."

Kay knew now who this man was, knew with sickening certainty he was the Pecos Kid, the notorious rustler captured by her father and Sheriff Harker.

"Luck's sure ridin' with me," said the desperado, with another low laugh. "Won't nobody try to stop me now I've got Cole Bannock's daughter for a nice little pal. Too bad for her if anybody tries to get me back into that gaol." A menacing press of the gun punctuated the words. "Come sun-up an' we'll be across the border, you and me."

Kay had no answer. She was too dazed to think coherently. She only knew that this desperate man planned to use her as a means of escape. There was ruthless determination in him. Nothing she could say would avail her, and the press of the gun against her back was making her sick. She struggled gamely to overcome her giddiness. This was no time to faint. It would be the finish. He was talking again, his voice as from a far distance, but thinly clear above the roaring in her ears.

"We're headin' up the left fork," he said; "there's a road the other side of Lobo Flats that runs down into Red Canyon. There's a feller there I know. He'll give us fresh horses—saddle horses."

Kay managed a brief, dry-lipped protest.

"What's the use, taking me with you? Let me out at the fork. You can make better time if you take one of the team horses and ride to wherever you want to go."

"I'm safer with you along with me right now," the Pecos Kid told her with his ugly laugh. "You're my passport to the border."

She drove on, slim body rigid against the press of the gun. The dark tides of night flowed in, made mighty imprisoning walls of the towering canyon cliffs. Kay wondered if she dared keep on past the left fork. Every mile beyond would bring them nearer the ranch—deliverance.

It was soon apparent that her captor was familiar with the country. At his terse command she obediently swung the team into the left fork. It was a seldom-used road, narrow and deeply rutted by the rains. Kay could hear the waters of the Little Toro down

in the black deeps of the canyon. She thought she heard another
sound. Her heart leaped, and for some reason the paralysing horror
fell away from her. The hands gripping the lines were no longer
clammy and limp but cool and firm. Courage was suddenly flowing through her, a clean, energizing tide that kindled new hope and
sharpened her senses. Kay found herself straining for a repetition
of that sound, so like the distant hoof-beat of a galloping horse. She
wondered if the man had heard. His next words informed her that
his ears were on the alert.

"Faster," he said. He reached over and slashed at the horses with
the whip.

Kay sensed a growing uneasiness in him. There was a sharp,
startled rasp in his voice.

"I can't see," she protested; "it's so dark—and I hardly know this
road." She spoke coolly, hands imperceptibly drawing on the reins
and slowing down the team. "We'll go over the cliff," she pointed
out.

"Faster," repeated the Pecos Kid harshly, "sounds like a horse—
down the road behind us."

"It was a rock—tumbling down the slope," Kay said. She drew
again on the reins.

"It's a horse . . ." The man's voice was a fierce snarl in her ears,
and then suddenly she felt his hard body crowding over the seat and
wedging down close to her side. He tore the reins from her hands
and cut the whip savagely at the horses. The forward rush of the
startled team flung the girl hard against the back of the seat. She
lay there, sprawled low on the leather cushion, feet pressed against
the dashboard, breathless, terrified, expecting every moment to hear
the crash of wheel splintering against a boulder, or the sudden,
sickening falling away of the ground beneath them as the buckboard
plunged over the precipice.

To her surprise nothing happened. The road had levelled out in
a long straight-away between tall cliffs and was fairly smooth. Kay
struggled to an upright position. For a moment she had a wild
impulse to jump headlong from the careening vehicle. She forced
the idea from her. It was not possible to leap over those
high, spinning wheels. She would be hideously mangled,
killed.

Again her straining ears caught the muffled thud of galloping hoof-beats. It was a chase, and the lone horseman was drawing steadily nearer. The Pecos Kid muttered an oath, and he suddenly swung the winded team sharply to the left. The man had the eyes of a cat. He could see things in the darkness not visible to Kay.

He pulled the blowing team to a standstill behind a great clump of ragged manzanitas. He leaped out, turned, and fastened strong fingers over Kay's wrist. She half jumped, half fell from the buck-board as he pulled. Again she felt the press of his gun against her side.

No need for words. Kay knew life depended on her silence. An outcry meant instant death.

She stood tensely by the man's side, stirringly aware of those approaching hoof-beats. Her wrist ached under the fierce clutch of the Kid's fingers. Kay marvelled at his coolness. His breathing was unhurried, his lean, hard body a coiled spring, ready for instant action.

She was suddenly conscious of a deep stillness in the night. Only the quick beat of her own heart, the gentle blowing of the horses. She realized the drumming of galloping hoofs no longer touched her ears. The pursuer had halted down the road.

The Kid's disappointed oath enlightened her. The unseen horse-man suspected a trap. He no longer heard the rattle of the buck-board's wheels, the pounding hoofs of the team. Kay's heart quickened. She lifted a look at the grey blur of the Kid's face.

"You'll have a better chance to escape if you leave me here. You can unhitch one of the horses and ride away." She spoke in a low whisper.

The man shook his head, and again the quick press of his gun warned her to silence.

"Not leavin' you yet," he muttered. "I'm needin' you plenty. It's you—or me—if it comes to the show-down with this feller that's picked up the trail."

Kay repressed a cold shiver, and then suddenly a voice spoke from the dark blanket of the night.

"Turn the girl loose——"

Amazement held Kay Bannock rigid. Not the words, not the nearness of the voice, were the cause of her stark surprise. The unseen speaker, crouched somewhere close in the impenetrable night was Allan Rand.

The tall Texan's voice sliced through the darkness.

"Turn her loose, Seely. I've got you covered—and you know I don't miss my shots."

Something like a startled snarl frothed from the rustler's lips.

"Where in hell did *you* drop from, Rand?" He spoke hoarsely, like a man in the grip of a terrible fear.

"Never mind about me. I'm telling you to let the girl go."

"Like hell, I'll let her go." A brittle laugh came from the Pecos Kid. "I'll blow her to pieces if you pull trigger on me, Rand."

There was a brief silence. Kay sensed that Rand knew the outlaw would fulfil the threat to kill her. He would pull the trigger of the gun thrust against her side even as he fell, riddled with Rand's bullets. She stood, incapable of speech, frozen with horror. Suddenly Rand was speaking again.

"I'll trade with you, Seely, your life for the girl. Turn her loose —and you can go where you will. I won't try to stop you."

"You mean that, Rand?" The Pecos Kid's tone was thoughtful.

"You know a Rand keeps his word, Seely." The tall Texan's voice had a razor-edge to it.

"Yeah—that's what I'm thinkin'." The outlaw spoke gloomily. "I'm rememberin' you promised to see me dangle at the end of a rope."

"We'll let that ride for another day, Seely," rejoined Allan Rand grimly. "Right now I'm giving you a chance to hit the trail for the border."

"How do I know you won't start shootin' quick as I turn her loose?" grumbled the Pecos Kid.

"I'm giving you my word," reminded Allan tersely.

"Yeah, I was forgettin'." Kay felt a lessening of the press of hard metal against her side, heard the outlaw's quickened breath. His decision was made—he was going to turn her loose. Allan Rand's quiet voice came again from the darkness.

"Don't waste time, Seely. They're buzzing like angry hornets back in the town. Take one of the horses and hit the trail for the border."

Kay was suddenly standing alone in the black night. She could vaguely discern the outlaw working feverishly to free one of the team horses from its harness. She made no attempt to stir from the spot. The man would strike with the deadly swiftness of a rattlesnake if she aroused his fears.

"You can pick up a saddle somewhere down the line," Allan called out. His voice held a lighter note.

"Won't be the first time I've picked me up an outfit," the Pecos Kid answered dryly. He swung up to the horse, and in a moment was lost in the deeps of the night. Kay waited, breathless, ears delighting in the quickly fading hoof-beats, and then, with a start, she saw the tall shape of her rescuer, a vague shadow in the darkness.

"An Indian couldn't make less sound than you," she said as he came up to her. She was striving to keep from tears. "No wonder we didn't dream you were so close until you spoke."

He sensed that her light greeting was an attempt to keep from an emotional let-down. He gave her a grave, approving smile.

"I was scared to death you'd hear me," he chuckled. "Every step I took sounded like a herd of cattle stampeding through the brush, I was thinking."

Her laugh came naturally. "I didn't hear a twig stir," she declared, "and I was listening!" Her tone sobered. "You—you were awfully brave. I—I'll never forget . . ."

"It was luck," he said quickly. "It was luck—picking up the trail."

"Not all luck," she told him simply. "You—you must have followed me for some reason. I don't understand just why you followed me."

"Agee Hand told me you'd just left town," Allan said. "It seems the man broke gaol shortly before you left. He was on foot."

Kay interrupted him. "You guessed what might happen—if he caught me alone on the road." She shuddered. "Well—you made a good guess."

"Agee told me of the short-cut," Allan explained. "I couldn't have caught up with you if Agee hadn't told me of that. It was luck," he repeated.

Kay shook her head, eyes intent on him as he pulled the harness from the lone mustang hitched to the buckboard. "Not luck," she insisted. "You thought of what might happen to me the instant you knew the Pecos Kid was loose. It was wonderful of you. None of the others had any thought of me."

"There was a lot of excitement in town," Allan told her. "It seems the Kid pulled a trick on Steve Starr. There was a big crowd at the gaol, getting the details from Billy Hall and Starr." He gave her the little he knew from Agee Hand of the escape.

"It's a good thing for me *you* were in town." Kay made the assertion soberly. "You were the only one who had a thought of me." She lifted her face in a faint smile. "You have a fast-working brain."

Allan chuckled, shook his head. He knew the real reason that had prompted him to such swift action. He could not explain that she had been in his thoughts constantly since the moment of meeting her at Agee Hand's livery barn. He turned to the immediate problem of getting her home.

"You can ride my horse," he suggested.

"Bess isn't broke for riding," worried Kay. "She's gentle enough, but dreadfully rough. She'll jar you to pieces, especially riding bare-back."

"I'm tough," grinned Allan. He glanced inside the abandoned buckboard. "Anything here you want to take with you?"

Kay considered a moment, shook her head. "Only a few things I got from Rankin's. They'll be safe enough until Dad sends a man for the rig."

They found the buckskin horse where Allan had left him, hidden behind a thick clump of piñons on the slope above the road. Kay climbed into the saddle.

"Don't trouble to shorten the stirrups," she protested, when Allan began to tug at the buckskin thongs.

"You may as well be comfortable," he told her.

She made no further objection, and in a few minutes the stirrups were adjusted to the right length.

"I shouldn't let you take me all the way home," the girl worried. "It's an hour's ride and more." She laughed nervously. "I'm afraid I'm going to let you come, though."

"You've nothing to say about it," Allan told her a bit grimly. "I'm not leaving you until I turn you over to your father."

"I don't want you to leave me," Kay confessed. "I'll admit that I'm—well, a trifle jumpy—plain frightened."

They went down the road at a jog-trot. Kay said curiously, "You seemed to know the Pecos Kid—spoke his name."

"It's not the first time I've run into him," Allan admitted. His tone was evasive. "Most cowmen know of the Kid."

She pondered his answer for a brief space. "Is he the reason that brings you up here to the Roaring River country?" Kay hesitated. "I mean, are you an Association man?"

"No." Allan's tone was curt. "I'm not a detective."

"Father belongs to the South-west Cattleman's Association," Kay told him half apologetically. "I happen to know he's been planning to get an Association man up here. Father's pestered to death with rustlers. He'll be wild when he hears the Pecos Kid is loose again, and after all the trouble he's had catching him."

"I'm thinking we won't see the Kid around these parts again for a long time," observed Allan.

Kay gave him a puzzled look. She was recalling the young outlaw's very real fear of the tall man riding by her side.

"He seemed afraid when he recognized your voice," she remarked.

"He has reason to be." Allan's tone was grim.

Kay repressed a shudder. "I've never been so completely terrified," she confessed. "He wouldn't have hesitated to kill me. I never dreamed any man could be so utterly ruthless—so cold-blooded."

There was no answer from the man riding by her side. The girl stole a quick glance up at his face. The harsh, implacable profile gave her a shock. Instinctively she knew the Pecos Kid could expect small mercy if he ever again encountered Allan Rand. She made haste to change to lighter matters.

"I like this horse of yours. He rides easy as a rocking-chair."

"Raised Buck from a colt," Allan told her. "Buck can do almost everything but talk. Got all the horse sense there is."

"I've a red bay mare at the ranch I'm crazy about," confided the girl. "I call her Chuparosa—means butterfly, and that's what she is, a dainty red butterfly."

The belated moon suddenly pushed over a saw-toothed ridge,

touched the rugged landscape with silver, etched the narrow mouth of the gorge where the road cut into the winding Toro grade. Allan pulled the mustang mare to standstill.

The sound was unmistakable. Horsemen—coming up the canyon road.

Allan smiled down at the girl.

"Agee's given the alarm about you," he guessed.

"It's all over now. I wish they hadn't troubled to come." Her tone gave him the impression she was not pleased.

A half-score riders swept round the bend. Shouts echoed from the canyon walls as the newcomers caught sight of the two waiting at the intersection. Old Agee Hand was the first to reach them. He drew his grey gelding to a halt, giving vent to delighted yips.

"Looks like you sure got to her in time, son," he chuckled. "Reckon you left the coyote layin' some place for the buzzards."

His fellow posse-men came up with a great noise of clattering hoofs. Allan recognized Steve Starr and Rod Bannock among them. The latter pressed his panting horse alongside the buckskin.

"Are you all right, Sis? The damn' skunk didn't hurt you, huh?" His voice betrayed that young Bannock had been drinking. His sister gave him a worried look, shook her head.

"I'm all right, Rod, thanks to Mr Rand." Her tone was cold.

Young Bannock stared at Allan. "Mighty fine of you, Mr Rand." He leered drunkenly. "I'm Kay's brother, and I'm declarin' loud it was damn' fine of you." He swayed unsteadily in his saddle, frowned owlishly at his sister. "Where's the buck-board, and how come you're ridin' that buckskin? Never saw that buckskin before."

"Don't get silly," retorted Kay. "The buckboard is somewhere up the road, in the chaparral. The Kid took one of the horses and that's why I'm riding Mr Rand's horse."

An exclamation dropped from Steve Starr. "You mean the Kid got clean away?" Something in his voice drew a sharp glance from Allan.

"Mr Rand let him go," admitted Kay. She looked distastefully at the Double Star man. "It was my life—or his, and what have you got to say about it, any of you?"

"You should have killed the skunk," hiccoughed Rod Bannock. He glared at Allan. "You're a hell of a fellow—lettin' him get away."

"You needn't swear, Rodney," flared Kay. "You're plain drunk, and I wish you'd go away. Mr Rand will take me home," she added. There was a droop to her slight figure, a note of weariness in her voice.

"Ain't drunk," denied young Bannock, "and Rand ain't takin' you home. I'm takin' you home. Agee," he added, "you give Sis your grey horse. Rand can have his buckskin back, and you can ride Bess to town."

"Sure she can have the grey, her or Mr Rand," agreed the livery man. He climbed down from his saddle.

"Thank you, Agee. I'll take your horse, and you can keep Bess until we send for her." Kay slid from the saddle.

"I'll fix the stirrups more comfortable for you," Agee said.

The girl nodded, stared up at her glowering brother. "You can go back to town with your friend, Rodney," she told him quietly. "Mr Rand will take me home."

"I reckon you'd better do like she wants, Rod," advised Agee, busy with the stirrups.

"Ain't lettin' no stranger take my sister home," shouted young Bannock.

"Mr Rand has just saved my life," retorted Kay angrily. "You can't call him a stranger."

"To hell with him," shouted her brother. He clutched at the saddle-horn, steadied himself. "Ain't I in the right, Steve?" He appealed to the Double Star man.

The latter shrugged, gave the girl an insolent grin. "I'll ride along with you, Miss Bannock, if you're worried about Rod's condition."

Kay ignored him, climbed up on the grey horse, settled her feet in the stirrups.

"Thank you, Agee." She looked at Allan, who was finishing readjusting his own stirrups. He nodded, swung up to his saddle, turned cold eyes on Rod Bannock.

"You heard your sister," he said in a flat voice; "she doesn't want you—and she doesn't want your friend."

Rod Bannock swore at him, reached for his gun. Agee Hand, the nearest to him, grabbed his wrist and wrenched the weapon from him.

A tired, drawling voice broke the brief silence that followed the short struggle between the two men. Kay uttered a relieved little cry.

"What's goin' on here?" Sheriff Harker reined his horse and stared with mild curiosity at the group of riders that filled the road. "On my way back to town from the ranch," he said to Kay. "Your dad was some worried at you bein' late."

"There's been some trouble," the girl explained in a low voice. "Rodney's been drinking," she added.

The sheriff nodded, keen eyes noting the gun the angry livery man was holding. His gaze went sternly to young Bannock.

"You get back to town, Rod. You ain't in no shape to go home. Your dad won't like it."

Rod Bannock glowered, but made no attempt to speak. It was plain he was afraid of the stern old sheriff.

"You can stay the night with Shawnee Jones," Ed Harker went on. "You mind me, Rod." There was a rasp in his voice, a cold look in his eyes as he finished.

Rod Bannock swung his horse. "Let's get out of here," he muttered to Steve Starr. He spurred down the grade.

The Double Star man grinned at the sheriff. "I'll see he gets to bed, Ed," he promised as he rode away.

The sheriff's frowning gaze followed him for a moment, then he turned and looked searchingly at Allan Rand.

"How come you mixed up in a fuss with Rod Bannock?" His tone was curt.

"It's not Mr Rand's fault," interposed Kay. "Rod was drunk—ugly, and—and anyway—Mr Rand has just saved my life." Her voice broke. "I wouldn't be here now if—if he hadn't been so brave—and—and fine."

Sheriff Harker narrowed puzzled eyes at her. "How do you mean —he saved your life?"

"The Pecos Kid broke gaol," Agee Hand informed him, not without some relish.

The sheriff dropped a startled grunt, wagged his head mournfully, but the others noticed that his keen eyes swept a sharp look at Allan Rand. The latter shook his head.

"Don't blame me," he said softly.

Sheriff Harker grunted, gave his attention to Agee's account of the gaol break. He scowled a bit at the part played by Steve Starr.

"Billy Hall had no business lettin' Starr talk to the Kid," he grumbled.

Kay gave him the details of the following events. The sheriff listened attentively, nodded approvingly at Allan.

"You done the right thing," he said. "Nothin' else you could do but bargain with the Kid like you did. No tellin' what would have happened to Kay if you hadn't got her away from him." A smile warmed his leathery old face. "I sure admire your nerve, son. Rod Bannock's goin' to feel mighty small when he sobers up and gets it into his head just what you done for his sister."

"Rod didn't want Mr Rand to take me home," explained Kay.

"Well," pondered the sheriff, "guess I'll ride back to the ranch with you, Kay. Your dad'll want to know about the Kid bein' on the loose again." He hesitated, stared curiously at Allan. "You can come along if you have a mind to," he added. "Cole Bannock'll be wantin' to thank you for what you've done."

Allan shook his head. He knew what was in the sheriff's mind. After all, he was a stranger, and the sheriff was dubious about letting a stranger be responsible for the girl's safe arrival home.

"No need for me to go now," he said. "I'm sure it's best for you to take Miss Bannock home to the ranch. See you in town later," he added.

"Not to-night," Sheriff Harker told him. "I'll be stayin' at the ranch to-night." He gave Allan a significant look. "Some time to-morrow mornin'," he added.

"I'll be at the Cattleman's Hotel," promised Allan.

Kay Bannock was frankly disappointed. "Dad will want to thank you," she said to Allan. "I'm sorry you won't come home with us." Her smile came back to him as she rode up the road with the sheriff.

4

A GNAWING emptiness reminded Allan of his promise to Poco Gato. He stabled the weary buckskin and proceeded on foot to the *cantina*, a low, adobe building set back from the street behind a row of big chinaberry-trees. Lamplight glowed dimly from narrow, curtained windows. There were horses drooping at the hitch-rail, and he heard the muted sound of a guitar—a man's voice lifted in a plaintive Mexican love song.

Allan pushed the door open and stepped inside. The song came to an abrupt end.

"*Amigo*—at last you come!" Poco Gato sprang from a corner bench, guitar clutched in a mighty paw.

"I could not help being late, Poco."

"*Si*, señor." The giant Mexican's tone sobered. "We know what happened. Soon we were riding to pick up your trail. . . ." He waved round the dimly lighted room, hazy with the smoke of cigarettes. "I sent the word—and behold my friends—ready to ride with me to the help of my señor."

Allan became aware of some half-score faces turned towards him from various tables, dark faces, shadowed by tall, steeple hats and lighted by the flash of white-toothed, friendly grins. His heart warmed to these fierce-eyed friends of Poco Gato.

"The affair is finished," he told them, "the señorita is in safe hands."

Poco nodded; grinned at a swarthy youth lolling lazily in a raw-hide chair. "Pepe has brought us the good news, señor. Pepe was with those who followed you, but unseen by them. He is of Apache blood and can follow the trail of a woodtick in the dark of the moon."

Allan smiled at the slim youth. "*Gracias*, Pepe. I am in your debt."

"Eet ees not'ing," replied Pepe, for some reason preferring to speak in halting English; "Poco 'ave tell us w'at you do for save ees life." He gestured grandly. "We your frien's, señor."

44

The quick beat of light feet on the hard-packed mud floor drew a short exclamation from Poco Gato.

"My señor has arrived," he said to the young woman who hurried up with a swirl of full skirts. "He will be hungry—ready for much good food."

The young woman—she was very good-looking—gave Allan an interested smile from dark and lustrous eyes. "You are welcome, señor. Pedro has told me of the brave thing you did. But for you he would not be here to-night."

"It is nothing," deprecated Allan, unconsciously echoing the words just used by Pepe. He smiled at her. "I have heard good things about your food, Señora Mendota. Shawnee Jones speaks in high praise."

Conchita dimpled. "I have a special dish for you," she confided; "*arroz con pollo*. I hope you will not be disappointed."

"Chicken!" exclaimed Allan, "with rice and onions and tomatoes and chick-peas and peppers. Ah, señora, my hunger grows ravenous."

"You will dine in the little room," declared Conchita, much pleased by his enthusiasm; "I have set a table for you and Pedro and me." She turned with a beckoning gesture.

Allan hesitated, smiled round at the steeple-hatted men. "I would be host to my new friends . . ." His glance went to the bar. "A little wine . . ."

"You cannot spend your money in my *cantina* to-night," declared Conchita firmly. She looked at Poco Gato. The latter slapped his pocket and strode to the bar.

"I have gold, thanks to the señor, and to-night it is I who buy the wine." A gold coin spun from his hand, fell with a tinkle on the bar. Conchita gave him an approving smile.

"The best in the house," she said to the paunchy, greying Mexican behind the bar as the steeple-hatted men crowded up with expectant grins.

Allan and Poco followed her into a small room with windows that looked out on a flower-filled patio now touched with moonlight. They took chairs at a round table spread with a bright red-and-white cloth. Señora Mendota clapped her hands smartly, and soon a middle-aged woman brought in a great, steaming platter of the promised *arroz con pollo*. Also came *enchilades* and *frijoles con queso*. Poco Gato beamed happily at his guest.

"We will not be hungry when these dishes are empty, señor," he prophesied.

"Not for days to come," chuckled Allan. "Señora, my compliments." He touched the glass of wine to his lips.

"You must call me Conchita," announced Señora Mendota. "You are Pedro's good friend, and so you are *my* friend."

Allan guessed from the look she gave the big Mexican that all was well between them. Poco had confided to him the story of his romance while they rode down the trail to Roaring River that afternoon. It was obvious that her suitor's virtuous conduct during the past months was to have its reward. His continued probity would no doubt result in his induction as mine host of the *cantina* and husband of its pretty owner.

Conchita plied him with questions about the rescue of Kay Bannock from the clutches of the Pecos Kid. She was very fond of the Bannock girl, and she was frankly disappointed when Allan admitted he had allowed the desperado to make his escape.

"You should have killed him," she asserted, with a shake of her head. "It is not murder to kill his kind of snake."

Poco Gato's frown reproved her. Death was reaching too eagerly for the Bannock girl, he reminded his inamorata. One could not blame the señor for using discretion.

"I myself will some day meet and destroy this snake they call the Pecos Kid," boasted the big Mexican. "I will bring you his ears, my pretty one." He laughed loudly. "His ears will look nice, pinned on the wall behind the bar."

Conchita shuddered, made a face at him. "You talk nonsense," she scolded; "you will not do any killing. I will not have my husband pointed out as one who kills other men."

Poco Gato rolled delighted eyes at his *Americano* friend. "Ha!" he exclaimed, "you know our secret now, Señor Rand."

Señora Mendota blushed charmingly. "It is true," she murmured, "I have told Pedro I will marry him now that he is following honest ways, but it must not be said of him that he is a killer." Her dark eyes danced. "Such tales would keep customers away from the *cantina*."

"God forbid," muttered Poco fervently.

Allan joined in the laughter and lifted his glass. "To your great happiness," he toasted.

"And to you—our friendship," chorused the happy bride and groom to-be.

Worry was suddenly mirrored in Conchita's eyes as she set her glass down. "Listen——" Her low whisper was tense with apprehension.

The street door banged noisily, and they heard the sound of heavy, lurching feet, a man's loud, drunken voice. Conchita sprang from her chair, stared at the others with scared, startled eyes.

"It's the young Señor Bannock," she whispered. "He asks for me——"

"*Por Dios*," muttered Poco, "he is very drunk, and the other man with him is Señor Starr." The Mexican's big face took on a greenish pallor, and he gave Allan an imploring look. It was plain that he dreaded an encounter with the owner of the Double Star. Only a miracle had saved him from death at the hands of Double Star men earlier that day.

The door opened, and they saw the frightened face of the barman. "They ask for you, señora——"

Conchita's coolness was returning. She gestured assent. "I will come," she said quietly. "Quick—close the door, Gaspar."

The barman's grey face vanished, and the door closed again softly. Conchita stood for a moment, gathering courage.

"I do not like this young Bannock," she told Allan in a hard, toneless voice; "he makes love to me, and I do not like his friend, who is sly and bad. He makes love to me, too, behind the other's back."

An animal-like cry of rage came from Poco Gato.

"Hush," reproved Conchita, "they must not know you are here."

"I do not fear them," muttered Poco.

"Do not make it worse for me," pleaded Señora Mendota. "Señor Rod already is jealous of you. No doubt he has heard you are in town and has come to pick a quarrel."

Allan shook his head at the big, glowering Mexican. "She is right," he said. "There'll be trouble if you go out there. Young Bannock is drunk, and the man with him has no love for you, Poco. Don't forget what his foreman tried to do to you this afternoon."

"Is it your command, señor?" Poco put the question simply, as though Allan's word was final.

"It is a command." Allan spoke firmly.

"*Gracias!*" Quick relief showed in Conchita's lustrous eyes. "I am not afraid of these swine," she added, with a cool little smile. She lifted her full yellow skirt, and the two men caught a glimpse of shapely leg—a tiny dagger clasped in a garter. The next moment the door closed behind her.

Poco stared unhappily across the gay red-and-white cloth at his patron. Allan's face was set in stern, hard lines, and there was an agate coldness in his eyes. Poco seemed to find comfort. He was not alone. This brave *Americano* was sent by the good angels to protect him and Conchita. Had he not already saved him from death only that day?

Rod Bannock leaned heavily against the bar, fist closed round the neck of a bottle. He was very drunk. Steve Starr lolled in a chair at one of the tables. A bottle of whisky stood in front of him, but, though he betrayed signs of drinking, he was not drunk. He watched with amused, sneering eyes as Conchita came with quick, business-like steps across the floor.

"Hello, señora." The cattleman got out of his chair, bowed with mock gallantry.

She gave him a cool, unsmiling nod, and went swiftly to the big man swaying unsteadily against the bar.

"You want me?" She flung the words at him like a cat spitting at a dog.

Young Bannock leered tipsily. " 'Lo, Con-conchita. Sure I wan' you . . . crazhy f-for you."

Conchita interrupted him with a fierce gesture. "You go way queek! I no 'ave you come my *cantina* drunk lak peeg." Indignation made her voice thin and nasal.

"Not drunk," hiccoughed the intoxicated young man. He put the bottle to his lips, gurgled noisily.

Conchita stamped a foot. "You go queek," she repeated. "I 'ave no time for talk weeth peeg lak you."

He turned on high boot-heels, regarded her with glassy eyes.

"Poco's here, huh?" His tone was ugly. "I'm goin' to throw that *hombre* out on his neck."

Her contemptuous silence seemed to infuriate him. "Ain't standin' for him makin' a play for you," he shouted.

"Peeg!" Conchita's voice was shrill, and with an angry gesture she turned to Steve Starr, again sprawled in his chair. "I wan' you both go queek," she flamed at him. "I no wan' you come mak trooble my *cantina*."

Starr got to his feet as she stood angrily by his table. "Maybe we can make a deal, sister." His eyes narrowed in a crafty look. "I'll get Bannock back to the hotel easy enough after he's downed a couple more drinks. He's due to pass out 'most any time."

"W'at you mean?" Conchita regarded him suspiciously.

Starr smirked. "I mean that I'll be headin' back here for a nice little time with you." His teeth showed in a fox-like grin that suddenly was an angry snarl as Conchita's hand smacked hard against his thin, high-boned cheek.

There was a stir at the tables behind them, a low, angry growl from the steeple-hatted men. Conchita flashed a warning look at the fierce, swarthy faces.

"Quiet, you," she said in Spanish; "do not make trouble for me."

"You little wildcat——" Starr spoke in a venomous whisper. "I'll be cuttin' your claws." His hand was on gun-butt, eyes suddenly intent on the glowering Mexicans. "You fellers clear out of here," he told them. "Señor Bannock ain't wantin' you here tonight."

They gazed at him in sullen silence. Starr growled out a malediction and jerked his gun from its holster. Conchita uttered a frightened cry, seized his wrist with both hands. There was a deafening report, the acrid smell of gun-smoke. Starr tore loose from the young woman, his own hand clutched her arm in a vice-like grip, swung her as a shield between the now enraged Mexicans and himself. The steeple-hatted men crouched at their tables, guns drawn, not daring to shoot for fear of harming the señora. Starr menaced them with his gun, his thin smile wicked.

"I'm takin' a kiss for that slap," he said to the helpless Conchita.

She kicked at his shins, struggled to break his hold. He laughed, drew her closer. Rod Bannock, somewhat sobered, lurched up.

"You ain't kissing my girl, Steve. Let loose of her, damn you——"

The street-door slammed open, and two men clattered into the long, dimly lighted room. Starr spoke to them tersely.

"Watch them Mex fellers, Selmo. Drop the first one that makes a move."

"Leave loose of her, Steve——" Young Bannock's voice was thick with drink and growing fury. He swung wildly at his friend, stumbled, and fell heavily to the floor. Starr laughed, holstered his gun and tried to slip an arm round Conchita's waist. She leaned away from the reaching arm, bent sideways in an attempt to snatch at her gartered dagger. Starr pulled her upright.

"I'm takin' that kiss—and more," he said gloatingly.

A door down the room suddenly flew wide open, revealed a tall man framed against the lamplight beyond. Smoke poured from the gun in his hand. Conchita felt Starr's hard grip on her wrist grow limp. He staggered, tripped over Rod Bannock's prone body, and fell backward with a crash. Selmo flung him a startled look, and as rapidly as he could pull trigger he sent three shots at the man in the doorway of the little supper-room. A fourth shot crashed out, but the bullet was not from Selmo's smoking gun. It sped with deadly accuracy from the weapon in the other man's hand. The Double Star cowboy crumpled to the floor. His companion took one hasty, horrified look and started backing towards the street-door, his gun waving wildly at the Mexicans. There was a sudden hush, broken only by the heavy, clumsy tread of the cowboy as he backed away, and the jingle and rasp of his dragging spurs.

"Let him go, boys." Allan's quiet voice seemed to hold the steeple-hatted men in leash. They stood, tense, furious-eyed, watching the scared Double Star man making his backward retreat to the street-door. Suddenly he whirled, vanished into the night.

The giant frame of Poco Gato filled the doorway behind Allan. The latter gave him an irate look. "Keep out of sight," he said sharply. Poco scowled, hesitated, then withdrew.

"Señor!" Conchita Mendota ran towards Allan with a swirl of yellow skirt. "The man is dead!"

Allan scarcely looked at her, and, gun in lowered hand, he went swiftly to Steve Starr. The cowman struggled to an upright position, stared at his bleeding wrist.

"Looks like you got in the way of a bullet," Allan said grimly.

"Your bullet," snarled Starr. He got to his feet, leaned against a table, a hand nursing the wounded arm.

"You can't prove it was my bullet." Allan spoke coolly, a hint of derision in his voice. "Lot of bullets got to flying in this room."

Starr was staring with startled eyes at the prone figure of Selmo. "You killed him, too," he said hoarsely. "You killed Selmo."

"You can't prove it," repeated Allan. He picked up Starr's fallen gun, whirled the cylinder. "One empty shell," he said. "You did some shooting yourself, Starr."

"Went off when the girl grabbed me," snarled the cowman.

"So you say," retorted Allan. "Anyway, what's a jury going to think when you admit the gun exploded while you were trying to attack a girl in her own house. Your story won't sound good, Starr."

The cowman smothered an oath, glanced uncertainly at Conchita. Her faint smile was mocking. Starr's gaze went to the dead man.

"You killed him," he said again in a thick voice.

"Maybe it was your bullet killed him when he tried to stop you from attacking the señora," countered Allan. "Who's to say differently—claim it wasn't your bullet?"

"Rod Bannock must have seen the killing," declared Starr.

"The peeg see not'ing," exclaimed Conchita, with a contemptuous glance at young Bannock's inert bulk.

Starr glowered at her. There would be no help from her. She would swear that she saw him shoot Selmo. Her triumphant smile told him enough.

"Rogan was here," he said to Allan; "Rogan saw the whole play, and what he can tell a jury will swing you."

"If you're talking about the man who just left in such a hurry, you're all wrong, Starr. He was too busy keeping his gun on the rest of 'em." Allan threw a brief glance at the cluster of steeple-hatted men.

"Rogan'll say what I tell him," blustered Starr. "You can't get away from the fact Selmo was shot dead in this woman's *cantina*." He stared for a moment at his wounded wrist. "Guess, I'll have plenty to say, too."

Allan gave him a cold smile. "You'll keep quiet, Starr. You're in a nasty mess. It's up to you to get your dead gunman away from

here and say nothing. You're well known as one of the big cattlemen in this country. You can't afford the publicity. You won't
like the story spreading that you were shot in a drunken brawl over
a woman."

"Who in the hell are you?" demanded the Double Star man.
"You know a lot more about me than I know about you."

"You'll find out who I am if you don't keep your mouth shut
about this affair," drawled Allan.

Starr's gaze went to the dead Selmo. He had no feelings one way
or another for the slain man. In fact, the unexpected arrival of
Selmo and Rogan had completely surprised him. He'd no idea they
were in town. His Double Star men were not popular in Roaring
River. The presence of Selmo and Rogan at the *cantina* of Señora
Mendota more than mystified the owner of the Starr ranch. Allan
could have enlightened him.

Allan said softly, "Better have a doctor fix up your arm, Starr."
He was watching the cattleman closely, sensed his indecision.

Starr muttered an oath. "Only a scratch. Can 'tend to it
myself."

Allan nodded. "Good idea, Starr. No sense starting talk."

The cowman stared worriedly at his slain rider. "We got a dead
man here to explain away," he grumbled. "What'll we do with
Selmo?"

Allan glanced at the Mexicans, grouped back at their tables. He
thought he saw a way to solve the problem of the dead
man.

"We can load him on a horse and carry him a mile or two out of
town," he suggested. "You can spread the story that Rengo's gang
ambushed him on the trail."

"How about Rogan?" The Double Star owner's tone was
thoughtful. "Rogan won't be backing up that story——"

"I reckon you can handle Rogan," Allan said with a careless
shrug.

The older man narrowed eyes at him. "Reckon I can"—
he spoke softly—"reckon I can handle Rogan."

"He's on your pay-roll," reminded Allan; "he'll say what you tell
him to say if my guess is right."

Starr's mirthless grin indicated louder than words that Allan's guess about Rogan was correct. The cowman's gaze went to Rod Bannock's inert bulk. He smothered another oath.

"Wouldn't have happened but for him," he said viciously. "Couldn't keep the drunk fool from headin' out here to the *cantina*."

Conchita received this with a derisive smile. "The fox lies," she said in Spanish to Allan, "he would have come alone if he could. He is always coming here, trying to make love to me."

Starr gave her a sulky look. His Spanish was too limited to get the full gist of her scornful comment, but her smile, the contemptuous lift of her shoulder, told him enough. His face darkened for a moment, then, apparently resolved to make the best of a bad incident, he gave the angry young woman a placating smile.

"Ain't claimin' it's all his fault. I've been drinkin' plenty myself, or I wouldn't have acted like I did, señora."

Conchita shrugged. "You go queek," she said shrilly; "you no come back my *cantina*."

"Reckon you'd better be on your way, Starr," broke in Allan. He jerked a nod at the heavily snoring Bannock. "I'll get him over to the hotel."

"Suits me," grunted Starr. He turned towards the door, halted with a backward look at Allan.

"You might as well take your gun," the latter said. He proffered the weapon.

Starr took the gun with an ungracious nod and went on his way. Allan spoke again, his voice hard.

"Remember, Starr—no talk, unless you want more trouble than you can take."

The owner of the Starr ranch paused in the doorway, turned his face slowly.

"I'm remembering," he said in a choked voice, "but I ain't forgetting. What's more, you'll make yourself scarce in these parts if you've got good sense, stranger. You lock horns with plenty trouble when you lock horns with me." The door slammed behind him.

Conchita Mendota was frankly worried by the threat. "I am full of sorrow," she told Allan tearfully. "This would not have happened if you had not come here to dine with Pedro and me."

She shook her smooth, dark head. "Señor Starr is a powerful man. He can do you harm. Your life will not be safe."

His smile was enigmatic. "I'd have run into Starr sooner or later," he rejoined. "You run along, Conchita. Tell Poco all is well."

"He will feel terrible," Conchita said unhappily. "It is the second time you have saved him to-day. You must not think Pedro is a coward," she added. "He would have faced these men. He is truly a lion for courage."

"I told Poco to keep out of sight," reminded Allan. "It would have been bad for Poco if Starr had seen him here. You know what Starr's men tried to do to him this afternoon."

"Poor Pedro——" Conchita spoke sadly. "It is so easy for Señor Starr to make trouble for him." She held her gaze for a moment on the slain cowboy, and in a harder tone she added, "We can guess what brought this rascal and his friend to my *cantina*, señor."

Allan nodded. "Poco's gold——"

"*Si*. They planned to rob him, perhaps murder him, for the gold he made with his honest work." Her voice had the sting of a black-snake whip, and she added an epithet that would have made the ears of the dead Double Star man burn could he have heard.

Rod Bannock stirred, let out a low groan. Allan looked at Conchita. "You and Poco keep out of sight. No need for Bannock to know Poco is mixed up in this."

"*Gracias*." She gave him a grateful smile, sped away with a swish of full yellow skirt.

The Mexicans crowded up in obedience to Allan's quick gesture. He singled out the slim Apache youth.

"Get this dead one away, Pepe—some place across the river where his friends will find him in the trail."

"*Si*, señor. I heard what you said to the *Americano* fox and understand." Pepe's eyes narrowed mirthfully. "It must be thought the man was slain by the Rengo gang."

"I'm leaving it to you, Pepe."

"His horse will be close," Pepe said. Obeying his gesture, two of his companions dragged the dead cowboy into the darkness beyond the door. Allan followed, watched while the body was lashed to the saddle of Selmo's horse. Pepe swung into his own saddle.

"Have no fear, señor," he said confidently. "He will be found a long way from here. No one will suspect."

"Be sure you leave no tracks," warned Allan.

The Apache gave him a look of mingled indignation and amusement.

"There will be no tracks," he replied simply. In another moment the three riders and the led horse were lost in the blanket of the night.

Rod Bannock was struggling to an upright position on the hard mud floor when Allan came back from the entrance. He sat there, head bowed in his hands, apparently still in a daze and unconscious of his surroundings. Allan spoke softly to the scowling swarthy men grouped near.

"Go back to your tables, take no notice of him." Allan looked at the worried old barman. "Gaspar—serve wine to our friends."

There were pleased grunts from the steeple-hatted men, a noisy pulling out of chairs as they returned to their tables. Wine gurgled into glasses from Gaspar's bottle. Allan bent over the groaning man on the floor.

"Took a nasty fall," he sympathized.

"Sick as a dog," muttered the young man, "sick as two dogs."

Allan pulled him up to his feet. Bannock was a big man, as tall as his father but without the bulk the years would give him. Allan studied the large, high-boned face closely. It would have been a fine, strong face, but for the lines of dissipation. There was little in him that resembled rugged old Cole Bannock; also, somewhat to Allan's surprise, there was nothing in him that spoke of close kinship with Kay. She was so exquisitely made, so sharply in contrast with this hulking piece of sodden flesh. Her well-shaped eyes were beautifully hazel and her gold-brown hair was soft and fine, whereas this young man's hair was black and rather coarse, and his eyes were sunk deep in his broad face and heavily thatched. It was hard to believe that the same mother had borne these two.

Allan steadied the young man on his feet, aware of a growing dislike of him, but resolute in his purpose, which was to get him to the hotel and to bed. He was Kay's brother, and what he could do for Kay's sake he was determined to do.

Rod Bannock put a hand to his aching head. There was a wet stickiness there, and he stared with widening eyes at the red smear on his fingers.

"Who shot me?" he wanted to know.

"Nobody shot you," Allan said. "You knocked your head against the table when you fell down."

Memory was returning. Rod scowled. "Steve was tryin' to kiss Conchita," he grumbled. "Wasn't goin' to let him kiss my girl —him nor nobody——" He broke off, dawning recognition in his sunken, smoky eyes. "You're the jasper that got Kay away from the Kid," he mumbled. He pushed loose from Allan's supporting hand. "Where's Kay? What you done with my sister?" His voice lost its drunken slackness, was suddenly hard and bellicose. "Kay said you were taking her home—told me I was too drunk, and I'm wantin' to know what you've done with her—what you've done with my sister."

"Sheriff Harker took your sister home," Allan told him quietly. "The sheriff said something to you, Bannock," he added, "something about you getting over to the hotel and sleeping off your liquor."

"Harker ain't orderin' me round," growled young Bannock. He made a lurching step towards the bar. "I'm wantin' a drink, and I'm wantin' Conchita——"

"You're doing what the sheriff said." Allan seized him firmly, propelled him rapidly towards the door. Young Bannock's resistance was feeble. He was in no shape for a tussle.

One of the Mexicans came to Allan's aid, and between them they managed to get Rod to the Cattleman's Hotel. Agee Hand and Shawnee Jones were in the lobby. The former gave Allan a sharp look.

"Steve Starr come bustin' over to the stable and got his horse," he said. "Went off like the devil was chasin' him." There was lively curiosity in the old liveryman's tone. "Had his hand tied up in his blue silk bandana."

Allan ignored him. He was in no mood for explanations. He waited in grim silence while Shawnee took down a key from the board behind the desk.

"Second door down the hall from yours," Shawnee said laconically. "You'll see the iron plain—the Triple R."

Allan took the key and pushed his charge towards the stairs. There was no more resistance now from Bannock. He made his way up the stairs on unsteady legs, a hand on Allan's supporting shoulder.

Allan partially undressed him. Bannock sprawled heavily on the bed, went almost instantly to sleep. Allan found his way to his own room. He had been through quite a day of it. The bed looked good to him as he wearily got out of his clothes.

5

BILLY HALL was getting a mild going-over from the sheriff. The old law man's creaky swivel chair was tilted at a comfortable angle, his dusty boots on the office desk, his usual position when mulling over a knotty problem.

"You shouldn't have done it," he grumbled; "you shouldn't have let Starr nor nobody get to see the Kid."

A flush darkened the deputy's brick-red countenance. He was a short, plumpish man with a round, cherubic face that was completely deceptive.

"Steve was set on havin' a talk with him." Billy Hall's tone was defensive. "Steve figured he might get the Kid to loosen up some 'bout Rengo."

"Ain't for Starr to be questionin' my prisoners," complained the sheriff. He wagged his head gloomily. "Cole Bannock's fit to be tied, what with the Kid breakin' gaol and then his takin' off with Kay like he done."

Billy Hall stared unhappily through the open door. The mild reproach in his superior's voice made him hot and uncomfortable. There was cause for the sheriff to feel aggrieved. Billy was keenly aware that he had been at fault, but Steve Starr had made himself so agreeable, expressed such deep admiration for Sheriff Harker's capture of the desperado. When Starr mentioned his desire to have a look at the Kid, the deputy had acquiesced readily enough. It hadn't occurred to him that Starr would be so careless as to give the Kid a chance to grab his gun. There was nothing cherubic about the deputy sheriff's face as he reflected bitterly on the foolishness that had given the Pecos Kid a chance to break gaol. Serve him right if Ed Harker took his badge—gave him the sack.

The old sheriff seemed to read his thoughts. He wagged his head again.

"No sense weepin' over spilt milk, Billy," he reproved mildly.

"Won't blame you none if you take my badge," blurted the

deputy. "I ain't fit for nothin' 'cept playin' nurse to a bunch o cows."

"I ain't losin' the best deputy in the south-west," declared Ed Harker with a chuckle.

"You're sure one white man, Ed," mumbled the pleased Billy. "I've sure learned a lesson I won't be forgettin'."

"When a man admits he can still learn things he ain't got no cause to worry," observed the old sheriff dryly. "I've lived a long time, and I'm still learnin'," he added with a chuckle.

Billy Hall's eyes narrowed as he continued to stare into the sunlit street.

"There's that feller that got Kay Bannock away from the Kid," he muttered. "He's headin' across the street for the office."

The sheriff's eyes took on a sudden gleam behind their grizzled thatch. His deputy's gaze swung round to him.

"Who is he, Ed? What's his bus'ness here in Roaring River?" Billy Hall's voice dripped curiosity. "He's got nerve, and a greased-lightnin' brain," he added. "I'm sure grateful for what he done for Kay last night."

A black shadow cut across the sunlit doorway, which suddenly framed the tall form of Allan Rand. The sheriff returned his cheerful greeting with a laconic "Mornin', Rand." The toe of a dusty boot upturned on the untidy desk inclined slightly towards his assistant. "Meet Billy Hall—he's my deputy."

Billy thrust out a hand. "Glad to know you," he declared. "Reckon there's a lot of us are mighty glad you was in town last evening." The deputy sheriff spoke with sober warmth.

Allan's answer was a slow, good-natured smile. He dropped into a chair and fumbled tobacco and cigarette-papers from shirt-pocket. The sheriff watched him for a moment, a speculative gleam in his eyes. He liked this young man's style. He was as careful with his words as he was quick to act.

"Billy"—the old law officer's gaze shifted to his deputy—"might be a good notion for you to mosey over to the hotel and have a look at Rod Bannock. Reckon he's sobered up by now, and if he's got sense he'll hightail it for the ranch before his dad comes lookin' for him. Cole's some peeved," he added dryly.

Billy Hall scowled a bit. "I ain't playin' nurse to that fool pup," he began; then, catching the significant look in Harker's eyes, he broke off with a sheepish grin. The sheriff was wanting to have a talk with Rand and didn't want him listening in. "I savvy, boss," he said briefly. Throwing Rand a friendly nod that held a hint of curiosity, the deputy clattered out to the street, taking care to close the door as he went.

"Don't come better deputies than Billy," Sheriff Harker deposed. He slid booted feet from the desk and let the creaky swivel chair resume its normal position.

"Looks a bit easy-going," commented Allan, "sort of angel-faced, with those round blue eyes and the way his mouth turns up at the corners."

"Billy's all hard steel underneath," confided the sheriff placidly. "He's got guts."

Allan nodded. "I know that kind. You can count on 'em till hell freezes. They don't back up."

"It ain't a man's looks that count," the sheriff asserted. "It's the heart he's got inside of him." Harker chuckled softly. "Right now Billy's fit to be tied about lettin' the Kid break loose from gaol. He's sure peeved at Steve Starr, playin' the fool like he done."

Something in the sheriff's voice drew a keen look from Allan.

"Starr must have been awful careless," he observed, after a brief silence.

The sheriff looked down his bony nose. His expression was both troubled and grim. Allan sensed a reluctance to comment further on Steve Starr's strangely careless ways when paying a call at the sheriff's bastille. He waited patiently for the latter to speak.

Harker's gaze suddenly lifted in a long, penetrating look.

"Got a letter here from Truman about you," he said softly. He fumbled in a desk drawer and fished out an envelope. "Truman don't say nothin' about what brings you to Roaring River, but says you own the Circle R ranch down in the Pecos country and that he's known you since you were a kid."

"I've owned the Circle R since my father died," confirmed Allan. "I asked Sheriff Truman to write you the letter," he added.

The sheriff nodded, absorbed in rereading the letter. "He says for me to give you any help you want, but dang it, he don't say what kind of help."

"You've helped me a lot already," reminded Allan with a brief smile. "Good thing you and Cole Bannock rode up the trail just when you did, yesterday afternoon."

Sheriff Harker's chuckle was grim. "Been lookin' for you ever since this letter come in on the stage several days back." He shook his head. "Wasn't figurin' to run across you with a rope round your neck."

"Was kind of surprised myself," admitted Allan ruefully. "Those Double Star men don't seem to care much who they hang so long as they can hang somebody."

The sheriff frowned. "Reminds me of some news that come in to the office this mornin'," he said; "one of them fellers was found layin' dead in the chaparral across the river. Shot between the eyes."

Allan exhibited proper interest. "Murdered, you mean?"

"Looks like he was dry-gulched," admitted Harker. "Some feller was layin' for him in the brush. Selmo was the dead man's name, and he ain't no loss; a bad, gun-slingin' hombre like most of the fellers Steve Starr has on his pay-roll."

"Any idea who shot him?" queried Allan.

Harker shook his head. "No, and I ain't troublin' to find out. The killin' was across the river and that ain't in my county." He was silent for a moment, brows wrinkled in thought. "Most likely it was Rengo's gang. Rengo holes up some place across the river, worse luck. Makes it hard for me to go after him and his gang. Not in my jurisdiction."

"Why don't you make a deal with the sheriff across the river?" Allan asked. "The two of you should get together on this Rengo business."

Sheriff Harker gave him a surprised look. "Hell's bells, son, ain't you knowin' who's sheriff across the river?" He let out a mirthless laugh. "Steve Starr's sheriff over yonder," he went on, not waiting for an answer. "Steve and me don't see eye to eye about nothin' and never will."

The revelation that Starr was the sheriff of Puma County completely astonished Allan. The loquacious Shawnee Jones had not mentioned the fact, and Conchita Mendota had spoken of him only as one who was rich and powerful. He began to understand Cole Bannock's none too thinly veiled animosity to the man. It was

obvious that he resented Starr's apparent indifference to the depredations of the Rengo gang, especially when on the south bank of the
river. He also more clearly understood why Starr had so readily
fallen in with the plan to hush up the affair of the *cantina* the previous
night. Such a story about the sheriff of Puma County would have
been disastrous. To begin with, the affair had taken place on the
wrong side of the county line for Starr. His version would have
received little credence from Ed Harker. The sheriff of Roaring
River would have jumped at a chance to throw his detested fellow-
sheriff in gaol on the charge of threatening violence on the person
of the *cantina's* comely proprietor. His drink-befuddled brain had
been no match for Allan's shrewd wits. Starr knew he could not
prove whose bullet killed Selmo. The latter's death would likely
have been pinned on him. He would have been up to his neck in
trouble, and with a rope perhaps reaching perilously close for the
self-same neck.

Another aspect of the matter struck Allan. He looked thoughtfully at the sheriff, who was watching him with lively interest.

"You seem some surprised at Starr being sheriff of Puma," he
observed mildly. "Got you to thinkin' powerful hard, from the
look of you."

"I was thinking about Starr's part in that business at the gaol,"
Allan returned. "Come to look at the thing, you can't blame Billy
Hall for letting Starr have a talk with the Kid. Starr's a sheriff, an
officer of the law. His request would seem natural to Billy."

"In a way it was natural," admitted Harker cautiously. He
frowned, hesitated. "There's one thing about it that got me peeved.
Billy knowed Starr and me don't play good in the same yard. He
should have put Starr off, made him wait till he could see me first,
even if Starr is sheriff in his own county."

"Maybe Starr really *did* think the Kid could give him a tip about
where the Rengo gang holes up." Allan watched the sheriff under
lowered lids, saw the officer's lips tighten grimly.

"Maybe he did, and then again, maybe he didn't." Harker's tone
was curt. "I aim to find out some day soon just what *did* happen
when Billy's back was turned." The sheriff looked at the letter in
his hand. "We're kind of forgettin' about the business that brings
you to this town, son. What is it you want me to do for you?"

"It's a queer business," Allan confided. "I'm looking for a man—an old friend of my father's when they were young."

"How far back does that make it?" inquired Harker. "I'm only some fifteen years here in Roaring River. Come up from the Nueces with a herd of longhorns for Bannock and stayed on with him as foreman. Was on the pay-roll five years and then got elected sheriff."

"Must be thirty-odd years since my father last saw Tom Sherwood," Allan said.

Sheriff Harker shook his head. "Don't recall ever hearin' of any Tom Sherwood in these parts," he regretted. "Reckon he was before my time." The sheriff pondered for a moment, added slowly, "Maybe he wasn't usin' the name of Sherwood."

"There's a chance he wasn't," admitted young Rand. "You see, he left just one jump ahead of the law."

Harker grunted, waited for more. It was an old story with him.

"It was worse than just the law after him," Allan went on, "a lynch mob was after him, and it was get out while he could or dangle at the end of a rope."

"Sounds like this Sherwood was in bad sure enough," commented the sheriff. "What was they wantin' to stretch his neck for?"

"A double killing," Allan told him, "a young girl and her mother. Tom Sherwood had no way of proving his innocence—at least, he couldn't stop long enough to prove it."

Harker lifted grizzled brows. "You mean he wasn't guilty?"

"Absolutely not," averred Allan. "A year or two later a half-breed confessed to the crime."

"Mighty tough on this Tom Sherwood," commiserated Harker. "Mighty tough your dad couldn't locate him—tell him he'd been cleared."

"My father never stopped trying to find him," Allan said. "Tom Sherwood was his best friend, prospectors together. He combed the whole south-west, trying to pick up his trail."

"Reckon he's dead, most likely," Harker observed.

"Dad heard from him twice, in a roundabout way," Allan continued, "once from some place below the Rio Grande, then later from the Indian Territory. That must have been twenty-five years ago."

The sheriff mulled this over for a brief moment. "Used his own name when he wrote?" he finally asked.

"Just his name, *Tom*," answered Rand. "He wrote in the letter he was going into the cattle business and was planning to trail-herd some longhorns up some place farther north. Didn't say where."

"Looks kind of hopeless to me," Harker confessed, and then, curiously, "What makes you so set on findin' this Sherwood?"

"I mentioned that my father and Sherwood had been doing some prospecting, looking for copper, mostly in New Mexico, some place near Silver City. After the trouble that sent Sherwood on the run to save his neck, my father went into the cattle business down in the Pecos country. He'd lost heart for prospecting, with Tom gone."

Sheriff Harker nodded sympathetically. "Wanted to get his mind off the thing," he commented. "Reckon it was up there the trouble happened."

"In Silver City," Allan admitted; "well, it seems that one of the mines they'd done some work on turned out rich and an Eastern syndicate wanted to buy it. Dad sold out to them, got a lot of money for the mine."

"Tom Sherwood was half-owner," objected Harker quickly. "A deal like that wouldn't hold water."

"The syndicate fixed that," explained Allan. "Sherwood was declared legally dead, and Dad was given permission to close the sale as sole owner. He'd done his best to locate Tom."

The sheriff mused a bit. "I reckon I get your drift," he observed presently; "your dad wants Sherwood to get his share of the money, huh?"

Allan nodded. "He's kept that money in trust for years, hoping that some day he'd get word from Tom. It's piled up to a real fortune, more than a quarter of a million."

"That's a heap of money," grunted the sheriff. He chuckled. "Looks like it's due to go into your own pocket, son. Not much chance this Sherwood feller is still alive."

"Maybe not," admitted Allan. He stared thoughtfully at the older man. "In that last letter my father had from him, Tom Sherwood said he was thinking of getting married."

"I get you." Harker's eyes narrowed in a sharp look. "You

mean that maybe there's children." He shook his head. "Like lookin' for needles in a straw pile, especially if Sherwood didn't use his own name when he married."

"I'm not thinking of *children*," Allan confided. "I'm thinking that maybe there's a girl who should have this money my father has kept in trust so long. It's *my* trust, now, and if there is such a girl, I've got to find her."

"No savvy," grumbled the sheriff in a perplexed voice. "How come you think there's maybe a lone girl who should be wearin' the name of Sherwood?"

"One of those queer things that happen," Allan said slowly. He was silent for a long moment, frowning gaze intent on a man across the street.

"Rod Bannock," muttered the sheriff, "headin' for the stable to get his horse." Harker's eyes twinkled. "Agee told me how you and a Mex feller lugged Rod over to the hotel last night. Found him at the *cantina*, I reckon."

Allan nodded, his expression bleak.

"The dang young fool," fumed the sheriff. "Sure is tough on Cole, the way that son of his is actin' up." He dropped the subject. "You was talkin' about a girl, Rand——"

"Isn't much I know," confessed Allan. "I was only a youngster and wouldn't know anything about it. Only I do remember a Salty Smith who drifted in one day and got a job riding for the Circle R. Of course Dad asked him questions, the way he always did when he took on a new man. Salty was a queer sort, not given to talk, and Dad suspected he was on the dodge from the law himself and had been for a long time."

"The brush is full of them hombres," murmured the sheriff.

"Salty let out one day, when he was talkative, that he kind of thought he might have known Tom Sherwood, only he wasn't calling himself Sherwood and that he was running a small bunch of cattle in the Roaring River country."

Sheriff Harker straightened up with a jerk that brought a protesting squeal from the swivel chair. "What name did this Salty Smith say the man was wearin'?" he asked with revived interest.

Allan's answering look was gloomy. "I only got it second-hand from Dad, but it seems Salty got scared for some reason. He wouldn't tell Dad the name of the man he thought might be Sherwood. Salty never got another chance to tell Dad the man's name. A rustler's bullet got him that same night."

"Don't make sense," grumbled Sheriff Harker. "What gave Salty the notion the feller might be Sherwood?"

"Salty claimed he'd seen a letter with the name on it," replied Allan. "My father was sure it was one of his own letters, one he managed to get to him before Tom made his escape from his room in Silver City. The hotel was surrounded by the lynch mob and Dad smuggled the note to him, telling him he'd a horse staked out for the getaway. It was the sort of letter a man would keep because my father said things a good friend would say, said he knew Tom was innocent and that he would stick by him."

"I get you," the sheriff said again in a gruff voice; "a feller would likely keep that sort of letter from his best friend." He wagged his head sadly. "Too bad Salty Smith went and took that rustler's bullet before he loosened up some more." Sheriff Harker's grizzled brows suddenly bent in a puzzled frown. "I'm still wonderin' about this girl. Did Salty Smith say there was a girl?"

"Only that the man had a little baby girl and that the mother died when she was born. Claimed he'd seen a squaw carrying her round the place when he was there one time."

"Seems like your dad would have done somethin' about it," mused the sheriff.

"He did what he could, but the Roaring River country was pretty remote in those days. No sheriff's office to get in touch with." Allan spoke defensively. "He never forgot, though, and told me the whole story shortly before he died."

"I'm the first sheriff of Roaring River," observed Harker with some pride. "Roaring River ain't so much like hell's backyard as she was, but she's plenty wild yet. We got a Boot Hill out yonder that's mighty well populated, son."

Rod Bannock, on a tall, bald-faced sorrel gelding, rode into view. He drew the horse to a halt in front of the office door.

"Hello, Ed——" He stared past Allan at the sheriff. "Agee says you took Kay home last night."

"She's safe and sound, Rod——" Sheriff Harker's voice hardened. "Kay was some worried about you, young feller."

"I wasn't letting no stranger take my sister home," mumbled Rod. "Kay'd no reason to get sore at me." He slouched heavily in his saddle, obviously still feeling the effects of the previous night's debauch. His eyes were puffy and there was a dark swelling high on his cheek. Sheriff Harker looked at him sorrowfully.

"It ain't that part of it, Rod," he said. "You know why Kay was worried."

"You can keep your nose out of my affairs, Ed," fumed young Bannock.

"I'll say this much, young feller"—the sheriff's tone was acid—"you're a plain, dang fool, and you ain't got the manners of a polecat. If you were half-way decent, you'd thank Mr Rand here for what he done for your sister. You'd ought to be mighty ashamed."

"Reckon Kay thanked him plenty," sneered Rod.

"That's about enough from *you*," Allan said quietly.

Sheriff Harker spoke angrily from his chair. "Don't you savvy nothin', young feller? I'm warnin' you now not to start ridin' me with your fool talk. I'm sure fed up with you and your drinkin'. You get out of town."

"I'm not taking orders from you nor nobody." Rod Bannock's tone was sullenly defiant. "You're getting too uppity, Ed Harker. If you don't watch your step there'll be a new sheriff in Roaring River."

"Yeah?" There was a cold gleam in the old law man's eyes.

"You bet your damn' boots," sneered the young man. "He'll do something else than keep that chair warm. He'll go get Rengo—clean out a few rustlers from this county." Rod flung a furious look at Allan. "I'll say this to you, Rand—don't get notions you'll be welcome out at the Triple R." His spurs savagely raked the gelding. Dust suddenly lifted, drifted down the street in the wake of horse and rider.

Sheriff Harker appeared to be in a brown study. He shook his head with an angry snort, like an enraged bull. "New sheriff, huh," he muttered. "Wonder what the young ape is fixin' to frame agin' me?" His look went to the tall young Texan sprawled lazily in the opposite chair. "Rod don't like you," he added. "Don't seem right or natural for him to talk like that to a man that's done what you did for his sister."

"He hasn't sobered up yet." Allan's tone was indifferent. "At that it doesn't mean a hoot to me what he thinks or says."

"It's danged unreasonable of him," grumbled the sheriff. "Must be somethin' back of his hostile talk." He stared frowningly down his bony nose. "Reckon Steve Starr must have said things after him and Rod left us up on the trail last night. Steve would be sore it was you that got Kay away from the Kid. He wouldn't like you gettin' in solid with Kay. Steve's kind of sweet on her."

The sheriff's deductions drew no comment from Allan. The latter stared thoughtfully at a poster on the opposite wall. He was thinking of the little scene he had witnessed from the window of his hotel room, Starr's attempt to speak to Kay Bannock—her rebuff and hasty retreat into the store. Suddenly the black lettering of the poster took coherent form. Allan straightened up, read the brief, laconic words carefully.

One Thousand Dollars Reward

FOR THE CAPTURE OF

RENGO

DEAD OR ALIVE

Description of this man is unknown. Any clue regarding his identity is worth fifty dollars to you.

SOUTH-WEST CATTLEMAN'S ASSOCIATION

Allan's gaze swung back to the sheriff, met the latter's wry grin.

"Won't do us a dang bit of good," he grumbled. "This Rengo's got the cunnin' of a coyote. He don't leave clues layin' round. Won't be nobody droppin' in to ask for that fifty bucks."

"The Pecos Kid could tell you." Allan's tone was musing. "Too bad the Kid got away from you, Sheriff."

Harker glowered, stared at him suspiciously, and then with an annoyed gesture he went back to the subject of Allan's quest.

"You might ask Shawnee Jones," he suggested. "Shawnee's an old-timer in the Roaring River country. Agee Hand's been here most as long."

"I don't know what name to give them," puzzled Allan. "It's

clear that Tom Sherwood wasn't using his own name. He kept his secret well."

"I guess you're plain stumped," agreed Sheriff Harker; "you're stumped as bad as I am about this Rengo coyote."

"I'm not giving up," Allan said. The hint of stubbornness in his voice drew an approving nod from the older man.

"That's the talk," the latter applauded. "I'm puttin' the same sort in my own pipe. I'll get Rengo, drag the coyote out of his hole." The sheriff's drawling voice sharpened. "I'll show folks there's plenty life in the old man yet."

"I'm betting on you," chuckled Allan.

"I'm up for re-election this fall," confided Harker. "It's get Rengo—or get out of this office." He shook his head. "One reason I been takin' the Kid's escape kind of hard." He broke off, his gaze on something in the street. "Here comes Cole Bannock," he added. "He'll be lookin' for you, Rand. Cole's mighty grateful for what you done last night."

The Triple R man's massive bulk suddenly shadowed the open doorway. The big, bearded rancher paused, penetrating eyes fastened on the young Texan.

"I was right about you, Rand." There was a hearty note in Cole Bannock's booming voice. "I said you're the kind of man I need out at the ranch." A smile warmed the rancher's bold-featured face. "Man—what you did for my daughter proved me right one thousand per cent."

Allan got out of his chair, his answering smile showing amused protest. "Any man on your pay-roll would have done the same, Mr Bannock. I can't take any credit for doing what any other man would have done."

"Kay told me what you did, and I'm declarin' loud that you've got guts, young feller."

"I was just lucky," demurred Allan; "the breaks were with me."

"Breaks or brains, you sure used 'em," laughed the big man. "I'm sure grateful, Rand." He stroked his iron-grey beard. "There's no room for you at Shawnee's hotel, young man. You're ridin' back to the ranch with me, and you're welcome to stay as long as you've a mind to, and if you still want a job you've got one with the Triple R. I can use your sort," he added, with a brief, hard glance at the Rengo poster.

"I'll think it over," began Allan, and then he looked at the sheriff. The latter was suddenly out of his swivel chair, inquiring gaze on a runty, sandy-haired man hesitating in the doorway behind Cole Bannock.

"You want to see me?" There was a sharp edge to Harker's voice, a frank suspicion in his probing eyes. "I've seen you some place," he added. "Sure, I remember your face. You're that nester over to Red Canyon——"

"I got me a place in Red Canyon——" The man's tone was sullen, tinged with defiance. "I ain't no nester. I got me a deed to my forty, and I guess that don't make me a nester."

Cole Bannock interrupted him. "Who was it sold you land in Red Canyon?" he inquired gruffly. "Triple R range takes in most of Red Canyon, and I don't recall deedin' any of my land away." The cattleman's face took on a dark flush. "Where is this land you say you own in Red Canyon?"

"Down on the west fork," answered the man sulkily.

Cole Bannock stifled an imprecation. "That's where the Double Star bulges round to my line," he muttered. "Guess that explains it."

"Mr Starr sold me the land," admitted the man. "He claimed the corner was no use to him because Triple R cows was always wantin' to water at the creek come dry seasons." The man's grin was frankly malicious. "I've run a fence across the bench," he added. "No way for the cows to get down to the creek now I've got that fence up."

"We'll see about that." Cole Bannock's tone was grim.

"I know my rights," muttered the man. "Anyway, I didn't come here to talk to you about my land." He looked at Sheriff Harker, then flicked a sly glance at the Rengo poster. "Guess my business is with the sheriff."

"You'll talk business with *me*," Cole Bannock boomed. "What's your name? I'm buying that west fork corner from you."

"You can't buy what's not for sale," grinned the man. He spat over his shoulder into the street and fished out a gnawed piece of plug tobacco.

"I'll give you twice what you paid Starr for the dad-blamed land," cajoled the cattleman. "I need right-of-way to that creek water. Got to have it."

The man shook his head, chewed off a piece of plug. "My business is with the sheriff here," he grumbled. His glance again went furtively to the Rengo poster.

There was a sudden hopeful glint in Sheriff Harker's eyes. He remembered this man now, Bert Nye, a comparative newcomer and an unsavoury character. He'd seen him in town several times in the company of Luce Henders, the Double Star foreman.

"All right, Nye," he said mildly, "I'm listenin'——"

"Don't know as I should let these folks hear what I've got to tell you," Nye demurred, with a shifty-eyed look at the other two men.

"I reckon I know what your business is." The sheriff flicked a glance at the big poster. "You think you maybe can make fifty bucks, huh?"

"I can use the fifty," admitted Nye. His look went boldly now to the poster. "I've got a good tip for you, Mister Sheriff."

"Let's have it." Repressed excitement took the drawl out of the sheriff's voice. "If it's a bony-fidy tip you'll get the fifty," he promised.

Nye nodded, hesitated, apparently was revolving in his mind the best way to convey his information. "It's like this," he began, "the Pecos Kid come bustin' up to my place last night——"

"How come you know this man was the Pecos Kid?" interrupted the sheriff sharply.

"I didn't know this feller was the Kid," sulkily returned Nye. "This feller—he come bustin' in, put a gun on me, and said he wanted the best horse he could get—wanted a full outfit, saddle, rifle, canteen. Said his own horse give out on him back on the trail."

The three men were listening attentively now. Allan glanced at the sheriff, nodded, as though in part confirmation.

"Miss Bannock said the Kid told her he would get fresh horses at some man's place in Red Canyon," he observed. "Ties up, so far."

"I didn't know he was the Kid," Nye continued. "Nothin' I could do but throw a saddle on my brown horse an' fix him up with a rifle and the other stuff he wanted." Nye paused, rolled his eyes at his audience, plainly enjoying his temporary importance. "Well, he rode off a piece, then called back to me. 'Want to make fifty bucks?' he asked me. I told him fifty bucks wouldn't pay me for the horse he was stealin' from me, but it was better'n nothin'."

"Hell's bells," grunted the sheriff, "I figured you was goin' to spill some news about Rengo." His tone was disgusted.

"Let me finish about this feller," protested Nye. "He went on talkin' from back there in the dark, told me he was the Pecos Kid and had just broke gaol, and then he said for me to give Sheriff Harker a message."

"I'm listenin'," prodded Harker impatiently.

Nye gave him a crafty look. "He said to tell you that he knowed Rengo like his own brother and that Rengo's real name was Allan Rand."

A startled grunt exploded from the sheriff's lips. He stood there, stared slack-jawed at Nye's grinning face. Slowly his gaze swung round to Allan. The latter was looking at Nye, his face a mask.

Cole Bannock's voice broke the stillness that followed the sheriff's amazed exclamation. A gun was in the big cattleman's hand.

"Reckon we've got you for sure, Rengo, Rand—or whatever other name you use."

There was no misunderstanding the deadly significance of the rancher's low, furious words, the menacing gun. Allan slowly got to his feet, lifted his hands. His face was very pale.

6

A MAN came running across the street—Billy Hall, his round, ruddy face pop-eyed with amazement. Three Triple R riders clattered at his heels. One of them, short, stocky, with bright, roving black eyes closely set in a hard, swarthy face, jerked his gun from holster as he ran. Cole Bannock's gaze swung to him briefly.

"Get his gun, Wirt."

The foreman of the Triple R moved deftly behind Allan. Sheriff Harker's voice, razor-edged, shorn of its customary mild drawl, stopped him in his tracks.

"Back up there, Wirt." The gun in the sheriff's hand punctuated the words in a way that made the Triple R man hold his out-thrust hand as if caught in an invisible vice. He looked round uncertainly at Cole Bannock. The latter was gazing incredulously at Harker.

"Are you crazy?" The words choked from him angrily. "This feller is Rengo!"

Sheriff Harker's brief glance told him that Billy Hall had his gun out, was covering the two Triple R men in the doorway. The deputy sheriff was not letting his bewilderment keep him from promptly backing up his superior officer's play. The stark threat in his blue eyes held them in suspended motion, widespread fingers rigid above gun-butts. Instant death was the unmistakable warning they read in that steady gaze.

"Drop your gun, Cole—you too, Wirt Gunnel——" The sheriff's usually mild voice had the rasp of a buzz-saw about to run wild. He had done some fast and furious thinking in those fleeting and tense seconds. There was something wrong, but the wrong was not in the cool-eyed young Texan, standing there with his hands lifted under the menace of Cole Bannock's gun. Lying on the desk was a letter from a man whose probity Sheriff Harker knew to be unquestioned. The letter stated that Sheriff Truman had known Allan Rand for years, since early boyhood. It was not possible to accept this wild tale brought by Bert Nye.

Perhaps something he read in the old sheriff's fierce glance at Nye impressed Cole Bannock. More likely it was something else that made the cattleman slowly lower his gun. He had known Harker for many years, knew the honest metal of the sheriff of Roaring River. There was a good reason behind Harker's defence of Rand. Cole Bannock gave Wirt Gunnel a look that made the latter reluctantly holster his weapon.

"All right, Ed." The cattleman's tone was gruff. "Looks like you think I'm some hasty——"

"You're barkin' up the wrong tree, Cole." Sheriff Harker spoke with his customary lazy drawl, and there was reassurance in the glance he gave Allan. "No need for you to keep your hands elevated, son," he added mildly.

"Thanks, Sheriff." Allan gave Bannock an amused smile. "*I'll* say you're some hasty, Mr Bannock, and I'll say too that I'm *not* Rengo."

"Don't need to tell *me*," chuckled Sheriff Harker.

The owner of the Triple R glowered at them. It was obvious that he was troubled in his mind, also suffering from twinges of remorse, recalling the story of his daughter's peril at the hands of the Pecos Kid, a peril from which she had been saved by the courage and quick wits of the man he had been perhaps too ready to believe was the unknown stealer of cattle he longed to see behind the bars.

"All right, Wirt," he growled, "reckon I'm not needing you."

"It's up to you, boss." The Triple R foreman gave Allan an ugly glance and shouldered his way into the street. The pair of cowboys followed at his heels, with hard glances over their shoulders at Billy Hall. They were puzzled by the affair, and plainly resentful of the deputy sheriff's strangely belligerent manner towards them. They wanted Billy Hall fully to understand his luck, and that it was only because of Cole Bannock's swift transition to pacifism that he had been saved from sudden death at their trigger fingers. They went away from there with a swagger of clicking boot-heels as became the breed that feared no odds when the boss decreed battle.

Sheriff Harker resumed his creaky swivel chair and bent a chill look at Bert Nye.

"Your tip don't make the grade, Nye. You don't pull down no fifty bucks this trip."

The man scowled, stole a furtive glance at the dark thunder-cloud that was Cole Bannock's face.

"I come all the way to town in good faith," he said defensively. "Ain't *my* fault if the tip's all haywire. I'm only tellin' you what the Kid said."

"The Kid's word don't make hay in this office," derided the sheriff. He shook his head. "Of course you don't know the facts, Nye. The Kid is sore at Rand 'cause of a mix-up they had last night."

"No!" Bert Nye gave him a startled look, then stared hard at Allan.

"The Kid was tryin' to get back at him," Harker said; "framed up a cock-and-bull story for you to bring me."

The Red Canyon man's ferrety eyes took on a hot glow. He spat out an oath. "Hooked me for a fool sucker," he snarled. "That's what the Kid done, hooked me for a damn' fool sucker."

"He sure did, mister." The sheriff's tone was dry, touched with frosty contempt.

"Held me up with a gun, stole my best horse—made a fool of me!" frothed Nye. Cole Bannock interrupted him.

"Red Canyon's no place for small fish like you, Nye," he sneered. "I'm telling you again that I'll take that forty off your hands—give you twice what you paid Steve Starr."

The man hesitated, shook his head. "No use your talkin'," he said sullenly. Throwing the sheriff a brief nod, he slouched into the street. Sheriff Harker's gaze followed him thoughtfully.

"I'd like to wring his skinny neck," fumed Bannock. "He's a no-count scallawag, Ed." The rancher scowled. "He's scared to sell out to me—scared of Steve Starr. I know his breed of skunk, and I'm betting he don't really own that corner down on the west fork. It's a bluff of Steve Starr's to keep me from that creek water. He's rigged up a fake sale with this Nye jasper and got him to build that fence."

"Looks that way, Cole," agreed the sheriff mildly. "Starr figures to use Nye as a sort of buffer between him and you. Starr knows you won't want to risk the sort of talk there'd be if you went and cut a little feller's fences."

"The country's going to pot," grumbled the burly owner of the

Triple R ranch. "Too many small farmers grabbin' up land round here. There's some I don't mind, but most of 'em are cheap crooks who figure to make me buy 'em out." Bannock snorted. "I'm fed up with 'em, Ed."

The sheriff nodded absently, his mind on another and more immediate problem. He looked at his deputy, lifted shaggy brows significantly at Bert Nye, who was climbing into his saddle across the street. Billy Hall returned him a brief, understanding nod and strolled out.

Cole Bannock's ill-humour was subsiding. He gave Allan a grimly amused look.

"This Rengo jasper's got me awful jumpy, or I wouldn't have gone off half-cock. Guess that low-down cow-thief's about got my goat. I'm seein' Rengos behind every bush."

"I'm not blaming you," Allan told him with a chuckle. "Nye's story sounded convincing. We knew for a fact that the Kid was heading for Red Canyon. He said as much to your daughter."

There was frank approval in the look Cole Bannock gave him. "You're a good sport, Rand." He held out a big, hairy hand, and the two exchanged a hearty grip. "I'm a stubborn cuss," Bannock went on; "I'm set on having you on the pay-roll. I need your sort out at the Triple R."

Something like a chuckle came from Sheriff Harker. He glanced briefly at a letter on his desk, gave Allan a dry, humorous grin. The latter's head moved in a scarcely perceptible negative shake. Harker's grin widened.

"You couldn't work for a better outfit in these parts, Rand," he said. "Of course, I ain't knowin' your plans. Maybe you'll want to be pushin' up north."

Allan frowned thoughtfully, giving a good imitation of indecision. His mind was already made up. He'd no intention of pushing on to the north or anywhere else. He wanted to see Kay Bannock again —in fact, was firmly resolved to see her often. A job with the Triple R offered agreeable opportunities, and it was plain that Kay's father had taken a genuine liking for him. He'd be a fool not to make the most of the chance. Also there would be opportunities for privately pushing his quest for the missing Tom Sherwood. Allan had come to believe there was something to old Salty Smith's vague story of the man who might have been Tom Sherwood. The letter Salty claimed to have seen was an interesting clue. Allan had a hunch that it was in the Roaring River country that he would eventually solve the mystery of Tom Sherwood. He realized, too, that a prolonged stay in the town in the role of a jobless cowboy would make him a mark for suspicion. Honest people liked to know the source of a man's income, and cowboys were not usually able to remain long in idleness. There would soon be dark surmises about him. A good job with a reputable outfit like the Triple R would vastly strengthen his position, increase his opportunities for picking up clues about the man for whom his father had searched for so many long years.

Cole Bannock was regarding him with growing impatience, not unmixed with annoyance.

"Well?" He spoke with restrained irritation. "How about it, Rand?"

"You've hired me," Allan said laconically.

"Good lad!" Bannock gave him a mighty slap on the back. "I'm putting you in charge of the Mesa camp," he said. "Takes in all my range west of Roaring River Creek."

"That's where Jim Stacy runs cattle, isn't it?" queried Allan, recalling what Kay had told him about the Stacys.

Bannock nodded. "Didn't know you was a friend of Jim Stacy," he said in a surprised voice.

"Stacy was in town yesterday," Allan explained cautiously. "Somebody was telling me he used to work for you and had a place over on Roaring River Mesa."

"Jim was one of the best hands ever rode for me," asserted Bannock. "I set him up with an outfit of his own when he married Nora Riley. You'll find him a good neighbour, and he'll tip you off to a lot of things you'd want to know about the Mesa country." Bannock scowled. "I'm telling you now, Rand, you won't have no easy time out there at the Mesa camp. You've got a lot of Mexican border slam up against you, and the Double Star lies east of you with a sprinklin' of no-count small fellers in between. It's a rough country with a maze of deep canyons and pot-holes and desert, and I reckon every damn' pot-hole hides a cow-thief."

Allan's eyes twinkled. "Sounds like you're handing me a man's job," he observed.

"That's why I'm sending you out there," gruffed Cole Bannock. "I figure you're the man for the job." He chuckled contentedly. "I'm riding back to the ranch inside of an hour," he added, with an inquiring lift of his brows.

"Can't make it so quick," Allan said. "I'll be out later, towards evening."

"Suits me." Bannock nodded, turned to the door. "So long, Ed——"

Allan's gesture halted him. "I'd like to ask a favour, Mr Bannock ——"

"Anything you want, Rand, within reason." The big cattleman was feeling benevolent. "You can have your pick of the remuda, and if you don't like the boys out at the camp, you can have your pick of the outfit."

"Thanks." Allan's tone was pleased. "I know horses and I know men. Maybe I'll be a bit choosy."

"That's the talk," boomed Kay's father. "What's this favour you want of me, Rand?"

"I can use a man like Poco Gato out there at the Mesa camp," Allan told him with a level-eyed look.

"Poco!" Cole Bannock drew down his brows in a protesting frown. "You don't know Poco like I do, Rand. He's a scamp."

"I want him out there with me," insisted Allan quietly. "I'm telling you now that I'd trust Poco with anything I have. All he needs is a chance to make good."

Bannock still hesitated, bent an inquiring look at Sheriff Harker. There was a quizzical gleam in the latter's eyes. He nodded thoughtfully.

"Poco's got good reason to play square with Rand," he commented. "I figure Poco's the sort that'll go to hell for Rand after what Rand done for him."

"I wasn't thinking of that exactly," hastily interposed Allan. "I said I know men, and I know there's good stuff in that big Mexican."

Bannock was visibly impressed. "Tell Poco he's hired," he surrendered. There was a hint of grimness in his voice. "Tell him if he so much as looks cross-eyed at a Triple R calf, I'll feed him to the buzzards." Chuckling at his sinister threat, Bannock strode briskly into the street.

Sheriff Harker gave Allan a long, curious look. "You've got me some stumped, son," he confessed. "Sure seems funny for you to hire out to the Triple R. From what you let slip about the money your dad got for his share from that mine, I reckon you could about buy Cole Bannock out lock, stock, and barrel."

"Most of that money went into the Circle R," Allan confided. "Plenty of cattle, not much cash."

"You'll get a lot more if you don't get trace of this Tom Sherwood," observed the sheriff dryly. "Plenty more cash, I mean."

"I've a hunch that Salty Smith's clue will turn up something big for me," Allan declared. "That's one reason why I took up Bannock's offer of a job. I need time, Harker, and some obvious reason to stay here in the Roaring River country. You know how people soon begin to wonder and talk if a stranger hangs around a town like this."

"Sure." Sheriff Harker smiled grimly. "Folks'd soon have you down for a train robber on the hide-out, or doin' spy work for rustlers, or somethin' crooked." He nodded. "It's a smart notion, son. Gives you a chance to get acquainted and ask questions natural like. Shouldn't be surprised but what you'll stumble on somethin' that'll put you on Sherwood's trail."

"It's my hunch," repeated the Texan.

"You didn't say what your *other* reason is," slyly prodded the sheriff. "Not that it's any of my business."

Allan's smile was non-committal. He spoke casually of reports he'd heard about placer gold up in the hills, said he guessed he'd inherited his father's leanings towards prospecting.

Sheriff Harker listened with a frank scepticism he made no effort to conceal.

"You don't need to keep on with that talk, son," he said gently. His shrewd eyes twinkled, and then, his tone grave, he added, "Cole Bannock's a man that likes his way, Rand. He's a bad man to cross, a bawlin', pawin' bull when he gets on the rampage."

"I'm under no illusions," Allan assured him, with a careless shrug.

"That's a good word," chuckled the sheriff; "means you ain't fooled none." He paused, frowned down his bony nose. "You'll understand what I mean, then, when I tell you not to think Cole Bannock wants you 'cause he likes you. He wants you because he can use you. His Mesa camp is about the toughest job a man ever had dumped on him. The last three men he put in charge over there didn't last long."

"Killed, you mean?" Allan's face hardened.

"Murdered." Sheriff Harker's tone was grim. "Shot in the back—all three of 'em."

"Doesn't sound promising," agreed Allan.

"Ain't too late to change your mind," suggested the sheriff, watching him closely.

Allan shook his head. "Thanks for the tip, though," he said gratefully from the doorway. "Maybe I'll be sending for you and Billy Hall to come on the run one of these days," he added over his shoulder. "So long, Harker."

"So long, son. Good luck to you." The sheriff's swivel chair creaked as he hoisted booted feet to the desk.

"A nervy youngster," he muttered, "cool as ice and sure a fast-thinkin' hombre. Wonder what that other reason is he said was keepin' him in these parts. Shouldn't be surprised but what it's a pair of pretty eyes—Kay's eyes." Sheriff Harker indulged in a long silent laugh that made the old chair quiver. "Don't blame him none. Good enough reason for any man." He fell into a brown study from which he was presently aroused by the brisk entrance of his deputy.

Billy Hall's cherubic face wore a satisfied smile. He plumped himself down in the chair vacated by Allan and fumbled tobacco and cigarette-papers from the pocket of his calfskin vest.

"I fixed it, boss," he said.

"Who'd you get, Billy?" Harker's eyes took on the little gleam that always came when he was most attentive.

"The Injun," answered the deputy sheriff. "Pepe'll stick to Nye like a burr to a bronc's tail."

"Pepe's smart," agreed the sheriff, with a pleased nod. "Nye won't never know he's being watched."

Billy thumb-nailed a match and lit his cigarette. "Something wrong with that Nye," he declared, blowing out a mouthful of smoke. "Wonder why he come here with that cock-and-bull story about Rand."

"Looks like somebody sent him," mused the sheriff. He leaned back in the swivel chair, stared with narrowed eyes at the poster on the opposite wall. "Maybe we'll some day get Nye to tell just how he come to rig up that story about Rand."

"Saw Rand talking to Cole Bannock down the street as I come in," remarked Billy.

"Cole's hired him to take charge of the Mesa camp."

It was news that made the deputy sheriff indulge in low, profane exclamations.

Allan was on his way to the hotel when he encountered his new boss in front of Rankin's big general merchandise store.

"How are you fixed for an outfit, Rand?" greeted the cowman. "You'll be needin' blankets and such."

"Was planning to get an outfit here at Rankin's," Allan informed him.

"Tell Rankin to charge 'em to me," boomed the owner of the Triple R, " anything you need, Rand. You're a cowman. I don't need to tell you about a cow camp."

"I've enough cash to get what I want," assured Allan.

"Suit yourself." Bannock spoke brusquely. "You'll want a pack-horse. Agee Hand will fix you up." With a parting gesture he went on his way.

The tall, angular Jim Rankin climbed down from the high stool in front of his desk and gave Allan a slow smile that spread in a warming glow over his gaunt, craggy features.

"I'm only one of many who owe you a big debt of gratitude, Mr Rand." The storekeeper had the rich, sonorous voice of an orator of the old school. "I am glad to know you, sir. I'm Jim Rankin," he added, offering his hand.

Allan shook hands with him and began to tell his wants.

"Cole Bannock said you'd likely be in for some camp supplies," Jim Rankin told him, reaching for an order pad. "Cole said to charge anything you got to the Triple R account."

"Won't be necessary, Rankin." Allan spoke firmly. "I'm getting a few things Mr Bannock mightn't think necessary. I'll pay the bill myself."

"Just as you say," acquiesced the storekeeper. "If you haven't ready cash your credit is good with me, after what you did for Kay Bannock. It was a brave deed, sir. I think more of that girl than I can express. I like your style, young man. You can count on Jim Rankin any time if you ever need help."

Allan thanked him. "You make too much of it," he protested. He chuckled. "I saw you making good time up the street with your gun," he added.

"It remained for *you* to think of the girl's peril," reminded Rankin with a shake of his head.

The purchases were quickly made, and included an extra bed-roll, two rifles, and ammunition in quantities that made the storekeeper look thoughtfully at his customer. He made no comment, and after checking the amount and receipting the bill, he added a dozen sacks of tobacco to the pile on the counter.

"A few smokes on the store," he said, with his benevolent smile.

Allan's heart warmed to him. "Don't know when I'll be back in town, Rankin," he said, "but I'll surely drop in to see you next time I'm in." He hesitated. "I'm wondering if you ever heard of a man by the name of Tom Sherwood in these parts."

Rankin shook his head. No, he'd never heard of the name.

"It may have been twenty or more years ago that Sherwood was here," Allan said.

"I've been here under ten years," Rankin informed him. His gaze went thoughtfully across the street. "You might ask Shawnee Jones," he suggested. "Shawnee's an old-timer here."

Allan said he'd try Shawnee's memory, and after arranging for his purchases to be taken over to Agee Hand's livery barn he crossed over to the Cattleman's Hotel to get his few things and pay his bill.

Shawnee Jones was not in his big porch chair, Allan noticed with some surprise. Nor was he behind the desk in the lobby. Evidently on the alert for arrivals, Mrs Riley quickly made an appearance, wiping moist hands on her apron.

"Shawnee's sick in bed," she told Allan. "He gets took with pains in his stummick at times, and Doc Stevens come and made him go to bed. You're leavin' us?" She looked questioningly at the gold piece he placed on the desk.

"Soon as I can get ready," Allan replied. "Sorry I can't say *adios* to Shawnee, but you tell him how it was, Mrs Riley.

"I'll tell him," promised the woman. "Shawnee'll feel bad to miss you. He just can't quit talkin' about the way you saved Kay Bannock from that dreadful Kid feller."

"I'll look him up next time I'm in town," Allan assured her.

"You're not goin' for good, then?" Mrs Riley seemed genuinely pleased.

"I've got a job with the Triple R," Allan told her with a chuckle. "A man can't lie around doing nothing, Mrs Riley. Living at a hotel eats up money."

"Shawnee feeds the boys, broke or not," smiled Mrs Riley. "You're always welcome here at the Cattleman's, Mr Rand, and you needn't ever worry about the bill."

"I'll remember," laughed the young Texan.

Agee Hand greeted him with a wide grin when he arrived at the livery barn a few minutes later.

"So you got a job ridin' for Bannock, huh?"

"You've guessed it." Allan's glance inside the stable told him that his horse was saddled.

"Told Diego to throw on your saddle," Agee cackled. "Knowed you'd be 'long for your buck horse right soon. Cole Bannock was in—told me he was sendin' you over to his Mesa camp."

Allan nodded. "Rankin's sending over some stuff from the store, Agee. I'll need a pack-horse."

"I'll fix you up," agreed the liveryman.

"Have the pack loaded soon as the stuff gets here," instructed the Texan. "I'll be back within an hour." He hurried into the stable for his horse. Agee followed, watched with musing eyes while Allan adjusted the bridle.

"Good outfit to work for, the Triple R," he observed. "Wirt Gunnel's some hard to get along with, the boys tell me."

Allan gave him a shrewd look. It was clear that he was being warned.

"Thanks for the tip, Agee," he said, and swung up to his saddle.

Poco Gato hailed him with glad cries when he presently dismounted under the great chinaberry-tree in front of the *cantina*.

"Señor!" Poco's shout brought Conchita to the doorway. She

waved a greeting. "You look like one who is in great haste, Señor," Poco's voice took on a note of alarm. "You are leaving us?"

"You bet, Poco, and so are you——" He swung from his saddle, followed them into the bar-room. "I've got a job for both of us, Poco, with the Triple R. You're going with me to the Mesa camp."

Poco Gato's face took on a greenish tinge. He stared with shocked eyes at his *Americano* friend and patron.

"The Mesa camp, señor!" He shook his head. "That is a bad place, Señor."

"For shame," scolded Conchita. Her eyes sparkled angrily. "All the more reason why you must ride with the señor, who is our good friend."

The giant Mexican gave her an imploring look. "But the Mesa camp!" he gasped. "The last three men Señor Bannock sent there were killed. And I do not like Wirt Gunnel—a dangerous man."

"You are going." Conchita spoke firmly. "It is my wish, Pedro."

"I will go." Poco surrendered with a sad shake of his head. "Alas, I do not like it, but I will go. It is a bad place, but I could not let our señor go alone and still call myself a man."

"You're all right, Poco," chuckled Allan. "I knew all the time you're the kind of man to ride the river with."

The look on the big Mexican's face was beatific.

7

MOON QUAN plucked a long black hair from his neatly braided queue and laid it across the edge of the gleaming meat-cleaver in his other hand. The hair halved without a quiver, thus proving the razor-keenness of the blade. His slant eyes sidled a sly glance in the direction of Rosaria. He resented the housekeeper's presence in the kitchen where for more than two decades he had reigned as cook. Rosaria's growing habit of peering into his cupboards and asking eternal questions annoyed Moon Quan excessively. Her constant intrusions were the cause of a long-standing quarrel between them, and there were times when the old cook's always brittle temper assumed apparently homicidal tendencies. At least Rosaria thought so. She was not aware that Moon Quan was play-acting for her especial benefit, or that he knew the terror aroused by his significant glances when occupied as at present. As a rule, Rosaria could stand her ground and give as good as she got when it came to loud and noisy vocal recriminations, but when the cook began to be morosely engrossed with his gleaming array of kitchen cutlery the housekeeper was convinced he intended diabolical mischief.

Moon Quan nodded, apparently satisfied with the edge he had put on the cleaver.

"You allee same cluck like fool hen," he said, with a hostile look at Rosaria. "Plitty soon I cut off head."

The housekeeper paled. She was a large, over-fat woman, and her unconfined bosom quivered easily under the stress of emotion.

"Peeg!" she shrieked, "the señor will 'ang you to tree like a low stealer of cows." Rosaria stole a wary glance at the open kitchen door, decided she could hastily beat a safe retreat if it came to the worst. "I tell you two chickens plenty for dinner."

"Foh chicken," Moon Quan shrieked back at her. "I cookum foh chicken."

"Peeg!" wailed the housekeeper. "I am boss! I tell you cook two chickens."

"You no boss me," declared the indignant cook; "you get out my kitchen. You go quick!" He brandished the shining cleaver.

Rosaria's courage deserted her. With a terrified moan she picked up full black skirts and waddled frantically towards the door. The cook started after her, stamping his feet to indicate furious pursuit and shouting rapid-fire threats in Chinese.

Kay Bannock heard the loud outcries. She knew there was no real danger, but Moon Quan was too realistic at times. She ran into the patio, waved her arms wildly at the spluttering cook.

"Stop it!" Her clear young voice rose sharply above the clamour.

"Señorita"—the housekeeper was breathless with mingled rage and fright—"the peeg try keel me——"

"Nonsense," scolded the girl. She gave the old Chinese an indignant look. "You shouldn't frighten her, Moon Quan."

"She allee time make me heap mad," grumbled the cook. He hid a grin. "Allee time talkee like damn' fool . . . allee time come my kitchen."

"It is my province, Señorita," Rosaria babbled in Spanish. "I only told him to serve two chickens for the dinner you plan in honour of the stranger who comes." She glared indignantly at her long-time rival. "This vile assassin insists he will serve four chickens, for what reason only heaven knows."

Kay repressed an amused smile. "It doesn't matter, Rosaria," she soothed. "Moon Quan has charge of the kitchen and you shouldn't interfere with him."

"It is a sinful waste," wailed the housekeeper.

"Moon Quan only wants to show Mr Rand how grateful he is to him for saving my life," Kay told her. "He wants to cook a fine dinner."

"You bet your life," asserted Moon Quan. "He vellee good man. I make vellee fine dinner foh him." He regarded Rosaria blandly and added in his own tongue, "Fat cow, you attend to your own affairs and leave me to mine."

Rosaria sensed she was being insulted, but, obeying Kay's gesture, she let the argument drop and went back to her own domain with as much dignity as her indignation and unwieldy person could manage. Kay shook her pretty head reproachfully at the triumphantly grinning cook.

"I know you didn't mean any real harm, Moon Quan, but I don't like your terrible play-acting."

The reprimand drew a low chuckle from the old Chinaman. "You mad, Missie Kay?" His tone was placid, indicated serene unrepentance.

"You scare me terribly," the girl told him aggrievedly. "It's mean of you to scare me."

Moon Quan fingered his cleaver for a moment. "No likee scare you, Missie Kay. I tell boss I quit. You get 'nother China-boy cook foh you."

"Don't be silly," scolded Kay.

Moon Quan gave her a bland, inscrutable smile. He knew he was forgiven.

"I go killum chicken," he said briefly, "foh chicken." He shuffled away towards the big barnyard.

Kay followed him through the patio gate and made her way to the corral, where a grizzled-whiskered, bow-legged man was saddling a trim red-bay mare. He looked round with a grin as the girl hurried up.

"Chuparosa's some frisky, Kay," he said. "Mebbe I'd best take the jumps out of her afore you fork saddle."

"Don't you insult me like that, Limpy Gregg!" Kay pretended vast indignation. "I can ride anything with the best of you, and you know it."

The chore man's grin widened. It was an old joke between them. "You sure can ride 'em," he cackled. "Like you say, I sure know how close you can stick to a saddle, seein' it was me that first put you in one." He wagged his head. "Seems like 'twas only yesterday I put you on that pinto pony the boss had me gentle for you— and now you're a grown young woman."

"Dad says you were the best rider in the outfit," Kay declared. She swung up easily into the saddle, and gave the chore man a fond smile.

"I wasn't one to pull leather no time," crowed Limpy. "Ain't no back-number to-day, nuther, even if I did get my legs busted in that dang stampede."

He watched as the girl rode away towards the avenue gate, an admiring gleam in his faded blue eyes. She sat her saddle with the

sure ease of a born horsewoman. The red mare arched sleek neck,
made dancing sideway steps, pretended she was afraid of a piece of
paper fluttered across the yard by the wind. Old Limpy Gregg
chuckled, then suddenly scowled. Rod Bannock was running across
the wide strip of Bermuda grass between the ranch-house and the
avenue. Limpy had no use for Rod.

"Looks like he's mad," muttered the chore man. "Can tell by
the look of the cuss he's goin' to pitch into Kay like blazes."

Kay greeted her brother with a doubtful smile. There was no
mistaking the black look on his face as he strode into the avenue.
She brought Chuparosa to a standstill.

"What's wrong?" Her tone was chilly. It was painfully
apparent that Rod was still in the throes of a bad hangover. There
was a tight, pinched look to his mouth, an ugly gleam in his blood-
shot eyes.

"I won't stand for that Rand bird, Sis," he exploded. "You and
Dad have sure gone crazy."

"You can tell it to Dad," retorted the girl. "I didn't hire Mr
Rand. Dad hired him, and it's Dad who said Mr Rand was to have
dinner with us to-night."

"I won't stand for him comin' here," shouted her brother.
"Rand's no good. I told him not to show his face here."

"You forget that Mr Rand saved my life," reminded Kay icily.
"He showed himself to be a man while you were carousing with
your friend Steve Starr."

"Starr and I would have done what he did, and you wouldn't even
have thanked us," sneered Rod. "At that we hit the trail soon as
we heard the Kid had broke gaol and that he might run into you
some place on the road."

"Mr Starr was there when the Kid broke gaol." The girl's tone
was furious. "You're still drunk, Rod. You don't even know
what really happened."

He was glaring at her suspiciously. "Where're you headin' for?"

"None of your business," retorted Kay. "Get out of the way!"
She gave the restive mare her head, and with a snort Chuparosa
went into a dead run down the winding avenue.

The forward surge of the mare had caused Rod to take a hurried
backward step. He tripped in the grass-grown levee and sprawled

his length. Muttering furious incoherencies, he picked himself up and stood for a moment, scowling gaze fixed on his sister as she fled through the lower avenue gate. One thought loomed large in his fuddled mind. Kay was going to meet Rand.

The brief, ugly scene between brother and sister worried old Limpy Gregg. He was ignorant of the cause of the quarrel, but he knew Rod had been drinking heavily, and when he saw him suddenly start on the run across the corral Limpy shrewdly guessed what was in the wind. Rod planned to get a horse and chase after the girl.

The old chore man muttered an angry exclamation and hobbled with surprising speed into the stable. Only one horse stood in a stall at the far end. The lower door was open. Limpy worked swiftly. It was up to him to give Kay a chance to put a lot of distance between herself and her drunken brother.

Rod hurried into the stable just in time to see the horse vanish with a flurry of gleeful up-flung heels into the pasture.

"Hey, you old fool! I want that horse!"

Limpy faced round slowly, stared at the angry young man with chill eyes.

"You nor nobody talks thataways to me," he rasped. "What's eatin' you, Rod?"

"I wanted that horse!" shouted young Bannock. He was breathing heavily.

"How'd I know you wanted him?" tartly rejoined Limpy Gregg.

"Well, you know it now," grumbled Rod. "Go catch him up—him or any other horse you can get a rope on quick."

"I ain't the horse wrangler on this ranch," protested the old chore man. "Go catch up your own broncs. I got other things to 'tend to." His calloused fingers closed over a long-handled pitchfork. "Got these stalls to clean out and bed down with fresh grass," he added.

Perhaps it was the knowledge that Limpy Gregg was one of the oldest members of the Triple R outfit and a man held in high esteem by Cole Bannock, or possibly it was the pitchfork that Limpy held like a great pronged spear in his hands. There was a cold gleam in the old man's eyes that spoke more loudly than words. Kay's brother flung him a black look, snatched a rope from a peg, and pushed his way into the pasture. Limpy grinned triumphantly at the disappearing broad back. Rod Bannock wouldn't have an easy time of it, catching up a horse on foot. Be another fifteen or twenty minutes before he could set out in chase of Kay.

Doubts began to trouble the girl as the ranch-house dropped from sight behind the ridge. She pulled Chuparosa to a halt and stared irresolutely down the long slope to the willow brakes that followed the twisting course of the turbulent Roaring River. She had not *really* intended to ride far enough to meet Allan Rand, but her brother's question, the sneer in his eyes, had crystallized a vague impulse into a definite resolve.

Kay's smooth brow puckered into a tiny frown as she thought the thing over. She was not so sure now that she wanted to meet Allan. He might think her over-anxious to see him, miserably misunderstand her. For some reason she unconsciously recoiled from doing anything that risked lessening his regard for her. If only her dreadful brother had kept his nose out of it. She was furious with Rod, wanted him to see her ride into the yard with Allan Rand. It would serve him right, give him to understand he had no authority over her comings and goings.

Her gaze went pensively to the rugged slopes of San Vicente rising sheer from the desert floor. Smoke-like clouds hovered above the snow-capped peaks; otherwise the sky was a faultless blue. The great mountain mass was fifteen miles beyond the river, and still beyond lay the remote Roaring River Mesa country. It was over there Allan Rand would be going, to take charge of her father's Mesa camp. The thought unpleasantly chilled the girl. She resented her father's queer way of rewarding the man for his courageous rescue of herself from a dreadful fate. She had heard tales of the Mesa camp, enough to know it was a place where death constantly lurked for the unwary. It was a good place to send a man one desired to be rid of. The thought horrified Kay. No such cold-blooded reason could be at the back of her father's plan to send Allan Rand to the camp. His motive was more simple, a bit grim but entirely practical. Cole Bannock needed a man of Rand's metal at troublesome Mesa camp. The problems there demanded both iron nerve and quick wits. Allan Rand had proved he possessed these needed qualities in abundance.

Something moved, down there in the willow brakes, held the girl's idling gaze. Her slim body went rigid in the saddle. A lone rider, leading a pack-horse, took shape, and for all the distance that lay between, Kay knew them for what they were. Her father had mentioned that Allan Rand would be packing in a new outfit from Rankin's.

She relaxed, hands resting on saddle pommel. Fate had made the decision for her. Given another minute, she would have turned Chuparosa up-trail for home. Kay knew now she would not return to the ranch alone. She would ride into the yard with Allan Rand. She hoped her brother would be there to see them.

Allan's keen eyes were quick to recognize her. The sight of the girl waiting up there on the rim-rock sent a warm glow through him. Kay Bannock had been in his thoughts almost constantly since he had set out from Agee Hand's livery barn, but not to the exclusion of certain hints dropped by the liveryman.

"Sure tickled you got you a job, son." Agee's tone had lacked enthusiasm. "The Triple R is a good outfit, only I'm thinkin' Cole has sure handed you a tough deal with his Mesa camp."

Allan grinned. "Don't be a croaker, Agee."

"Call it croakin' if you will, son, but I ain't takin' bets you'll be back this way." Agee's gloom was riding him heavily. "Fellers as rides to Mesa camp don't ever come back."

"Harker said as much," admitted Allan. "Harker told me the last three men Bannock sent out there were shot in the back."

"Rustlers lay round in yonder brush like rattlesnakes," declared Agee.

"I've good medicine for rattlesnakes," chuckled Allan. "No need for you to worry, Agee."

Agee refused to let go of his dire forebodings. "Maybe you didn't take in what I said about Wirt Gunnel awhile back," he went on. "Wirt's got a way of ridin' fellers he don't like, and from what he spilled when he come in for his horse this mornin' I'm guessin' he don't like you a-tall."

"You know what happened in the sheriff's office," reminded Allan. "He'll get over it."

"You're gettin' off to a bad start with him," asserted Agee.

"Maybe it was a mistake, but Wirt ain't one to ever blame himself for a mistake. He'll be layin' for you."

"I savvy his kind," Allan reassured the old man.

Agee Hand shook his head gloomily. "Young Bannock's cussin' you out, too," he worried. "Acts like he don't want you to see his sister ag'in. He sure won't like you showin' up at the ranch."

It was not until he was several miles out on the trail that Allan realized with some chagrin that he had not asked Agee if he had ever known of a man who might have been Tom Sherwood. His plan to question Shawnee Jones had been balked by the hotel man's illness. Both Shawnee and Agee were old-timers in the Roaring River country, according to Sheriff Harker. There was a possibility that either of them could have furnished him with a valuable clue. The matter would have to wait until he could see them again.

For a moment Allan half regretted the impulse that made him accept Cole Bannock's offer of a job with the Triple R. His business in Roaring River was to find some trace of Tom Sherwood. He firmly believed there was something to Salty Smith's tale of a baby girl. She would be a young woman now, and the rightful owner of all that should have been her father's. Old Salty Smith had been so positive about the letter he had chanced to see. The man carrying that letter addressed to Tom Sherwood could have been none other than his father's long-missing friend.

Thoughts of Kay Bannock returned, banished the momentary regret. Kay was a magnet that drew him irresistibly across the miles to her father's ranch. Allan made no attempt to deceive himself. Kay Bannock was the main reason why he was on the Triple R payroll. He knew too that Conchita had shrewdly guessed his secret.

"I fear for you," the young Mexican woman said simply; "I see dangers waiting for you, but not all of them at Mesa camp." Her dark eyes clouded. "It is said that Señor Starr is in love with the señorita, and he is close to her brother."

The warning was too unmistakable for Allan to misunderstand. Conchita wanted him to know that in Kay Bannock he would confront perils greater than he might find in the Roaring River Mesa country. His slow smile thanked her, but it was to Poco Gato he spoke.

"You will reach the camp at sundown to-morrow," he instructed. "If I am not there, do not show yourself."

"How will I know?" queried the big Mexican, frowning at him.

"What was that song you were singing as we came down the trail yesterday afternoon?" Allan's eyes twinkled.

"*La Paloma, si*. I sing *La Paloma*——" Poco rolled a languishing look at Conchita.

"Only you didn't call her La Paloma," reminded Allan with a laugh. "La Conchita was the lady's name you used."

"*Si*," grinned the Mexican, "always I call her my Conchita."

Allan gave the flushed Conchita a dancing-eyed look. "Listen, then, Poco," he said, "this will be the signal—my voice at sundown, singing *La Paloma*, only it will be as you sing the song. If you hear me call the lady La Conchita, you will know it is safe to show yourself. If I call her La Paloma, keep from sight until I signal as agreed."

"It is understood," acquiesced Poco Gato. He nodded, adding solemnly, "The song will be our password, Señor. It is good to have a password. *La Conchita* means all is well, but *La Paloma* warns of danger. My friends must know of this password."

"Your friends?" Allan's eyebrows lifted questioningly.

Poco exchanged looks with Conchita. The girl hesitated, said slowly, "We have good friends, Señor, brave men who, like you, are without fear. They are your friends, too. It will be a good thing for them to know the password."

Her words remained with Allan Rand as he journeyed from town to the Triple R ranch. A twist of fate had brought him a strange friendship that was bearing the rich fruit of devotion and loyalty. He felt he could count on the friendship of Poco Gato and his Conchita, whose friends were his friends too. For all the dark prophecies of Agee Hand his heart was light as he followed the trail through the thick willow brakes. At the end of the trail would be Kay Bannock. For a few hours at least he would be with her again, and when he pushed on to the rugged, danger-infested wilds of Roaring River Mesa he would carry with him refreshing memories of her delights. Only once did he have a disturbing doubt. Rod Bannock had warned him to keep away from the ranch, meaning, of course, from his sister. Allan shrugged the doubt aside. Something had happened to him that never-to-be-forgotten moment when he first looked into Kay's clear, honest eyes. No man, let alone Rod Bannock, could keep him from seeing Kay. Not even Cole Bannock could swerve him from his purpose. Only the girl herself had the power to bring his resolve to naught.

And so it was that Allan Rand's heart leaped when he glimpsed her waiting up there on the rim-rock. He knew as if she had called to him that she waited for him, had ridden down the trail to welcome him. He spoke curt, urging words to the pack-horse at the end of the lead-rope. Old Agee had picked him a good beast, nimble and willing. Buck fell into his swift running walk, a pace that kept the lightly laden pack-horse moving at a lively jog.

"Welcome, cowboy!" The girl's voice was cool, betrayed no hint of her own excitement and pleasure. "So you've hired on with the Triple R outfit, mister."

"Sure have, lady." There was a chuckle in Allan's voice. "Kind of bamboozled your dad into thinkin' I'm a top hand."

Kay laughed, let down her armour for a brief moment as she looked into his eyes. "I'm right glad to see you again, mister." And then, aware of the lilt in her voice, she flushed, lifted her chin, and pretended to study him with cool appraisement. "Dad is right hard to fool," she said severely. "I'm advising you to make dust away from this ranch if you're not what you've told him you are."

Her make-believe rebuff made no impression on him. He sat relaxed in his saddle, smiling contentedly at her, fingers busy with tobacco and cigarette-paper. He had seen enough in that brief, unguarded moment to know she was more glad than she dared put into words.

They had met for the first time only yesterday, in front of the wide doors of Agee Hand's livery barn. The yellowing late after-noon sun had put bright gold in her brown hair and made more lovely the hazel lights in her eyes. Later that same evening fate had brought them together again, drawn close in the bonds of perilous adventure. Common dangers shared make life run swiftly, and so at this third meeting on the rim-rock above the turbulent flood of Roaring River Allan and Kay felt more to each other than ordinarily possible in the space of some twenty-four hours. Events had rent apart the calendar for them. The years behind suddenly ceased to be of importance in their lives—shadowy, vague, empty years. Instinctively they knew, as they sat there on their horses, looking at each other, that a dawn of a new world was rising above the horizon of their lives. A strange, indescribably beautiful dawn that left them both breathless and filled their eyes with mingled wonder and fear. Wonder at the perfection spread before them, fear lest evil mischance should destroy a prospect so sublime.

Allan broke the silence that held them in thrall. He spoke lightly, and none would have guessed the thoughts that had moved him to an unwonted paleness.

"Your Chuparosa mare, I reckon?" he drawled, with an approving smile.

"Bred and raised on the ranch," Kay told him. "Limpy Gregg gentled her for me. Limpy's a wonder with colts." She spoke a bit breathlessly, acutely aware that her heart was going at an unaccountable rate. "Rod wanted to gentle her," she went on. "Dad wouldn't let him. Rod is rough with young stock, and Dad was afraid he'd spoil Chuparosa.".

"Speaking of your brother——" The bleak note in Allan's voice lifted the girl's chin in a startled look at him, and then, following his frowning gaze, she uttered a dismayed little cry.

"He's coming! Oh, Allan—it's Rod—and—and he's not himself."

He gave her a quick glance, thrilled at her unconscious use of his name.

"I can't run away." He spoke curtly, and then, seeing the distress in her eyes. "You want me to leave you, Kay?"

For a moment her look clung to his, and then, with another lift of her chin she said almost fiercely, "No—never—*never*——"

"I won't." Allan spoke quietly, but his voice was touched with hard steel. "I'll never leave you, *Kay*." His tone softened to an indescribable tenderness as he repeated her name.

She flung him a brief, tremulous glance, seemed to draw strength from the quietly efficient look of him. Her colour returned and the fear went from her eyes.

"I must tell you something," she said. "Rod seemed to suspect I was coming to meet you." Kay flushed as she realized her inadvertent slip, floundered helplessly. "I—I wasn't *really*—oh, well, what if it *was* in my mind? And anyway it was none of his business."

"He tried to stop you?" Allan's tone was hard.

"We quarrelled dreadfully," admitted Kay. Her glance went apprehensively to the approaching rider. "Oh, Allan—I'm afraid. Rod—he's been drinking."

There was no time for more. Rod Bannock's voice, drink-thickened, hoarse with passion, lifted above the clatter of galloping hoofs.

"I told you to keep away from the ranch, damn you, Rand!"

He jerked cruelly on the bit, drew the blown horse to a standstill. He was hatless, his big, sodden face streaked with sweat that trickled down his throat and made tiny, iridescent globules on the coarse black hair that showed above the open collar of his flannel shirt. Allan was struck with the look of Indian in him. Surely a strange man to be brother of the slim, finely made girl on the red mare, her eyes coolly defiant and unafraid now.

"I've a right on this ranch, Bannock." Allan purposely kept his voice down. For the girl's sake he must avoid violence if possible. "Your father hired me," he added, with a good-natured grin at the glowering young man. "He told me to come out to-night, and that's all there is to it."

"Not by a long shot," shouted Rod. "You're fired pronto, mister." He dragged at the gun in his holster. "I'm firin' you, Rand—and this backs up my say-so!"

"Rod!" Alarm sharpened Kay's voice. "Put that gun down!"

His eyes rolled in a resentful look at her. "Shut your mouth, Sis. Ain't you got any sense, ridin' out alone to meet this jasper? You need a damn' good spankin'—that's what you need, acting like a little fool."

"You're the fool," retorted the girl hotly, "a drunken fool."

Allan's cool voice broke in.

"Let's talk this over, Bannock," he said. "What is it you have against me?" Ignoring the gun in the other man's hand, he slid from his saddle.

"Keep back," snarled Rod Bannock. His gun lifted. Allan made no further move, stood motionless, his back to the buckskin. Rod looked at his sister. "Get started," he ordered roughly, "you make tracks back for home and leave me 'tend to this skunk."

"Let's talk it over," Allan said again. "What's it all about, Bannock?"

"There's nothin' to talk over," Rod told him. "I just don't like you, Rand, and I'm telling you to get out."

"Why don't you like me?" Allan shook his head wonderingly. "What have I done to you?"

"You're no good," blustered Kay's brother, "you're a rustler—a Rengo man."

"Who says so?" queried Allan. He was staring intently down at Chuparosa's right forefoot. "Looks like the mare's picked up a stone," he added. He was suddenly at the girl's stirrup and bending down, apparently examining the mare's hoof. The move presented his back to the gun in Rod's hand.

"Steve Starr says so," the latter was saying loudly. "He's got you spotted, Rand."

"Just a moment, Bannock." Chuparosa's foot came up lightly to the pull of Allan's hand.

"Quit foolin' with the mare and listen to me," grumbled Kay's brother. The gun in his hand wavered uncertainly. "There's more I don't like you for. You figure to get in solid with Kay 'cause of last night, and you've somehow managed to pull the wool over Dad's eyes—got him to give you a job with the outfit."

Allan slowly lowered the mare's foot and straightened up, and the move as he faced round brought him within a long arm's reach of the gun in the other man's hand. Suddenly Kay sensed his purpose. She stiffened in her saddle, sent a startled look over her brother's shoulder.

"Rod—those men—behind you——"

Young Bannock, taken off guard, swung his head for a look, and in that brief instant Allan's lightning reach had snatched the gun from his hand.

"We've had enough of you, Bannock," he said tersely. "I'm riding on to the ranch with your sister, and you've nothing more to say about the matter."

Rod stared in sullen silence at their cold faces. It was plain that his drunken courage was oozing with the loss of his gun.

"It's your own fault, Rod," his sister told him in a troubled voice. "Why don't you act decently?"

"Think you're smart," sneered Rod, "pullin' off that trick so as he could get my gun. I'll pay you back good for this, you little she-devil."

"Go back home and sleep it off," begged the girl. "You don't know what you're doing, Rod."

"I'll be back home when that Rand skunk has cleared out, or is dangling from a tree," Rod Bannock told her, with an ugly laugh. His horse squealed under raking spurs, went plunging down the hill.

Kay's face was pale as she silently watched him go. Allan climbed into his saddle, looked at her soberly.

"Do you believe Starr's talk about me?" he asked as she met his eyes.

Kay shook her head. "I'd never believe anything like that," she answered simply. "You know that, don't you, Allan?"

"Yes," he said, his voice a bit unsteady, "I know it, Kay."

They rode on, up the winding trail, towards the big ranch-house showing its red roof through the trees. And after them crawled the shadows of night. Kay wondered, and Allan wondered, if those swiftly creeping shades of darkness would overtake them, engulf them both in smothering blackness.

8

COLE BANNOCK saw them from the doorway of the ranch office as they rode into the yard. Something in the girl's face, lifted to the man on the tall buckskin horse, seemed to arrest his attention. He watched for a moment, his expression thoughtful, touched with displeasure. Whatever it was that disturbed him, he was agreeable enough to the newest member of the Triple R outfit at the dinner-table later that night. His jovial good-humour in no way deceived Moon Quan. The workings of the big cattleman's mind were no mystery to the astute old Chinaman. He sensed the false note in Cole Bannock's uproarious gaiety. There was a sly speculation in the rancher's eyes when he looked at Rand, the furtive wariness of an old wolf fearful of an unseen threat that the wind has brought to its nose. It was obvious to Moon Quan that something deeply troubled his boss.

The old cook was puzzled. He was keenly interested in any affair that affected the Bannock household. He felt that the cause of the boss's strangely masked perturbation was the new cowboy for whom Missie Kay had requested Moon Quan's best efforts for a fine dinner. His brief, sharp scrutiny of the young man had quite satisfied the wise old Chinaman. It worried him to feel that the stranger was the cause of Cole Bannock's mental disturbance. His shrewd guess was that the boss was not pleased at Missie Kay's obvious liking for the young man. Moon Quan's immediate reaction was to lend the girl his subtle support.

"I bling cake plitty soon now," he said as he shuffled round the table, removing the plates.

"Cake!" Cole Bannock's shaggy brows lifted in a surprised look at his daughter. "Some dinner we're gettin' to-night, Kay." His laugh boomed. "Wonder what's got into Moon Quan, givin' us chicken an' cake? This ain't Sunday."

"I wanted Mr Rand to have *one* good dinner before he went over to the Mesa camp," smiled Kay. "He won't get chicken and cake out at the camp, Dad."

"I'll say he won't," chuckled her father. "Pork and beans, and beans and pork, at a cattle-camp. Chuck-wagon fare don't include chicken and cake." His tone sobered. "Just the same, I reckon Rand is welcome to the best Moon Quan can fix up for him. Nothin's too good for the man who got my daughter away from the Pecos Kid, and not a hair of her head harmed."

"That's what Moon Quan said when I told him about it," Kay said, smiling brightly at the two men. "The cake is a surprise, though."

"Serve Rod right for runnin' out on us," declared Cole Bannock with another of his too-hearty laughs. "Wonder what's become of the boy. Went off without sayin' a word to nobody."

To Kay's relief, the cook came in from the kitchen, a three-decker chocolate cake on the platter in his hands. She had decided not to mention the meeting with Rod on the rim-rock, the near-tragedy averted by Allan's cool efficiency—and her own quick wits. She clapped her hands, exclaimed delightedly,

"Oh, Moon Quan, it's gorgeous—and a candle!"

The Chinaman placed the cake in front of her and stepped back, a bland smile on his face. The candle, hastily dug out of a kitchen drawer, was an inspiration of the moment, born from his resolve to show the boss his approval of young Rand.

"Foh celeblate Meester Land eat dinnah first time here," Moon Quan said placidly. "Maybe so next year we have two candle foh him." He gave Cole Bannock an inscrutable look from shoe-button eyes and made his shuffling way to the kitchen-door.

"The darn' old highbinder," muttered Cole Bannock. He stared at the tall candle, something like a frown darkening his face. "Candle, huh." He gave Allan a somewhat wry smile. "Looks like you've made a hit with Moon Quan."

"It was sweet of him!" cried Kay. "But it's awfully funny—a tallow candle. I wonder what made him do it! I'm sure he must have only just thought of it." She laughed softly. "It's a sign he likes you, Mr Rand."

Her father's high mood seemed to have become lost in the dark clouds of a deepening gloom. His morose abstraction was too obvious to be ignored. Kay gave him a worried look. She knew there was much to cause him anxiety—the drought, rustlers, and a natural concern about Rodney. The latter's tendency to wild ways had already been the cause of several violent outbreaks between them. The girl would have been astounded could she have divined the cause of Cole Bannock's curious distemper. Rodney was only indirectly involved in an affair that was far beyond Kay's wildest imaginings.

The rancher brushed his beard free of the crumbs from his hastily devoured cake and pushed back his chair.

"You'll be hittin' the trail at sun-up, Rand," he said curtly.

Allan nodded. Bannock's sudden transition from benevolent good-humour to a morose, almost antagonistic manner vaguely perturbed him. He put it down to the rancher's secret annoyance over his son's unexplained absence.

"You said I could pick my own men," he reminded, "and I'll want to look over the remuda."

"The wrangler'll have plenty horses in the corral for you to look over," assured Bannock. "Wirt'll be in late to-night. You can thresh things out with him in the morning." The big cattleman smiled grimly. "There'll be no trouble choosin' a crew, Rand. Any man that draws pay from the Triple R has got to stand ace high. You can pick 'em blindfold and any one of 'em top-hand."

"There's more to it than that," Allan commented dryly.

"Well"—Cole Bannock shrugged wide shoulders—"it's between you and Wirt, and if Wirt tries to hold out on you, I ain't buttin' in. Wirt's a good cowman, knows his business." He drew a pipe from a coat-pocket. "I'm going over to the office," he added, looking at his daughter; "got some tally-sheets to check up."

His heavy tread died away into the night. Kay looked across the table at her companion. "The Stacy ranch is over there, in the Roaring River Mesa country," she said thoughtfully. "You'll like Jim and Nora."

" I'll look them up," promised Allan.

"I hope you will. I'm awfully fond of Nora, and—and, Allan" —she gave him a shy little smile as she used his name—"perhaps Jim can be of help to you."

"I'll remember," he promised again.

"Jim Stacy is the sort of man I think was in your mind just now, when you said what you did to Dad."

"You read my thoughts easy as that?" His smile was quizzical. "I'll have to mind myself." And then, softly, "I can't help it, Kay, if my thoughts are about—*you*——"

She was silent for a long moment, fingers playing with the cake-crumbs on her plate, her eyes downcast, and then suddenly her look lifted to his.

"I don't mind," she said simply; "I—I like you to think of me."

The kitchen-door pushed open, and Moon Quan shuffled into the room. He gave them a bland smile.

"You likee cake?" His bright shoe-button eyes played sharply over their faces.

"You bet," grinned Allan.

"I makee him celeblate foh you," chanted the cook. "You good fliend Missie Kay—you save her life—you vellee good man, I think so."

"The candle was lovely," broke in the girl; "it was sweet of you, Moon Quan."

The old Chinaman chuckled. "She vellee good—allee same angel." He looked at Allan. "Maybe so you think she vellee nice —like angel."

"Moon Quan!" Colour waved into the girl's cheeks. "Don't be silly."

"I vellee smart man," asserted the cook blandly. "I savvy lots." He shuffled to the window, peered into the night. "Plitty soon vellee nice moon. I think so Missa Land likee see moonlight in garden."

Kay gave the man opposite a shy, confused look. "He wants to get rid of us," she declared with an embarrassed laugh.

There was a satisfied gleam in the cook's eyes as he watched from the window until the darkness under the trees hid them from view.

It was not really a garden, but a large grove of tall trees that reached several hundred yards down to a little creek. The sound of running water came to their ears and the low, eerie call of an owl. Behind them twinkled the ranch-house lights, and other lights from the office and the bunk-house. They walked slowly, without words. Both of them were afraid of words just then. It was enough that they were alone together in the blanketing darkness of the great trees that here and there let down a shimmering patchwork of stars. And when finally words came, the talk was of little things. Chuparosa,

Limpy Gregg, the never-ending feud between Moon Quan and Rosaria. Old Shawnee Jones and his insatiable curiosity, the generosity that made his hotel a haven for many a jobless cowboy.

Allan came to a standstill. "Horses coming," he said. "Wirt Gunnel, I guess."

"He's back early." Kay shook her head. "I don't like Wirt Gunnel—much. He—he's so hard."

The promised moon was up now. Allan saw they were close by a picket-fence overgrown with some sort of thickly brushed vine.

"Grape-vines," Kay said, noticing his look. "Our little grave-yard," she added.

The fence only enclosed a few square yards, a small, weed-grown plot with a large oak-tree in the centre. It was a very private cemetery, Kay told Allan. Only one grave.

"Rob Hood's," the girl said. "Rob Hood was an old friend of Dad's. I don't remember him. He was killed by border raiders, and Dad buried him here."

They wandered on, suddenly espied a speck of red fire moving towards them, and then the big, vague shape of Cole Bannock, framed in pale moonlight between two huge-girthed oaks.

"Here we are, Dad." Surprise, a touch of nervousness, gave sharpness to Kay's voice. "Are you looking for us?"

"Yeah." Her father removed the cigar from his lips. "Moon Quan said you were out here some place." There was a brusqueness in his voice that hinted of repressed annoyance. "Wirt got in some early, Rand. I figured it would be a good idea if you talked things over with him to-night. Save time in the mornin'."

"Suits me," assented Allan (which was far from the truth). He'd no wish to see Wirt Gunnel just then. He wanted to be with Kay Bannock these last moments. Something in the girl's rigid body as she stood there told him the same desire was in her.

It was obvious that Cole Bannock had no intention of giving them any moments alone. He moved out of the path, indicated with a gesture for them to precede him.

"Looks like Kay's been showing you Rob Hood's grave," he said as he followed at their heels. "Saw you come out from there." His heavy voice took on an oddly softened note. "Robin was a pardner of mine in the old days. A hombre to ride the river with, he was. Killed in a scrap with raiders from across the border."

"Your daughter was telling me," Allan commented.

"Thought an awful lot of Rob Hood," Cole Bannock said. "That's why I had him buried here on the ranch. Must tell Limpy Gregg to clean out those weeds," he added.

They reached the patio gate. The girl hesitated. "I won't be seeing you again," she said, lifting her face to Allan.

"Not unless you're out of bed awful early," laughed her father.

Kay held out her hand. "Well, perhaps it's *adios*," she said. "Don't forget the Stacys, Mr Rand——" There was a tremor to the firm little hand she placed in his. Somehow Allan managed to keep his voice quietly casual. Cole Bannock was watching him closely.

"I'll look them up," he promised.

"Won't be much time for visiting round," Cole Bannock said curtly. "I'm tellin' you now, Rand, you've got a job of work, out there at the Mesa camp."

Kay paused, one hand on the gate, her face showing distress under the lantern of the moon as she looked back at the two men.

"I—I hate you sending him out there." She spoke with a bitterness that drew her father's brows down in a black frown. "It—it just doesn't seem fair, after what Mr Rand did—for—for me." The gate swung shut behind her, and they heard the quick beat of her feet up the flagged walk.

Cole Bannock broke the brief silence. "Womenfolks don't savvy these things," he said heavily. "Kay don't savvy why I'm sending you over to the Mesa camp." He chewed savagely on his cigar. "I'm sending you there because it's only a man like you can clean up that backyard of hell. It ain't that I'm not almighty grateful for what you did last night. I make up my mind fast about a man, and I figured you're the one for the job. I reckon you savvy even if she don't."

"You're maybe rating me too high," Allan commented dryly, as he followed the older man into the office. Cole Bannock lowered his big frame into the desk chair and gave him a wintry smile.

"I don't make mistakes—much," he said, and then, his voice a low growl in his throat, the menacing, warning rumble of an aroused mastiff. "I'm figuring you won't make no mistakes, either, Rand. Maybe you savvy what I mean."

"I don't." Allan's tone was curt. "I don't know what you mean, unless it concerns something that's none of your business."

"I'll give you plain talk," Cole Bannock said gruffly. "Anything that's to do with my daughter is sure my business." He puffed vigorously at his cigar for a moment. "Kay's took a fancy to you. I ain't blind."

"We like each other," admitted Allan cautiously. "We're good friends, I hope."

"So long as it stands that way, I don't give a hoot." The rancher's tone was grimly significant. "Reckon you savvy what I mean."

"Seems to me you're jumping pretty far ahead of things," suggested Allan, with an amused smile. "Let's wait until there's something for you to worry about, Mr Bannock."

"You act like it's funny," grumbled Kay's father, staring at him suspiciously.

"Your daughter would think so," laughed the young man. He put a match to his cigarette. Not even Cole Bannock's probing gaze could detect the hot anger seething behind the cool mask of his unperturbed manner. The rancher's fears appeared to subside.

"Forget it," he said brusquely. "I always sort of warn off any likely young fellow that turns up. You see, I've got plans all set in my mind for Kay." He went back to the vexing problem of the Mesa camp. "Big leak there," he grumbled. "Tally-sheets show close on three hundred head gone since last round-up, mostly calves." He shook his head gloomily. "Too much to lose, Rand. The Triple R'll go broke."

"Sounds like the work of an organized gang," mused Allan.

"Rengo's got the cunning of a wolf," grumbled Bannock.

"If your trouble *is* Rengo . . ." Allan's tone was speculative, and then, a bit grimly, "It's up to me to find out."

"You bet," grunted Bannock.

Allan hesitated. "Your daughter said something about you sending for an Association man——"

"I sent for him all right——" The Triple R man's tone was harsh. "Peters—Val Peters."

"I've heard of him," Allan murmured, "a first-rate man."

Bannock shook his head gloomily. "He went out to the Mesa camp—and that's the last I've seen of him." He broke off, glanced at the door. "Here's Wirt," he added. "Wirt can tell you about Peters."

The short, stocky foreman of the Triple R darted a sharp look at Allan as he clattered into the office. His boss jerked a sideways nod at Allan.

"You've met Rand, Wirt."

The foreman grunted, sank into a chair. He was dusty and sweat-grimed, his swarthy face badly in need of a razor.

"Yeah." He gave Allan a grin in which his bright, hard black eyes took no part. "Sure—you the feller was in the sheriff's office."

"I'm sendin' him out to Mesa camp."

"You was tellin' me——" Wirt Gunnel dragged a sack of tobacco from his shirt-pocket and dribbled a thin stream of yellow flakes into cigarette-paper. His fingers were steady, Allan observed. Not a single fleck spilled from the thin brown paper. "Yeah—and you know what I told you." The foreman's fingers flipped the tobacco-filled paper into a neat roll, lightly sealed it with the tip of his tongue. "I said the Mesa's no place to send a greenie. Look what happened to that Peters hombre."

Allan interrupted him. "What *did* happen to Peters?" he asked in a lazy drawl.

"Reckon the buzzards can answer *that* question," returned Wirt Gunnel. He stared at Allan, a challenging gleam lurking in the back of his smoky eyes. "You'll have a good chance to ask 'em."

It was obvious that the brief encounter in the sheriff's office still rankled in the hard-bitten foreman's mind. For some strange reason he chose to regard Allan as responsible for the humiliation of himself and his two men. Cole Bannock seemed to sense the man's animosity. He frowned, shook his head.

"Don't hold it against Rand for what happened at Harker's this morning," he said with a show of irritation. "Nye's yarn was all poppycock, and so don't you get fool notions about Rand." He paused, drummed big fingers on the desk. "I told Rand he could pick his own men," he added. "You two can fight it out."

Gunnel got out of his chair, looked at Allan. "Most of the boys is over at the bunk-house," he said grumpily.

Allan followed him across the yard to a long, rambling building mid-way between the house and the corrals. A huge cottonwood-tree stood in front of the door, shading a dug well and windlass. A tin cup with a long handle hung from a nail on the tree, and there was a bench with an array of upturned tin wash-basins. Water simmered in a big iron kettle over a bed of glowing wood, and an old Mexican was washing dishes stacked on a rough, home-made table. The latter gave the stocky foreman a wary, sideways glance as the two men passed him. Allan sensed he both disliked and feared Wirt Gunnel.

Some half-score men lounged at their ease in the long room. It was obvious that Cole Bannock made some attempt at rude comfort for his outfit. There were large, rawhide-bottomed chairs, home-made but comfortable; a long table, littered with weeks-old newspapers, and some smaller tables, at one of which sat three cowboys absorbed in a card game. In a far corner of the room a slim, red-haired youth sprawled indolently in one of the big rawhide chairs, head resting against a folded sheepskin pelt. A guitar lay across his knees, and he was singing softly in a high, nasal voice to the accompaniment of lazily plucked notes.

"Oh, bury me de-eep—on the banks of the cre-eek,
    Where the green wil-lows my see-cret will ke-eep."

"Shut up, Boone! I got bus'ness with you boys." Wirt Gunnel threw an irate glance at the red-headed troubadour. One of the men at the card-table swung his head and glared indignantly at the fore-man. He was a grizzled-whiskered old man who bore all the ear-marks of a veteran of the range.

"No call to bawl thataways at the kid, Wirt," he protested in a shrill voice. "He sings real good, an' I like that there song."

"You can shut up too, Limpy," rasped Wirt Gunnel.

"Dang your mangy hide!" The old man got to his feet, stood on wide-apart bow-legs. "I don't take slack talk from you nor nobody."

Allan looked at the irate old-timer with interest. Kay had told him about Limpy Gregg, his devotion to her. Instantly he was all sympathy for the man whom age and disability had relegated to the lowly post of chore man.

It was obvious that the old man's outbursts were amusedly taken for granted by the members of the Triple R outfit. Grins went round the room, and after a moment Wirt Gunnel said placatingly, "Now, don't get your back up and go on the prod, old-timer. I sure apologize for talkin' out of turn like I did."

Limpy appeared mollified, withdrew gnarled fingers from the butt of his ancient six-gun and gave Allan a grin of recognition.

"Howdy, young feller. So you've done joined up with the outfit, huh?" He chuckled. "Seen you come in with Kay."

"Rand's figurin' to take you along to the Mesa camp with him," Wirt said, with a short, hard laugh that was a thinly veiled sneer.

"Maybe I will." Allan turned a steel-hard look on the foreman. "Any objections, Gunnel?"

"Hell, no!" ejaculated the foreman in a startled voice. Perhaps it was the warning gleam in Limpy's eyes that restrained him from expressing astonishment. "It's up to the boss about Limpy goin' over there with you." Wirt's gaze travelled slowly round the room. "Brazos an' Gus Silver maybe will suit you," he went on, with a gesture in the direction of two men who came tramping in from the bunk-room corridor.

Allan's quick glance told him he had seen the pair before, only that morning, framed in the doorway of the sheriff's office. They were lean, hardy-looking men, poker-faced and cold-eyed. Every effortless, unwasted motion of them spoke of cool efficiency. Nevertheless, he shook his head. He was obeying a hunch that warned him to be wary of this unfriendly foreman's suggestions. The fact that Gunnel wanted him to take Brazos and Gus Silver was one very good reason for him to turn the men down.

"Reckon not, Gunnel," he said mildly.

The foreman showed signs of irritation. "The boss'd say you're loco," he grumbled. He shrugged his dusty shoulders. "Suit yourself. Won't give you another chance at 'em." His glance went briefly to the old Mexican who was carrying an armful of dishes into the kitchen. "Maybe you'd fancy Miguel Cota, there," he added, with a sneering laugh. "No cook out there at the camp."

Again Allan followed his hunch. "I'll take Miguel," he decided, "and"—his look went to the red-headed youth lolling in the rawhide chair—"and I'll take Boone." There was a touch of grim humour in Allan's smile. "Limpy Gregg likes his music," he added dryly.

"You ain't takin' Custer," growled the foreman. "Got a bunch of broncs I want him to bust."

"Bannock said I could have my pick." Allan spoke firmly. "I'm taking Custer Boone." He smiled at the redhead. "All right with you, Boone."

"Sure." The cowboy got out of his chair, revealed some six feet of lean, hard body. "Just as leave go as stay," he laughed.

Allan liked him, liked the frank eyes so startlingly blue in the sun-browned face.

Wirt Gunnel's swarthy face was like a thunder-cloud. He flung the red-headed cowboy an ugly look. "All right," he muttered, after a moment's frowning thought. He shook his head. "You sure got me stumped, Rand. The boss said you was wantin' the best in the outfit, and you sure pick 'em like you ain't got good sense. I ain't sayin' another word to help you."

Unperturbed by the foreman's ill-humour, Allan selected a fourth member for his crew, a short, black-haired youth who had the name of Stumpy Hill. There was an air to Stumpy that caught his attention, a dour look that spoke of unshakable tenacity.

Followed by the men he had selected, Allan made his way back to the ranch office. Cole Bannock, still mulling over tally-sheets at his desk, widened his eyes in a surprised look at Limpy Gregg and Miguel Cota.

"Limpy's too old," he objected. "Miguel's good enough for the chuck-wagon, but you're crazy—picking Limpy."

The grizzled old range veteran reached for his gun. "Them there words is a dang insult, Cole Bannock" he shrieked. "I ain't so old an' stove up but what I can pull trigger fast as any of you hombres."

"I don't give a hoot if you stay or go," shouted Cole Bannock. "You're an ornery old sidewinder, that's what *you* are, Limpy Gregg. If I'd any sense I'd have booted you off the ranch long before this." His sly wink told Allan that his anger was only simulated. "One of these days you're goin' to pull that trigger accidental and blow a hole in somebody."

The mutual blast at each other seemed to satisfy the veteran cow-boy. He shoved the gun back in his belt and gave Allan a triumphant look. "Reckon that settles it, young feller. When do we hit the trail?"

"Soon as it's light enough to pick our horses from the remuda," Allan told him.

"Won't take us no time a-tall," Limpy assured him. "I savvy every horse that's wearin' the Triple R brand like I know the nose on my face. Don't you worry, son. I'll pick you a remuda for us to take along that can't be beat."

Bannock gave Allan a puzzled look as the two made their way through the moonlit patio to the house a few minutes later.

"Custer Boone's first rate, knows his business," he said, "and Stumpy Hill is the fastest man with a gun I ever saw." He shook his head. "I just don't savvy why you want old Limpy."

"He's got something I want," Allan told him. "I know what I'm doing."

The cattleman seemed to divine his meaning. He nodded. "Limpy's a loyal old cuss," he observed. "He'll never quit on the job."

"That's how I sized him up." The grimness in Allan's voice drew a quick glance from his companion. "Loyalty is what's needed out there at the Mesa camp, I'm thinking. I've an idea that young Boone and Stumpy Hill will show the same stuff."

Limpy Gregg's knowledge of the Triple R horse herd proved a time-saver. Dawn was only faintly flushing the mountain ridges when Allan and his crew rode out of the big corral, each man with a string of four horses. Miguel Cota followed with two laden pack-animals, one of them carrying the supplies Allan had purchased from Rankin's. The pack-horse loaned by Agee Hand was to be sent back to town.

Allan's faint hopes that he might see Kay before leaving seemed destined for disappointment. He ate a solitary breakfast in the dining-room, where Moon Quan had lighted the big swing lamp. The cook seemed a little out of sorts. He disliked being routed out so early.

"I could have eaten with the men," Allan told him apologetically. "Was on my way over there when you stopped me."

"Missie Kay—she tell me you eat bleakfast here," Moon Quan said a bit peevishly. "She tell me cookum fine bleakfast foh you." He slammed down a large platter of bacon and eggs, a pot of coffee, and crisply baked biscuit.

It was a good breakfast, the coffee hot, the biscuit fresh from the oven. Moon Quan presently brought in a dish of canned peaches.

"You're one top-hand cook," praised Allan.

"I vellee smart man." The cook's tone was grumpy, despite the momentary gleam of pleasure. "Maybe so you likee peach. Miss Kay—she put up peach. Heap good."

"You bet," ejaculated the young man. "Some peaches! Never tasted better canned peaches."

The old Chinaman regarded him with frowning eyes. "Missie Kay—she velly smart girl," he said. "You likee her, maybe so?"

Allan gave him a level-eyed look. "You claim to be a smart man," he said laconically.

The cook nodded, apparently satisfied. "Maybe so she likee you, huh?"

"There's a chance she does—a little," admitted Allan cautiously.

"What foh boss no likee you?"

"No savvy." Allan's tone was impatient. The cross-examination was becoming irksome.

"Boss no likee you." The cook shook his head sadly. "Maybe so you watch out."

The old Chinaman's vague warning was in Allan's mind as he rode across the yard towards the avenue gate. Moon Quan knew the boss better than most. He wanted Allan to be on his guard. Allan's faint smile was grim. Cole Bannock had already put up a "no trespass" sign. His words of the previous night had been plain enough. His plans for Kay were all set in his mind, the rancher had bluntly told him.

Something moved under the trees that grew below the ranch-house, scarcely discernible in that deceptive, greying dawn. Allan would have missed it save for his longing looks in that direction. He pulled his buckskin to a halt.

"You and the boys keep going," he said to Limpy Gregg. "Something I—I forgot."

"Sure," Limpy assented. "We'll mosey along slow."

Allan waited until a bend in the avenue hid the riders from view, his gloom suddenly replaced by an exultation that made his heart pound. "Something he'd forgot," he'd told Limpy. Something he unutterably longed for, he should have said.

He climbed from his saddle and dropped the buckskin's reins. The well-trained horse would not stir from the spot, Allan knew.

Again that slim, pale shape moved under the trees, came towards him swiftly.

"I wanted to say *adios*," Kay said as they met there in that vague, grey dawn.

He looked at her, for the moment too stirred for words. She seemed indescribably lovely in her short white skirt and blouse, opened low at the rounded neck, a picture he would take away with him—and cherish. Her smile came, shy, a bit confused under his look.

"I've startled you," she said. "I—I'm being bold—you think."

Allan shook his head. "I was hating to go—without seeing you again." He drew a deep breath. "Kay—I wanted more than I can tell—to see you."

"Dad's been acting queer," the girl told him in a troubled voice. "He—he said I wasn't to see you again, Allan." She moved closer, her face lifted to his. "I—I don't understand Dad." And she added a bit wildly, "I'm afraid I don't understand myself, either—behaving like this."

"Let me do the understanding for both of us." Allan spoke huskily, and suddenly he was drawing her into his arms, only to release her as she frantically pulled away.

"No—no!" Kay flung a startled look over her shoulder. "I hear Dad! He's looking for me. Oh, Allan, I'm afraid he—he's watching."

"Let him watch," fumed Allan. "I'm not afraid of your father." He took a step towards her. "Kay—I want to tell you something. Kay—I——"

"No, not now." She stood, poised for flight, the wind fluttering white skirt, slim, vibrant with life, a faint little smile curving her lips. "I'm glad you said that, though—I'm glad you're not afraid of him. And Allan—just to say *adios*." She was suddenly close to him, the scent of her hair sweet to him, the quick, light press of her lips on his. The next instant she was gone, was an elusive shape that vanished into the darker shadows of the trees now taking form in the paling greyness of the early morning.

Old Limpy Gregg gave Allan an inquiring look as the latter over-took the outfit on the ridge.

"Get what you went back for?" he wanted to know.

"Yep." The supreme contentment in the laconic response made the old cowboy look at him again, this time quizzically.

9

THE harsh green branches of the greasewood made good cover for the man crouched in the cleft of the giant boulder at the rim-rock's edge. Numerous cigarette-stubs indicated he had been there for a considerable length of time.

The slope dropped steeply beneath him in a series of ledge-like formations of reddish-brown slab rock. From an occasional crevice showed the grey-green of an incense bush in golden-yellow bloom, vying with the tiny yellow blossoms of the greasewood in touching with beauty the harsh face of the desert landscape. Wild bees droned in and out of the bush behind which the man crouched like a patiently watchful spider. There was nectar in the little yellow blossoms, a far different distilling from the venom in the hard, unwinking eyes of the lone watcher. Now and again he dropped a low curse, flinched at the too-nearness of one of the buzzing honey-seekers. He was too wise to do more than scowl and curse at them. Leave them to their business and they would leave him to his, which was alertly watching for signs of life down there on the grass-grown mesa where a shack stood mid-way between the little creek and a large pole corral.

The mid-afternoon sun was a blinding, molten disc in the hot turquoise sky. An eagle swooped low across the watcher's vision, swung in a circuit above the deserted cattle-camp, then with a quick beat of powerful wings sought frantically for altitude in great soaring sweeps until lost to view against the cool, dark blueness of the San Vicentes.

The eagle's sudden alarm was not missed by the lone man ensconced in his brush-concealed eyrie five hundred feet above the mesa. He hastily stubbed out cigarette and fastened expectant gaze on the mouth of a narrow canyon that cut down the rugged, boulder-strewn flank of the opposite ridge.

Something moved, took shape against the brown hills. A horseman, and suddenly three more riders, at a standstill now and scarcely discernible from the dark clumps of brush that covered the wide, sandy wash of the creek. Presently a fifth rider, leading two pack-horses, slowly emerged from the shadowed gorge. Apparently the others had been waiting for the man with the pack-animals. They were moving again, following the trail that took the twisting course of the creek across the mesa towards the cattle-camp.

The lone man on the rim-rock watched for several minutes, until a thicket of alder-trees hid the approaching riders from view. With a satisfied grunt he backed cautiously out of the crevice and wormed his way across the boulder-covered ridge to a big clump of grease-wood that filled the gap between two giant slabs of rock tumbled from the cliff above by the erosion of wind and rain. There was no visible passage through the thick tangle of brush, and the huge segments of reddish-brown decomposing granite stood several times higher than the man's head.

He came to a standstill, his hard eyes in close scrutiny of the immediate landscape, then quickly began pulling at the tough green brambles. They came away easily in his hands, indicating they had recently been cut and then replaced. In less than a minute he uncovered an opening and pushed on through to a tiny open space behind the cleft slab to a bald-faced horse that looked at him with nervously twitching ears.

The man grinned. "Wasn't likin' this hole much, I reckon." He seized the dragging reins and led the animal from the place, pausing only long enough to pile the brush back hastily in the opening before leaving the scene of his long vigil.

Something stirred in the shadowed crags above him as he rode away. A swarthy face pushed into sight, fierce gaze following the man on the bald-faced horse. A long minute passed, and then the unseen watcher slid down from the crags with the ease of a cat and went swiftly to the ledge overlooking the mesa. The horsemen were within several hundred yards of the cattle-camp now.

The slim Apache youth watched intently through the opening in the greasewood. From his expression it was evident he recognized the man on the tall buckskin horse. Five minutes later he was back in the boulder-tumbled clearing and scrambling up the jagged sides of the cliff to the flat top of the ridge where great fallen slabs of rock lay in a riot of confusion as if thrown down by giant hands from the higher peaks. A reddish roan horse was grazing the sparse drying grass that had found root in the crevices. The Apache youth unfastened the long, rawhide rope, hastily coiled and tied it to the saddle, and in another minute was riding across the rocky backbone of the ridge and down the steep slope into a gorge. Here he halted the horse and carefully scrutinized the waste of boulders and sand. Apparently what his keen eyes detected satisfied him. He continued along the gorge which twisted up through the maze of barren hills.

Suddenly the almost invisible trail he was following cut sharply to the left, down a steep gully. The Apache halted, and, leaving the red roan concealed in the brush, he made his way cautiously along the shouldering ridge that followed above the course of the gully.

A few minutes brought him to cliffs again. The Apache flattened down, crawled on hands and knees to a mass of boulders balanced precariously on the rim. Below him, several hundred feet down, spread a small, basin-like valley.

Cattle grazed at the far end, where green fringing willows indicated a creek, and beyond the creek was a small shack and a pole corral. Thin blue smoke lifted lazily from a fire some yards from the shack, and a man was stirring something in a kettle that hung above the blaze.

The Apache's gaze fastened on a lone horseman who rode out of the gully below him. The animal under the rider was a bald-face.

The slim, dark youth wasted no more time. He hurried back to his horse and rode for several hundred yards down the gorge, then cut into a ravine that twisted sharply up into the bleak hills. There was no trail for ordinary eyes to see, but the young Apache rode with a careless confidence that denoted an amazing knowledge of his surroundings.

The detour brought him to the deep canyon from which the five horsemen had emerged some two hours earlier. Sunlight still lay on the upper slopes, but the shadowed twilight already mantled the rugged canyon floor.

It was apparent that the Apache had arranged a rendezvous in this dark and forbidding defile. He left the trail, fairly well marked here, and struck across the dry wash of the creek towards a thick willow brake. Twice he halted the red roan, to scrutinize closely the silver-grey trunks of sycamore-trees that had their roots deep down in the rocky bed of the wash. Each tree bore a freshly broken twig that hung suspended by a shred of bark. These signs seemed to increase the Apache's confidence. Nevertheless, his alert eyes constantly raked his surroundings as he neared the willow brakes. Suddenly a voice hailed him softly, in Spanish.

"You come, at last, Pepe!"

"*Si!*" The Indian drew his horse to a standstill, slid lithely from saddle, and pulled tobacco and a book of brown cigarette-papers from the pocket of his fringed buckskin shirt. "Our señor is now at the cattle-camp," he added.

"You saw him?" Poco Gato's huge frame pushed into view from the willow brakes. One hand held the bridle reins of the horse following at his heels.

"I saw him, and four others, one of them with two pack-horses." Pepe put a match to his cigarette, exhaled contentedly. "Another was watching from the cliff when I came. So I watched him. He was the man they call Bert Nye."

Poco Gato dropped a low, startled exclamation. "That is bad," he muttered, frowning at the Indian. "Already the wolves gather for another kill."

"There was time before the hour to meet you here," Pepe went on in his careful Mission-school Spanish. "I followed Nye to the secret lair of these wolves."

Poco Gato was all eager attention. "That was good work, Pepe," he congratulated.

"It is a bad place," Pepe told him solemnly. "Long ago, before the white men came, many of my people were surprised there and slain by enemies. It is said that when the two big stars come close to the moon the voices of the slain warriors can be heard lamenting their lost scalps."

"Such tales are silly," declared Poco peevishly.

The young Apache's half-grin indicated some scepticism on his own part. "I only know what I have been told," he said, "and it is true that my people avoid the place."

"Where is this secret hide-out?" asked the Mexican.

"You know it as the Poison Sinks," Pepe answered. "There is grass when the rains come, and always a little water in the creek, but on the south and west slopes there are deep pot-holes and springs of water that are death to man and beast."

"Poison Sinks," muttered Poco Gato, "*si*—I know the place. The water in those sink holes looks sweet to a thirsty man, but a drink of it will tie him up in knots and turn him into rotting flesh for the buzzards to fatten on."

"It is close to the border," Pepe went on, "and beyond the creek there is a secret pass through the hills, in some places less than ten feet wide and never less than a hundred feet to the top of the cliffs. It is like the deep channel of a river that no longer runs there."

Poco Gato nodded thoughtfully. "A fine highway for stolen cattle to be rushed unseen across the border," he declared. "I must tell our señor of this hidden rustler's trail, Pepe."

"The secret is guarded day and night," murmured the Indian. "Others have learned of Poison Sinks Pass, but they have not lived to carry the tale to Señor Bannock."

"Three men have died in less than three months," muttered the big Mexican. He scowled, shook his head. "What is Nye's business in the Poison Sinks? He works for the Double Star, whose owner is also a sheriff."

"There is only one answer." Pepe's tone was significant. "He is a Rengo man."

"Señor Starr, who is also the sheriff of Puma County, would laugh at us for fools if we took him such a tale," grumbled Poco; then, with a shrewd glance at the Indian's inscrutable face, he added, "Or have us killed—for knowing too much."

"He would have us killed," muttered Pepe, after a long silence.

"You know more than you will tell," accused the Mexican in an aggrieved voice.

Pepe's answer was a bit vague. "I watch another man for Sheriff Harker," he said. "He is now down there in the Sinks—with the others."

The sunlight was fading from the hilltops. Poco Gato swung up to his saddle.

"You are our señor's eyes and ears too," he reminded, with a stern look at the youth. "Do not forget, Pepe, that our señor's affairs are more important to us than watching a man for the sheriff."

"It is quite possible that their business is the same," Pepe said pointedly.

Poco Gato gave him a startled look. "We are good friends," he grumbled, "but there are times when I do not understand you, Pepe." He gestured. "I must ride if I am to be in time to hear the señor give me the sun-down signal as agreed." The Mexican chuckled. "I will give you the secret password, Pepe."

"A good idea," said the Apache. "I may need such a password."

Poco Gato's smile broadened. "You know the little song I sometimes sing?"

"Your friends have heard the song from you until they weary of it." Amusement flickered like a beam of light across the young Indian's impassive brown face.

Poco ignored the gentle derision. "When one sings of the little dove it warns of danger, but when you sing of my Conchita all is well. It is the señor's password."

Pepe nodded. "I fear that we will sing more often of La Paloma than of your Conchita," he said gravely.

The two men stared at each other, and Poco said worriedly, "It is possible, Pepe." His gigantic frame straightened up in the saddle, towered above the slim youth on the red roan horse. "Our señor saved my life. I cannot do less than use my life in his service. I fight for him, but the danger is great. We must have help, and so, Pepe, you ride with the password to our friends, Pablo and Fernando and Pancho and Domingo—all the others."

"The password will reach them before the dawn," promised Pepe.

"You will be our eyes and ears," again said the Mexican. "You have the cunning of a coyote, Pepe, and the eyes of an eagle—the courage of a grizzly bear. None knows when you come—or go." Poco Gato's tone was deeply admiring. The descendant of Apache warriors shrugged lithe-muscled shoulders. The virtues extolled by the Mexican were his natural birthright.

"*Adios,*" he said simply. His glance went to the sunlight on the mountain ridge, now in fast retreat before the upward climb of the drawling shadows. "*Vamos!* We have work to do, you and I." He whirled his horse, and in another moment the willow brakes hid him from Poco's eyes.

The big Mexican started his horse across the sandy wash towards the trail down the canyon. There was need to make haste if he would be in time to reach the alder thicket below the camp before the going down of the sun. A buzzard soared against the pale patchwork of sky above the canyon cliffs. Poco crossed himself, muttered a prayer to his saint.

STEVE STARR's smile was amiable enough as he rode across the yard and drew rein close to the corral gate. There was nothing in his expression to indicate he harboured ill-will towards the man who had bested him in the *cantina* a few nights earlier. Three other riders came up through the dust that drifted in billowing clouds from the corral where some hundred head of cattle made resentful clamour in protest to the expert ministrations of Stumpy Hill and Custer Boone who were singling out calves and dragging them from the corral at the end of a rope.

Limpy Gregg, eyes bright with excitement and pleasure at finding himself again in active service, was ready with the red-hot irons as the cowboys dragged the bawling victims up to the fire and turned them over to the mighty arms of Poco Gato, who held them helpless for the brief space of time needed for Limpy to do his work. A puff of smoke, the smell of burned hair and hide, and the calf would stagger away to join the growing number of young fellow-initiates of the Triple R herd.

The unexpected appearance of the Double Star men shocked a startled grunt from Limpy Gregg. He dropped the branding-iron and grabbed frantically for the gun in his holster. Stumpy Hill and Custer Boone were a shade faster in making similar motions, but Poco Gato made a slow fourth in getting his gun out, his attention for the moment being entirely on the unruly young bald-face he was holding down on its side.

Allan slid from his perch on the corral fence. There was amusement, a grim satisfaction, in the smile he gave the owner of the Double Star. The prompt reaction of his small, hand-picked outfit pleased him. He had been aware of the approaching horsemen, had recognized Starr, and purposely waited to see the effect of surprise on his men. Allan recalled Cole Bannock's words. "Stumpy Hill is the fastest man with a gun I ever saw." Allan was of the opinion that Custer Boone was just as fast. The only difference between them was that Stumpy had a gun in either hand.

Allan's slow, humorous glance at the visitors told him they were deeply impressed.

"The boys are a bit jumpy," he said to Starr. "Can't blame 'em, after what's happened at this camp."

"I'll send notice, next time I drop in," grinned Starr. "Don't want to be on the wrong end of some lead-throwin'." His tone sobered. "Can't blame 'em for not taking chances. Been too many killings out here in this man's land."

"You bet we ain't takin' chances!" There was a rasp in Limpy Gregg's high, shrill voice, an unfriendly gleam in his eyes as he stared at the four Double Star men. As a loyal member of the Triple R outfit, he was in no way shy about expressing his hostile sentiments regarding his boss's detested neighbour. "Speakin' for myself, I ain't trustin' none of you fellers further'n I can throw hot lead."

A derisive laugh came from the riders grouped behind Starr.

"The ol' coot's sure warlike," one of them chuckled.

"You bet I'm warlike, Luce Henders!" shouted the irate old-timer. "I've got about as much use for you as I have for your smooth-talkin' boss, an' that's the same use I've got for a polecat."

"Your fire's getting low, Limpy," mildly interposed Allan. His look went to the two younger members of his outfit. "All right, boys—don't keep Limpy waiting too long with his irons."

Custer Boone and Stumpy Hill turned their attention back to the milling herd, ropes swinging in slow motion at their selected victims for the branding-irons. Starr broke the silence that had followed Limpy's hostile comment.

"Was heading for the Cottonwood Flats ford when we saw signs of life down at the camp here," he told Allan. "Didn't know Bannock was working cattle out this way, so we figured we'd ride over and find out what's going on."

"Thought maybe a gang of rustlers had holed up at the camp—eh, Starr?"

Allan's laconic comment drew a shrug from the Double Star owner.

"Plenty of rustlers in this hell hole," he observed. "Fact is I'm trailin' a couple of fellers Luce claims have been working on my side of the river." He tapped the star pinned to his shirt. "Luce claims a private little necktie party is good enough for a cow-thief, but now I'm a sheriff I've got to make him leave such things as hanging rustlers to the law." Starr threw his lanky, hard-faced foreman a sardonic grin. "Luce ain't strong for this law-and-order business, claims it cramps his style, having his boss turn sheriff on him."

"Sure does," grunted Henders. He was staring at Allan, startled recognition in his eyes. "Say, feller—seems to me I've saw you before."

"One of your private little necktie parties," chuckled Allan. "You'd have pulled it off, only another sheriff happened along in time."

The Double Star foreman had the grace to show signs of embarrassment.

"I was mebbe some hasty," he admitted. His glance flickered in Poco Gato's direction. "I'm not claimin' for certain the Mex is one of the Rengo gang, but there's been talk he ain't above pickin' up a cow when nobody's lookin'." Luce Henders scowled. "Has a way of butcherin' a cow in some gully and sellin' the beef to his Mex friends."

"Poco's on the Triple R pay-roll now." Allan spoke slowly, a note of warning in his voice. "He'll maybe butcher a cow once in a while, when the cook wants beef for the camp. Don't you be too quick to say he's a thief, Henders."

"So long as he butchers Triple R cows it ain't *my* worry," retorted the Double Star foreman. He grinned. "If I catch him on our side of the river, I'll turn him over to the boss here."

The sheriff of Puma County stared at the big Mexican, wrestling another calf down for Limpy's hot iron.

"I've got a gaol he won't break out of, like the Kid did in Roaring River," he sneered.

"I'll tell Harker what you say," promised Allan unsmilingly. "By the way, Harker'll want to know what you're doing, over here in his bailiwick."

"I told you I'm trailin' rustlers," grumbled Starr.

"It's up to you to notify Harker," Allan coldly rejoined. "He's the law on *this* side of the river."

"Harker's a hell of a sheriff," jeered the Puma County law officer.

"He caught the Pecos Kid," reminded Allan.

"And let the Kid walk out of his gaol," grinned Starr.

"Say," broke in Luce Henders, "speakin' of the Kid, he's a dead ringer for you, feller." He stared intently at Allan. "Reckon I wasn't so awful to blame for tryin' to swing you the other day, findin' you with Poco, and you lookin' enough like the Kid to be him." The foreman's smile was wintry. "Lucky for you Harker an' Bannock come up the trail when they did."

"Proves it's best to leave rustlers to the law," observed Allan good-naturedly. He was inclined to like the outspoken cowman, despite the unfortunate episode referred to. Henders was not much different from most of his kind. His bitter hatred of cattle-thieves was naturally come by.

"The only way you don't look like the Kid is you don't wear his dinky black moustache," chuckled the Double Star foreman.

"You didn't let my not having a moustache stop you from trying to hang me and Poco," reminded Allan curtly.

"You being with Poco kind of fixed it in my mind," explained Henders, with an embarrassed grin. "I said at the time you looked like the Kid."

"I remember," admitted Allan, and, his voice hardening, "I'm trying to forget it too, Henders."

Henders nodded gloomily. "Reckon it's up to me to act more slow," he admitted. "At that, how was I to know but what the Kid had shaved off his moustache?" The possibility seemed to comfort the foreman. He grinned cheerfully. "Ain't never saw the Kid face to face," he confessed. "Only seen his picture in the sheriff's office. Could pass off for a Mex dandy, with his black moustache and that fancy rig he wears."

"I'm no Mex dandy," protested Allan in an injured tone.

The Double Star riders exchanged amused grins, and Henders said in his slow drawl, "Wasn't meanin' the Pecos Kid ain't one fightin' fool. He's sure the toughest gent as ever smoked guns at a sheriff's posse." He nodded, eyes approving the tall young boss of the Mesa camp outfit. "I ain't forgettin' the way you come bustin' in on our necktie party with Poco Gato. I ain't never saw a more salty gent than you, young feller." Henders glanced at Steve Starr. "That's the truth, Boss. Reckon old Bannock's sure got him a good man to clean up the rustlers down here in the Mesa country."

Starr's sour smile told Allan that the sheriff of Puma County had kept discreet silence about the affair in the *cantina*. Rogan too had been told to keep his mouth shut. It was obvious that Luce Henders had no knowledge of the truth regarding the circumstances of Selmo's death. He would not have been so friendly.

"Well"—Starr swung his horse—"let's be on our way, fellers." He jerked a nod at Allan. "Wish you luck, Rand. If old Harker sticks too close to his arm-chair, you give me a call if you're needin' a sheriff on the job in a hurry."

"Just a moment, Starr." Allan gestured in the direction of the desolate hills to the west. "What do you know of that outfit camped over in the Sinks yonder?"

Starr appeared to ponder for a moment, and then with a shake of his head, "I wouldn't know about any outfit in the Sinks, Rand."

"Used to be a couple of prospectors over there," put in Luce Henders. "Built theirselves a shack and hung round there for years." Henders chortled. "Seen 'em one time I was lookin' for strays. Couple of old desert rats, whiskers an' all."

Starr was giving Allan sly, speculative glances.

"How do you know there's an outfit workin' in the Sinks?" he asked, when Henders had finished his story about the prospectors. "Been over that way?"

"No." Allan shook his head. "Happened to hear there was a shack over there. Thought maybe you could tell me who was camped in the Sinks."

"Who told you about the shack?" Starr asked softly.

"Why—I wouldn't remember." Allan was suddenly cautious. No use telling the man about the spy Pepe had trailed to Poison Sinks. The spy was Bert Nye, and probably in Starr's pay. The Double Star man was apparently friendly enough, but Allan was recalling the cattleman's threats at the *cantina* after the killing of Selmo. Starr had promised to make things too hot for him in Roaring River. Starr was not forgetting the rough treatment handed him that night in the *cantina* of Conchita Mendota. Allan was reasonably certain there was a connexion between the spy seen by Pepe and this apparently casual appearance of Starr and his men at the Mesa camp. He was not for a moment believing Starr's tale about looking for rustlers. He had come for the purpose of looking things over. In fact, save for the presence of Luce Henders the purpose may have been murder. Allan's shrewd sizing up of Henders spoke loudly in the man's favour. Henders was hard and ruthless when it concerned matters of the range. He had all the typical cowman's intolerance of nesters and cow-thieves, but he was not the sort who would stoop to murder. Allan was sure of this, despite the Poco Gato affair. Henders had been quite convinced that he was taking the cattleman's way with a pair of cattle stealers. His presence at the camp with Starr was proof that the latter was not contemplating any immediate violence. He would not have brought his hard-bitten but likable foreman with him had murder been in his mind. Allan came back to Starr's question.

"I wouldn't remember," he repeated, brows wrinkled thoughtfully, "Cole Bannock maybe. Doesn't matter who told me, Starr. Took on this job sort of sudden, and Bannock told me a lot of things, and maybe I got it from him about the shack." Allan swung his head in an amused smile at Henders. "Likely enough it's your pair of desert rats Bannock was telling me about," he added.

"If it ain't them, it's more of the same breed," Henders suggested. "Nobody with good sense would want to be in a hell hole like the Sinks." He grinned round at his companions. "Ain't never saw a prospector that wasn't loco," he declared.

Allan watched until lifting dust veiled the departing visitors from view. They were heading south-east across the Mesa in the direction of the Cottonwood Flats ford, about the only safe crossing of Roaring River for miles, old Limpy Gregg had told him. The turbulent stream was the dividing line between the two big ranches. Miles to the south would be Red Canyon, where a portion of Double Star range sprawled across the river. It was in Red Canyon that Bert Nye ranched, on the land he claimed to have bought from Starr. The man was a long way from home, according to the story told by Pepe to Poco Gato. No question but what Nye's presence in the Poison Sinks had something to do with the Triple R outfit's arrival at the Mesa camp. His report was causing Starr anxiety. There was more to it than Starr's personal grudge because of the affair at the *cantina*.

Limpy Gregg came up, sweat running down the creases of his dusty, leathery face.

"All done, Boss," he announced, "thirty-seven more of 'em wearin' the Triple R on their hides. Purty good count for our first day's drag of them brakes." Limpy shook his head doubtfully. "We'll be needin' a lot more hands, if you ask me," he added. "That is, if all we're here for is to comb out this hell's back-yard for Triple R cows."

"What do you know about the Poison Sinks?"

The abrupt question drew a sharp, quizzical look from Limpy that indicated an almost comical satisfaction.

"I take it that chasin' cows out of the brush ain't *all* we've come out to the Mesa for," he said.

"I was asking you about the Poison Sinks," Allan reminded dryly.

"It ain't called Poison Sinks for nothin'." The old range man wagged his head. "It's Triple R range, but the boss don't like his cows roamin' over that way. Ain't easy to get down into—mebbe some half-dozen draws an' gullies, an' the boss has got each one of 'em stopped with bob wire. No chance for cows to stray down to them poison water-holes onless some skunk goes an' cuts the wires on us."

Allan nodded, musing gaze on the spirals of dust falling into the distance. His next question drew another sharp look from Limpy.

"What do you make of Starr's visit?"

"Don't savvy a-tall—him an' his bunch droppin' in like they did," grumbled the old man. His eyes narrowed to gleaming slits as he stared thoughtfully at the pale, pluming dust lifting in the wake of the distant horsemen. "Double Star cattle don't cross the river no place near here, not for miles up or down. Them fellers wouldn't be lookin' for strays over this way."

"Cattle could cross over at the Cottonwood Flats ford," suggested Allan.

"Ain't likely," demurred Limpy. "There's bob-wire wings strung both sides the river that turns the cows off from the crossin', an' there's bob wire strung between the wings." Limpy paused, pondered for a moment. "Course there's a chance some feller might leave the wires down when he makes the crossin'," he finally admitted. "'Tain't likely, onless the feller is too lazy to climb down from his saddle, but as a rule cow-hands is careful about closin' gates. Save's 'em plenty trouble goin' after strays."

"Starr didn't say they were looking for strays," reminded Allan.

"I heard him," Limpy snorted. "Claimed they was lookin' for rustlers."

"You don't believe him?"

"No more than you do," declared the old man. "He was after somethin', but it wasn't rustlers, an' it wasn't stray cows."

Miguel Cota appeared in the doorway of the shack and banged a tin plate against bare knuckles.

"Tellin' us to come an' git it," grinned Limpy. He hurried off, to be first at the wash-basin.

Poco Gato had opened the corral gate, and the cattle were streaming out, moving in a long line across the Mesa, eager to get back to the willow brakes. Custer Boone and Stumpy Hill stripped off saddle gear from their sweating horses and turned them loose in the smaller corral used for the remuda.

"We're going for a ride this afternoon," Allan told the pair of cowboys as they clattered hurriedly up on their way to the cook-house.

They sensed something beyond the ordinary in his voice, came to an abrupt halt, dusty hot faces turned towards him inquiringly.

"We're going to take a look at this Poison Sinks place," Allan said a bit grimly.

The youthful pair exchanged ecstatic grins. They knew the purpose that had brought them to the Mesa camp, knew they were not there merely for the routine work of a cattle ranch. Allan had told them just enough and no more.

"Never was over in them Sinks," Custer Boone admitted. He grinned. "From what I've heard I reckon it's a right smart idea to pack your own canteen of water along."

"Me too," grunted Stumpy Hill. "Maybe we'll need to pack more than water with us, huh, Boss?" He slapped a well-filled cartridge-belt, and stared at Allan intently, an expectant gleam in his smoky eyes.

"No telling what we'll run up against," admitted Allan. He looked at Poco Gato, who was listening with gloomy attention.

"I'm curious about those cattle Poco says a friend of his saw over in the Sinks."

"*Por Dios!*" The big Mexican spoke worriedly. "We will find more than cattle in that place, Señor."

"I'm hoping we will." Allan's smile was grim. "We're not here to work cattle. You boys know that." He gestured at the herd stringing across the Mesa. "We had to make a show at it, after what Poco told us about the spy up there on the bluffs."

"We get you, Boss," muttered Stumpy Hill. "Guess we savvy why them Double Star fellers was nosin' round this mornin'."

"I'm not certain about it, Stumpy, but I've a good notion they wanted to make sure it was only round-up business that brought us here."

"Reckon they went off satisfied," chuckled Custer. "They sure caught us hard at it. That bunch of bawlin' wild beef we had in the corral sure didn't look like we was play-actin'." His frank, boyish face took on a perplexed look. "I'm sure up a tree, though, just why you'd want to fool Steve Starr. He's a big cattleman, and sheriff of his own county to boot."

"I was expecting callers," Allan told them. "I didn't know who, and I'm just about as surprised as you that our callers were Double Star men."

"It's awful puzzlin'," observed Stumpy Hill. "I ain't figurin' it out any more than Custer."

"You've said it," agreed Custer Boone. "A sure enough picture puzzle—that's what this doggone business is."

"We'll have to put the pieces together as we find them," smiled Allan. "Maybe we'll find a few pieces in the Poison Sinks that will make good sense."

11

THE buzzard rose heavily from the coulee, drove upward, higher and higher, and was suddenly a black speck floating against the torrid sky.

"Somethin' dead down there," Limpy Gregg muttered; "that buzzard was stuffed so full, could hardly get off the ground."

Allan's eyes narrowed in a thoughtful look down the rugged slope. The shimmering heat waves made him squint. "Let's have a look," he said.

The two men rode slowly, let their horses pick their way through the maze of slab rock. A hundred yards brought them to the scene of the carrion bird's ghastly feasting.

Limpy muttered a low imprecation as he stared at the remains of the dead horse. A bridle hung loosely to the shrivelled head, and the shocked men could see the saddle protruding from the grease-wood under which the unfortunate animal's dying struggles had plunged it.

Ignoring the stench, Limpy made a hasty examination.

"Two bullet-holes," he announced, "first bullet broke a leg an' looks like the feller ridin' him put another bullet into the critter's head to end its sufferin'."

"The rider was hurt too," Allan said. "The sign's plain to read, Limpy."

"He wouldn't be gettin' far," muttered the cowboy. "Went off crawlin' on hands an' knees. He's layin' somewheres close."

Leading their horses, the two followed the pitiful trail down the coulee and suddenly sighted a small spring that trickled from the side of a cliff. Limpy stared gloomily at the dead man lying there.

"Wasn't knowin' it for poison water." He wagged his head. "Sure is bad medicine, this here Poison Sinks water. How you figger it gets that way, Boss?"

Allan shook his head. "You're an old-timer in these parts, Limpy. You know more about the Poison Sinks than I do."

"Ain't got your eddication," reminded Limpy tartly.

"I've heard of these so-called poison pools in Death Valley," Allan continued. "Scientists claim the water contains large quantities of sodium and magnesium salts, dangerous for even a strong, healthy man. Wouldn't take much of the stuff to kill a sick, wounded man like this poor fellow here."

"I've seed plenty dead cows layin' round the pools afore we fenced 'em off," commented the cowboy. "Sure is bad medicine."

"It's quick death for 'most any poor thirsty devil who fills up on it," agreed Allan. He forced himself to bend low over the stiffened corpse. He straightened up with a grunt, stared grimly at the small, silver-plated badge in the palm of his hand.

"The Association feller." Limpy spoke gruffly. "It's Val Peters, Boss."

Allan nodded gloomily. The story was plain. Val Peters had followed the trail into the Sinks, met death at the hands of the desperadoes he was pursuing. The mystery of the missing Association detective was solved.

In grim silence the two men did all that was possible for the unfortunate's remains, and when they rode away a cairn of stones marked the last resting-place of Val Peters.

They kept an alert watch as they followed down the gully. No telling but what sharp eyes were observing their movements.

The gorge deepened near its mouth, and they found themselves between closely pressing cliffs. Allan produced cutters and snipped the barbed wires strung across the narrow portal.

For the moment the two men were content to remain in the shadowed entrance. A quarter of a mile of open country lay between them and the fringing willows that lined the twisting course of the creek. The cabin described by Poco Gato from the story related by Pepe was not far beyond the willow brakes.

"About time Custer and Stumpy is showin' up," Limpy Gregg speculated. "That gully they took was some longer, and they'd have to circle the ridge where we left 'em, but we got delayed findin' Val Peters."

Allan was studying the landscape with frowning intentness. He wanted to get into the cover of those green willows, and Limpy, sensing what was in his mind, was suddenly silent. The cleft that broke out of the gorge offered possibilities.

"Makes a double hitch like the tracks of a crawlin' sidewinder, then heads through them willows for the creek," the old range man finally observed. "We could easy git into them willows if we go afoot. That barranca's deep enough if we keep our heads down."

"I'm going over there," Allan said. "You're right about the barranca, Limpy; only you're not going to try it."

"I can do it better than you," protested the old man. "I ain't so tall. I can make it easy without showin' my head."

"You'll stay with the horses," Allan told him with an amused grin.

Limpy accepted the decision with an annoyed grunt; then, "What'll I tell the boys, when they git here?"

"Tell them to wait here with you until I give you a signal, or until I get back."

"What if you don't give us a signal—or come back?" Limpy's tone was significant.

"You boys can work that one out for yourselves," grimly replied the younger man. In another moment he was in the barranca.

The twisting course of the dry wash considerably lengthened the distance to the creek willows. The some two hundred yards between the mouth of the gorge and the brakes became nearly half a mile. There were places where the barranca widened out to shallow banks that forced him to crawl on hands and knees. In one of these spots a sinister whirring sound brought him to a halt. Crouched there on hands and knees, he swung his gaze from side to side, suddenly located the rattlesnake, a big, reddish, desert diamond-back that had sought the shade of a boulder.

Allan stared at it for a moment, hand on the butt of his gun, then with a grin he made a cautious detour. The rattlesnake was more of a gentleman than most of the killers that infested the Poison Sinks. The reptile had given warning, which was more than the human variety would trouble to do. A shot in the back was their way.

He succeeded in reaching the willows without further incident and straightened to his full height with a sigh of relief. It was unbearably hot down in that sandy, boulder-strewn barranca. He could feel the sweat running down his back and chest, and the salt of it stung his eyes. He wiped his dripping face with shirt-sleeve and stared back across the narrow strip of valley to ascertain if Limpy Gregg was making himself too visible. No sign of man or horses showed at the dark entrance to the gorge, but farther down the sweep of hills Allan thought he detected a movement in the mouth of the coulee that Custer Boone and Stumpy Hill were to follow into the Sinks. He half wished he had made old Limpy Gregg accompany them. Limpy was a shrewd veteran campaigner, wise to all the hidden dangers of such a place. His experience would have been valuable to the boys.

As he stood there, troubled gaze on those too obvious stirrings in the mouth of the coulee, Allan became vaguely aware that something was missing in the picture. Poco Gato had spoken of cattle in this narrow strip of valley between the creek and the western rim of the hills. Pepe had told Poco he had seen cattle grazing the parched grass.

For a long minute he scrutinized every shadowed draw that opened down from the surrounding hills. Unless the cattle were now across the creek, on the side where the shack stood, it was apparent that they had been moved out of the Sinks, probably were already on their way to the border.

Allan recalled Pepe's story of the secret pass through the hills. The whole set-up was ideal for the rustler gang that was playing such havoc with Cole Bannock's range. It was odd that the owner of the Triple R seemed to be unaware that the answer to his troubles was likely to be found in the grim basin of the Poison Sinks. It came to Allan that there was a sinister reason for the old cattleman's ignorance. Too great a confidence in the loyalty of his men. Allan thought uneasily of Wirt Gunnel. He did not trust the dark-visaged foreman of the Triple R ranch.

He worked his way cautiously through the thicket and reached the creek, a clear, shallow stream flowing over a gravelly bed. Below him the trampled bank showed that cattle had recently watered there.

He crossed over, was confronted by a heavy growth of cat's-claw that forced him to turn down stream for some hundred yards. Here he struck a path, obviously used by the occupants of the shack. The hard-packed sand at the water's edge showed the imprints of boot-heels. There was a deep, clear pool here. Allan surmised that the place was the source of the camp's water-supply.

He scrutinized the footprints closely, saw they were not fresh.

Nobody had been there to fill his water-bucket that day. Only the quiet murmurings of the stream, the faint rustle of wind in the brakes, touched his ears. The rustlers were away on some business, probably were hurrying the cattle through the secret pass that led to the border.

In a few moments he was looking at the shack several rods beyond the outmost fringe of willows. It was a crude structure of roughly hewn logs, chinked with mud, and the pole roof was thatched with willows. Near by was a great butte that threw a dark shadow across the shack, adding a sinister look to the place.

Allan, crouched behind the covering tangle of bushes, absorbed the details of the desolate scene. The only sign of life was a lone jack-rabbit ambling lazily near the corral. Suddenly it sat up, ears rigidly erect, then was gone with startled bounds into the brush.

Allan waited, grimly expectant. The rabbit's frantic flight was a warning not to be ignored. Another moment would have found him in the open, a target for the guns of the men who suddenly rode round the base of the big butte.

The features of the three riders were darkly shadowed by the butte as they swung in from the bright glare of the sun, and for a brief moment Allan thought the taller of the horsemen was Poco Gato. He towered above his companions.

Allan was conscious of mingled dismay and bewilderment. Poco was supposed to be at the Mesa camp, waiting for news from Pepe.

A closer view of the approaching horsemen quickly told Allan the big man was not Poco. Nevertheless, he continued to watch with ever-increasing bewilderment. The tall rider was Rod Bannock, and it was obvious that he was a prisoner. His hands were bound to the horn of his saddle.

The newcomers made straight for the shack. One of them swung down from his saddle and began to loose the prisoner's hands from the saddle-horn. Allan's eyes widened a bit as he recognized Rogan. He had last seen the Double Star cowboy the night of the shooting in Conchita Mendota's *cantina*.

Rod Bannock got down awkwardly from his saddle and went into the shack. He moved slowly, like a man riddled with fear. Rogan's gaze followed him, then swung to his companion, still slouched in his saddle. The latter nodded in response to something

Rogan said and rode off to the corral with the three horses. Rogan vanished into the shack, but in a moment or two was back at the door, a demi-john in either hand. He placed them on the ground and again disappeared.

The other man was returning from the corral where he had left the horses. Something familiar about his appearance awakened Allan's memory. Rogan's companion was Choctaw, the swarthy half-breed. He still wore a bandage on the wrist Allan's bullet had gashed the afternoon Luce Henders and his crew had attempted their lynching party.

Allan's eyes hardened as he watched the half-breed. These men seemed to know their way around in the Poison Sinks. Both were Double Star men. The conviction grew in Allan's mind that Luce Henders had done some lying to him that morning. The Double Star foreman had professed ignorance regarding any activities in the Sinks. The evidence unrolling before Allan's eyes indicated that Luce Henders was mixed up in lawless operations that perhaps had some connexion with the notorious Rengo. Another thought made Allan's heart skip a beat. It was even possible that the Double Star's trusted foreman was himself the arch-rustler.

Choctaw was standing in front of the door, lighting a cigarette. Rogan appeared, and his voice, loud and peevish, drifted on the wind to the ears of the watcher behind the bushes.

"Git a move on, feller, an' fill them jugs. I'm sure cravin' a drink of that cold creek water."

"Me too," grinned the half-breed. He picked up one of the demi-johns and started along the path leading to the creek. Allan held his breath. The man would pass within a scant three yards of his hiding-place.

His fingers itched for the gun in his holster as Choctaw clattered past. For a moment he was tempted to follow the man. He would have the advantage of surprise. Allan resisted the impulse. He wanted to find out why Rod Bannock was the prisoner of these men, and what they proposed to do with him. He sensed their loudened voices was a bit of by-play, intended to impress the prisoner. They wanted him to know that Choctaw was filling the jugs with fresh, cold water from the creek. Rogan had spoken loudly about the *jugs*. Allan was conscious of a cold, prickling sensation that ran down his spine. The half-breed was carrying only *one* of the demi-johns to the creek.

He waited, tense with growing apprehensions, hoped the half-breed would not notice the fresh imprints of his boot-heels. Apparently Choctaw was not in a suspicious mood. There was no reason for him to be on the alert for footprints. He presently returned, the filled jug swinging in his hand.

To Allan's increasing mystification he put the demi-john down near the door and picked up the empty one. Allan's puzzled gaze followed him, saw that he went towards the big butte. For a few moments he was lost to sight, and then suddenly he was hurrying back to the shack. Allan knew by the way he carried the jug that it had been filled. His perplexity increased. One demi-john filled at the creek, the other jug filled from some source at the great butte —a spring that trickled from the rocks.

Horror swept Allan in a chilling wave. He knew now the sinister purpose of the two demi-johns of water. One of them was for the unsuspecting, thirsting Rod Bannock. Why these men planned to murder him was a mystery he had no time to puzzle out. It was a cunning thing, diabolic in its perfection. The dead youth would be found in the shack, the jug of poison water at his elbow, all the signs indicating he himself had filled it at the poison spring, or the plan might be to carry the body to one of the poison springs, to be left lying there, mute evidence of the way of his death. Some unknown enemy with the cunning of a fox was responsible for thus concealing a cold-blooded killing.

The cowhide stretched on willow poles that did for a door flapped shut on the half-breed as he went inside with his jugs of water. Allan's coolly functioning brain reacted with lightning speed. This was his chance to reach the shack unseen. Gun in hand, he moved swiftly and soundlessly, in a moment was crouching close to the one small window. There was no glass in the two-foot-square opening, only a piece of cowhide, now drawn aside to admit light and air.

Cautiously he peered into the room, glimpsed Rod Bannock slumped on a crude bench against the opposite wall. The youth was plainly in a semi-stupor, partly from fright and perhaps partly because of some crushing blow on his head. Allan's quick look saw the coarse black hair was matted with drying blood.

Rogan and Choctaw occupied rawhide chairs on either side of a small home-made table. The former had a demi-john tipped to his lips. He drank deeply, noisily, dropped the demi-john on the table and pushed it across to his companion.

"Sure good an' cold, that creek water," he said loudly. His gaze swung to the dazed prisoner. "How you feelin', feller? You sure took a mean bump on your head."

Young Bannock looked at him with lack-lustre eyes. "I'm sick," he muttered; and then, more loudly, "what are you going to do with me?"

"Nothin' a-tall, 'cept kind of nurse you some," Rogan answered. Evil amusement was in the grin he gave his companion. "We found you layin' there in the brush an' fetched you over to our place here." Rogan spoke soothingly. "Some fellers was down the trail, an' we figured they was lookin' for you—mebbe was fixin' to kill you—so we sneaked you away from 'em."

"Don't seem to remember," muttered Rod Bannock. He put a hand to the lump on his head. "I'm sick," he repeated. He stared thirstily at the demi-john on the table. "I—I'm thirsty."

"Give him a drink." Rogan grinned at the half-breed. "That there fresh jug you just filled at the creek," he added.

Choctaw got up, reached for the demi-john on the floor near the door. He jerked upright, turned a startled look at the window.

"Thought I seen a shadow move," he muttered uneasily.

"Nothin' but the wind blowing that piece of cowhide," Rogan told him.

The freshening wind was lifting the stiff cowhide drawn back from the little window. It billowed for a brief instant, fell back against the wall with a sharp, scraping sound. Reassured, Choctaw picked up the demi-john and slouched over to young Bannock. The latter was speaking again in a low, mumbling, puzzled voice.

"What was I tied up for?"

"You was actin' kind of loco," Rogan explained. "We had to rope you to the horse to keep you from lopin' off into the chaparral. When a feller acts loco like you done, he's got to be tied up."

"Don't remember nothin'," mumbled the dazed youth. He reached for the demi-john in the half-breed's hands.

Warned by Choctaw's startled exclamation, Allan had ducked low beneath the window, his ears tense for signs of further suspicion. He heard Rogan's voice reassuring the half-breed, the latter's tread as he crossed the earthen floor. Again he dared to lift his head for a cautious look, grimly aware now that the crisis had come for both Rod Bannock and himself. The demi-john was already in the youth's hands, was tilted to parched, thirsty lips.

Absorbed in watching their unsuspecting victim, Rogan and Choctaw failed to notice the shadow darkening the window at their backs.

"Take a good swig, young feller," the former was saying, "make you feel better——" He broke off with a startled oath, suddenly aware of a movement behind him.

Surprised to see Rogan tumble sideways out of his chair, the half-breed whirled, hand jerking at his gun as he glimpsed the face at the window.

The gun in Allan's hand exploded twice. The first bullet smashed the demi-john Rod was holding to his lips, the second bullet took Choctaw between the eyes. The half-breed was dead before he crumpled to the floor among fragments of broken glass, the gun in his hand exploding as he fell.

The triple blast of gunfire lifted Rod Bannock to his feet, face and shirt drenched with water. For a moment he stared stupidly around the smoke-filled room, then shudderingly collapsed, lay sprawled across the prone body of the slain half-breed.

Allan continued to crouch at the window in a futile effort to locate Rogan. Acrid gun-smoke eddied through the window, stung his eyes. A gun crashed, and he heard the vicious spat of a bullet in the log above his head. For the moment the advantage was Rogan's. The man was lightning fast with his gun.

There was a silence, broken by the sound of a voice reaching from the haze of smoke that curled from the window.

"Let's call it quits, feller. You go your way, an' I'll go mine. No sense us smokin' our guns at each other on account of a drunken bum."

There was no hint of fear in Rogan's voice. His tone was coolly matter-of-fact.

Allan ignored the offered truce. With the stealth of a stalking cat he edged away from the window and reached the cowhide flap over the door. He straightened up, stood there, gun ready, ears keyed for any movement beyond that piece of sunbaked hide. Rogan spoke again, his voice surly, heavy with growing menace.

"Bannock ain't dead, but he's due for a quick check to hell if you don't make it a deal awful fast."

No answer from Allan. His gun hand lifted, and slowly his free hand fastened on the stiff hide. He knew the purpose behind Rogan's talk. The man hoped to catch him off guard long enough to get in the first and fatal shot.

"I'm all set to pull trigger." Rogan's snarl betrayed growing desperation, a real panic. Allan's continued silence worried him. "I ain't foolin'. Bannock's due for a dose o' hot slugs if you don't spill out some peace talk."

Anxiety suddenly beset Allan. He had small reason to grieve if Rogan killed Cole Bannock's detestable son, but Rod was also the brother of the girl he loved. Allan knew he would never forgive himself if he let Kay down in this dreadful moment of life or death. Rogan was desperate. He would not stay his hand in reaching for any sort of revenge. Once he knew escape was impossible, Rogan would keep his promise to kill Rod.

Allan's mind and body shifted into high gear, a perfectly co-ordinated, smoothly functioning dynamo of cool and resolute action. His outstretched hand dropped from the cowhide that covered the doorway, and in the same swooping motion seized a battered zinc water-bucket that lay on its side close to the shack. The bucket soared into the air, descended with a loud, tearing crash on the willow-thatched roof. An oath exploded from the man inside, the quick stamp of his booted feet. In that same instant Allan reached again for the cowhide flap.

Startled by the crash over his head, Rogan stood with his back to the door, a gun in each hand, gaze roving up furiously for sight of the enemy he thought was trying to get a shot at him from the roof. The harsh creak of the cowhide as Allan tore the thing aside swung Rogan round.

The latter had no words now, only bullets for the tall, grim-faced man framed in the narrow entrance. Flame and smoke belched from the guns he held low at either hip, and then, of a sudden, he was reeling sideways in a half-spin, guns clattering to the mud floor from nerveless hands.

Allan watched him from the doorway, his own gun lowered. He knew that his single bullet had found its mark. Rogan was dead before his hard body hit the floor.

Allan continued to stare at the slain renegade, his face a grim mask. He detested this business of killing, but it was Rogan's life or his life —and Rod Bannock's.

New sounds broke the silence as Allan stood there. Horses, coming on the run, old Limpy Gregg's shrill war-cry.

Something like a grin broke the taut lines of Allan's face as he glimpsed three riders bursting from the willow brakes. Custer Boone and Stumpy Hill in a neck-and-neck race, with Limpy a poor third, but his voice lifted in wild rebel yells to let Allan know he was on the way. The trio had crossed the creek some quarter of a mile above the water-hole and must have heard the gunshots.

It was in Allan's mind that his bullet had not smashed the demi-john quickly enough. Rod Bannock lay like a dead man across the prostrate body of the slain half-breed. Allan bent down for a closer look. Custer and Stumpy hurried into the room, came to a shocked standstill.

"My gawd, Boss! What's been goin' on here?" Custer Boone's sunburned face took on a greenish pallor. "Looks like a slaughter-house."

"Shut your mouth," rasped Limpy Gregg from the doorway behind him. His look went to Allan, read the torture behind the set mask of his face. "It was them, or you, Boss. 'Tain't murder, killin' sidewinders like Rogan an' Choctaw."

Between them they lifted the unconscious Bannock to the bunk.

"He's sure a mean pup, but he's Kay's brother and I reckon we've got to do what we can for him," muttered Limpy.

"What's he doin' here?" wondered Stumpy. "Don't make good sense, Rod Bannock—here in the Sinks."

"Wish I knew the answer, Stumpy," Allan replied. He gave the deeply puzzled Triple R men a brief account of the affair. "Don't think Rod got more than a swallow or two of that water," he finished.

"Been swillin' whisky like a hog," Limpy commented. His eyes narrowed as he stared at the senseless man. "Looks like he's been gun-whipped by the signs of that gash in his head.   Guess it's more'n that swaller o' poison water that's troublin' him."

"He's coming out of it," muttered Allan.

Rod's eyes fluttered open, and he began to retch painfully.

"Best thing he can do," observed Limpy. "That poison water ain't mixin' with all the whisky he's soaked with."

Custer Boone stared at the two dead Double Star men. "Looks like we're collectin' some pieces of that picture puzzle," he observed. "Sure crave to know how come two Double Star fellers an' Rod Bannock was holed down here in the Poison Sinks." The red-headed cowboy gave Allan a perplexed look. "Don't put it past Rogan an' Choctaw to do some cow-stealin', but I sure cain't figger how Rod fits into the picture."

Rod was suddenly sitting up, something like sanity in his staring eyes, a dawning recognition in the look he fastened on Allan.

"Rand," he muttered, "*Rand——*" His breath came in long, painful gasps. "He's pullin' off a raid to-night! My God, Rand—he's raiding Stacy—*to-night!*"

Allan bent closer to him. "Who's raiding Stacy?" Excitement made his voice brittle.

"Rengo——" Rod's head went down on his chest. He was visibly struggling to hold on to his senses. "Tell Harker . . . tell him to get to Stacy before it's too late.   Jim will be killed, and Nora . . . burned out."

Allan tried another question. "You know who Rengo is, Rod?"

"Rengo's a devil . . . he—he——" The sick man's voice trailed away in a long, sighing gasp.

Limpy Gregg's disappointed voice broke the sudden silence.

"Looks like Rod won't be tellin' what he knows about Rengo." He bent close over the inert form on the cot, pressed his ear to Rod's chest. "Heart's workin'," he added, "awful feeble, though."

"We've got to keep him alive." Allan spoke fiercely. "We've got to keep him alive, if it's only long enough for him to tell what he knows about Rengo."

Limpy slowly turned and looked at him. "You ain't forgettin' what he said about Jim Stacy." His tone was grim. "They don't come better than Jim Stacy."

"No," answered Allan. "I'm not forgetting what he said about

Jim Stacy." He glanced at Custer and Stumpy. "Get those dead men out of here. Don't waste too much time with them."

"What'll we do with Rod?" queried Limpy Gregg when the two cowboys had dragged out the slain Double Star men. "He ain't in no shape to fork a saddle."

"Somebody's got to stay here with him," Allan told the old man. "You're elected, Limpy."

"I was figurin' to ride to Stacy's with you." Limpy's tone was aggrieved. "Dang the luck!"

"Rod is your job," Allan pointed out. "If there's a chance to pull him through, you can do it. He'd probably die if we left it to Custer or Stumpy." Allan paused, stared intently at the glowering Triple R veteran. "It's an important job, Limpy. Don't forget that Rod can tell us what he knows about Rengo."

Limpy brightened. "I savvy, boss," he said laconically. "Leave it to me."

"Get word to Sheriff Harker if Rod tells you who Rengo is," instructed Allan. He turned towards the door.

"You bet," grunted Limpy.

Allan paused in the doorway, his expression suddenly rueful. "What did you do with my horse, Limpy? I left him with you back in the gully."

"Your buck horse trailed along with us when we come kitin' to see what kept you so long." Limpy grinned. "We got some uneasy when you didn't show up." He chuckled. "You said for us to work things out for ourselves if you was gone too long," he reminded.

Allan nodded. "I was depending on you," he told the old man soberly. "I knew you'd be johnny-on-the-spot, Limpy."

He broke into a run towards the corral. He could see the tall buckskin there, standing with the other horses. It was a long, hard ride to Jim Stacy's S Bar ranch. He prayed they would be in time. Custer and Stumpy were also on the run for the corral, from the hastily fashioned grave with its scant covering of stones.

Allan's eyes took on a steely look. There was a picture in his mind, a bronze-faced young man in a buckboard, a fair-haired girl by his side, a little baby in her lap. "The Stacys . . . they've got the sweetest little baby." Kay's low voice was in Allan's ears as he ran.

12

THE red mare disliked Wirt Gunnel. She laid ears back, snorted nervously as the foreman approached. Wirt had a peculiar rolling, choppy walk and a way of holding his arms slightly crooked that made him seem in a perpetual state of belligerency. Kay gave him an impatient look across the saddle she was easing down on the mare's back.

"Don't come too close, Wirt," she said. "Chuparosa's afraid of you." She reached for the dangling cinch, drew it tight with deft fingers.

"Limpy never broke her right," commented the foreman. "She needs a good bustin' . . . take some of the hell out of her."

"She's gentle enough with me," asserted the girl. "Don't you ever dare to rough-ride Chuparosa."

He ogled her boldly. "Been hearin' talk that Steve Starr is swingin' his loop for you," he said. "Don't blame him, Kay. You've growed up pretty as they come." His swarthy face creased in a teasing smile.

Kay gave him a level-eyed look. She had always been the least bit afraid of Wirt Gunnel. She was like Chuparosa. He frightened her. Wirt was always respectful enough. He no longer attempted his clumsy fondlings, not since her fifteenth birthday. Wirt's gift was a Mexican quirt, and, suddenly enraged by his accompanying kiss, she had used the whip on his face. She had always resented the feel of his hands. Looking at him now, the girl sensed that Wirt Gunnel was remembering that blow. The man hated her.

She made no attempt to conceal her annoyance at the coupling of her name with the owner of the Double Star.

"You say that just to be mean," she charged hotly.

"Only tellin' you what Rod says," grinned Wirt. "Rod says Steve Starr is sweet on you. Reckon Rod knows, him bein' so thick with Steve."

The mention of her brother brought a worried look to the girl's eyes. Rod's continued absence both alarmed and angered her father.

"Do you know where he is, Wirt?" Kay forced a more friendly tone into her voice. "I'm riding to town to ask Shawnee Jones if he's seen him."

The foreman shook his head. He had no idea of Rod's whereabouts.

"Ain't seen Rod since the night Rand stopped here," he told the girl. "Met him down on the river flats, said he was headed for town." Wirt hunched a shoulder. "Like as not he's layin' round drunk some place. He was sure red-eyed about the boss givin' Rand a job with the outfit."

"It's Steve Starr's fault!" flared the girl. "Rod didn't drink so dreadfully until he began running around with Steve Starr."

"Rod's a weak sister." Wirt's smile was a thinly veiled sneer. "He needs the hell busted out of him—same as your mare does."

"I hate you!" Kay told him furiously.

"You need a man to bust you good," retorted the foreman.

"You—you——" Kay snatched her quirt from the saddle-horn and slashed at the sneering face. Wirt dropped an oath, sprang aside, and the twisted rawhide thong slid harmlessly down his shoulder. "I'll tell Dad!" stormed the girl.

"Maybe your dad thinks the same as I do," grinned Wirt. He backed away, wary of the quirt in her hand, and now his tone was suddenly friendly, placating. "You're sure one little piece of dynamite, Kay. Feller tries to joke you and you explode right in his face."

"Didn't sound like a joke," fumed the girl. "I don't like your idea of a joke."

His grin widened. "Maybe I was some rough," he continued to placate. "Tell you what I'll do, Kay. I'm ridin' over Red Canyon way this mornin', and I'll take a look in at the Double Star and ask Steve if he's seen Rod." The foreman nodded. "Like as not Rod is layin' over in Steve's house, sleepin' it off. Steve would be takin' care of him if he run across him in town."

"Oh, Wirt, I'll be so grateful." There was a hint of repentance in Kay's voice. "I—I'm sorry I got so mad."

"Forget it." Wirt shrugged dusty, compact shoulders. "Ain't likin' you less for actin' spitfire."

She frowned, again suddenly resentful. "Send word to Shawnee Jones if you find Rod at Starr's place." Kay forced a smile, managed to keep a friendly note in her voice.

"I'll do that," promised the foreman. He went off with his swaggering boxer's walk. Kay's gaze followed him, saw that Brazos and Gus Silver were waiting with their horses in the shade of a big cottonwood-tree near the yard gate.

The girl was aware of a troublesome dissatisfaction as she watched the three Triple R men ride away. Brazos, Gus Silver—and Wirt Gunnel. Of the score or more riders on her father's pay-roll, these three were the only men she disliked. Why her father tolerated Wirt Gunnel she could not understand. The man was hard, openly insolent at times. Cole Bannock had shown grim amusement at her veiled hints that he should discharge Wirt Gunnel. Bossing the Triple R outfit needed a hard man like Wirt, he would tell her curtly. Wirt was a first-rate man with cows—knew his business. Kay was beginning to wonder if her father's estimate of Wirt was right. If the man knew his business, why was the ranch losing so heavily to rustlers. Her intuitions were entirely against her father's faith in the swart-faced foreman. She distrusted Wirt Gunnel, and she heartily disliked Brazos and Gus Silver. The pair bore the mark of the killer breed, were obviously hireling gunmen. But perhaps men of their stamp were needed on the ranch. Rustlers made a problem that called for ruthless action.

Kay stepped into her saddle and rode slowly across the big yard towards the ranch office, a vague wish in her mind that she could be boss of the Triple R, at least long enough to send Wirt Gunnel and his two cronies packing. She'd put Allan Rand in charge as foreman of the outfit. The old ranch would be a different place. Allan was a good cowman too, and he could be as hard as Wirt Gunnel, only in a different way. She was conscious of a wild longing to see him, hear his quiet, reassuring voice. There was something so competent in the steadfast look of him.

Her father spoke to her from his office doorway as she drew rein. "I want to talk to you, Kay," he said. "Climb down and come in."

His solemn tone startled her. She slipped out of her saddle, followed him into the office. There was a grey look about Cole Bannock's face. Kay was conscious of chilling apprehension. Only something dreadful could have brought that ominously grim look to her father's face. She sat down, stared at him with frightened eyes.

Cole Bannock pulled a cigar from his shirt-pocket, looked at it gloomily for a moment, then flipped it to the desk. There was a perceptible tremor to his fingers.

"Ain't easy to tell you what's on my mind," he began slowly. "Sooner face a loaded gun an' me empty-handed."

"Why, Dad!" Kay managed a light laugh. "What in the world's got into you?"

"Never thought I'd be telling you," Cole Bannock went on. "Maybe I acted wrong from the start. Wasn't that I meant any meanness . . . just didn't seem necessary to—to tell you the truth."

Kay stared at him, bewilderment, growing fright, in her eyes. She made no attempt to speak. Words were futile at that moment. His distress was too apparent to ignore. He began again, his voice gruff.

"I ain't your dad really . . ."

The confession wrung a startled cry from the girl. Cole Bannock's big, sunburned face broke out into beads of sweat.

"Guess it's some shock, hearin' me say I'm not really your own father." He shook his massive head. "Don't make things any different with me, Kay. I love you like you're my own daughter."

Kay found her voice. "I—I just can't believe it." She tried to speak calmly, managed a faint smile of mingled amusement and concern. "You're not yourself, Dad, talking so queerly."

"I ain't crazy in the head," he reassured her. "It's the truth, Kay. I'm not your father."

She saw now that he meant it, gave him a wild look.

"Who *is* my father?" The question came from her in a scarcely audible whisper.

"He's been dead since before you were a yearlin'," Cole Bannock told her. "Killed in a raid." His voice hushed, and then, very gently, "You've seen his grave often enough, Kay."

Her eyes widened in a quick, understanding look. "You mean Rob Hood's grave? You—you mean he—he was my father?"

"Robin was my best friend." There was emotion in the big cattleman's voice, a hint of lingering affection. "That's why I took you when he died, raised you like you was my own daughter." He paused, added softly, "That's why I buried him out there in the garden. Thought he'd maybe rest more peaceful, with you close to him."

Kay was silent. She was too moved for words. It was her father, lying out there in the neglected old grave. If only she had known the truth no weeds would now be growing over Robin Hood's grave. The thought of that neglected plot behind the vine-grown picket-fence sent hot shame waving over the girl. She should have cared for it, no matter whose grave.

"I wish I'd known," she said miserably.

"Didn't seem necessary," repeated the rancher.

She saw he misunderstood her. With an effort she pushed the picture of the neglected grave aside. There were other things she must know.

"My—my mother?"

"She's dead too," interrupted Bannock. "Died when you was born." His voice softened. "A right pretty girl, your mother was. Don't know much about her, only that her folks was killed by Indians. Was headin' for Oregon from Kentucky when a war party jumped the wagon train."

Kay repressed a shudder, and after a moment she said thoughtfully, "Then my name is not really Bannock. I'm Kay Hood."

"No reason for you to stop being Kay Bannock," protested her foster-father. "No need for changin' your name, 'cept for the plan that's in my mind. If you do what I want, you can keep right on bein' Kay Bannock."

"I—I don't understand," puzzled the girl. She shook her head. "I'd want to use my father's name."

"I've a reason for telling you about Rob Hood," rumbled the cattleman. He paused, stared at her intently. "It's got to do with Rod."

She tensed in her chair, paled under his look. His voice took on a harsher, almost defiant note.

"Maybe you can guess why I want you to know you and Rod are not really brother and sister."

"Please"—Kay sprang to her feet—"please, Dad—don't say any more!" She gave him a horrified look.

"I've got my reasons." His tone was stubborn. "Been in my mind for most a year that I want you and Rod to marry. I love you, even if you ain't my real daughter, and if you marry Rod you'll be fixed comfortable for life."

Kay listened in aghast silence. Out of the confusion his words caused stood one clear thought. She understood now his attitude towards Allan Rand. He feared Allan as a possible obstacle to his plans for her. Until Allan's advent she had given him no cause for such fears.

"I've got my heart set on this thing," he went on more gently, almost pleadingly. "Rod's playin' the damn' fool. You can straighten him up, make a decent feller out of him."

She found her voice, said faintly, "Rod doesn't like me. He's always trying to pick a quarrel. He won't want it any more than I do."

"Rod'll change his mind when he knows you ain't his sister." Cole Bannock smiled. "You're mighty pretty, Kay. Won't be no trouble about Rod. He'll look at you the way any man looks at a pretty girl."

"I can't bear it," she said desperately. "I—I could never think of him in that way, as a girl thinks of a man she—she might marry."

He shook her protests aside. "You'll come round to it. Rod's a good-lookin' feller." He paused, added slowly, "Rod'll have the ranch after I'm gone, Kay. When you marry him, I'll fix it so you'll be half-owner."

"I'd rather starve to death," Kay told him with a despairing gesture.

"You'll come round to it," he repeated. "I'm set on this marriage. I like my way about things, and I ain't goin' to let any foolish notions beat me."

There was a long silence. Cole Bannock watched her, his expression a mixture of tenderness and hard resolve. "It's the best way to settle things that have worried me a lot," he said finally, and then, with a quick, almost sly look at her, "I mean it'll make a man out of Rod and fix things so you can stay on here at the ranch. You'll still be Kay Bannock—and half-owner of the Triple R."

She gazed at him, unpleasantly impressed by that oddly furtive look. It was unlike him. She had never seen any hint of slyness in Cole Bannock before. The conviction grew in the girl's mind that he was holding something back. Cole Bannock had not given her *all* his reasons for wanting this marriage. Kay had no doubts of his affection. Cole Bannock loved her as a daughter. His wish was not unnatural. She would be his son's wife and more than ever his daughter. She found no flaw in his reasoning, realized with some pity how painful the effort to make the confession. For the sake of this marriage he had been obliged to tell her the amazing truth, admit he was not her father, nor Rod her brother. It all sounded reasonable enough, and yet Kay found herself vaguely conscious of disturbing doubts. Cole Bannock was keeping something back. There was another and more vital reason for his wanting her to marry his son.

He broke in on her distracted thoughts. "You can think it over," he said with a gruff kindliness. "I'll break it to Rod when he gets back."

"He won't like it, any more than I do," Kay said bitterly.

"I'm used to havin' my way," reminded Cole Bannock. He leaned back in his chair, narrowed his eyes thoughtfully. "We'll fix to have the weddin' soon as you can get ready. No sense waitin', now you know the truth. You'll be happy enough, Kay. Don't you worry about Rod. He'll buck up, quit his fool ways. All he needs is a good woman like you." The cattleman spoke confidently. Now that the worst was over he was again his jocular, booming-voiced self. "We'll have a bang-up weddin', with all the fancy trimmin's," he chuckled.

Kay felt she could stand no more. She flung him a piteous look and fled out to the sunlight to her waiting mare.

She was half-way down the long, winding avenue before her confused mind began to function with something like coherence. She drew Chuparosa to a standstill under the shade of a chinaberry-tree. One thought was sharply clear. She was not going to marry Rod Bannock. She would run away.

For long moments she sat there, slumped despondently in her saddle, her tortured mind turning this way and that for some answer to the dreadful surprise Cole Bannock had sprung on her. She was in a trap. Her only escape lay in flight. She had no idea where to go. Cole Bannock was not one to accept defeat without a struggle. He would find ways of forcing her to bow to his will. Kay held no illusions about the man who had been the only father she had ever known. He was the ruthless despot when he chose to be. His voice spoke the last word in the affairs of the Roaring River country. She dreaded his rage. To run away was easier said than done. It meant horseback or the stage. Cole Bannock's word would travel faster than either of these only means of escape. He would have her back at the ranch long before she could reach safety.

She thought wildly of appealing to Sheriff Ed Harker. The veteran law officer was kindly, her friend since she was a small girl. Kay reluctantly dropped the idea. The sheriff would not oppose Cole Bannock. He would doubtless advise her to marry Rod Bannock.

The rattle of buckboard wheels brought the girl out of her frantic conjecturings. Her eyes widened. Sheriff Harker—and looking very solemn as he pulled his team to a halt.

The sheriff's first words made Kay temporarily forget her own troubles.

"Nora's baby is awful sick," he told her. "Got the measles bad, from what Doc Gary says."

"Oh, Uncle Ed."

"Nora's sick in bed, too," went on the sheriff. "Slipped on something in the kitchen and broke her arm. She sent word for Doc Gary to tell her mother, but Mrs Riley went to Shoshone yesterday. Won't be back for a couple of days."

"I'll go!" exclaimed the girl. "I'll go, Uncle Ed."

"I figured you'd maybe want to go." The sheriff's face crinkled in a pleased smile. "Told Doc Gary he could bank on it." He picked up a small package from the seat. "The doc give me some medicine for you to take along."

Kay slid from the mare and unfastened the flap of her small saddle-pouch. Sheriff Harker watched her with benign interest as she tucked the bottle of medicine securely inside.

"You sure look like a boy in them pants—almost." He chuckled.

"Dad roared all over the place when I told him I was done with riding sidesaddle," laughed Kay.

"You've got plenty good sense," approved the old sheriff.

The girl swung back to her saddle, gave him a thoughtful look. "You're going on up to the house, Uncle Ed?"

"Was figurin' to see your dad," admitted Sheriff Harker. "Got some news for him." His voice took on a harder note. "I'm thinkin' it's news that won't surprise him much."

"Uncle Ed——" She spoke quickly. "You tell Dad about Nora Stacy . . . tell him where I've gone."

The sheriff looked at her doubtfully. "Don't know as you should ride over to the S Bar by your lonesome, Kay."

She derided his fears. "I've done it lots of times by myself. The S Bar isn't so far if you know the short-cuts."

"Ain't feared of you gettin' lost." The sheriff spoke worriedly. "You know the trails good enough. Don't like you ridin' over to the S Bar alone. Too close to the Poison Sinks country. No tellin' but what you might run into trouble."

"I'm not afraid," scoffed the girl. "Anyway, I'm going, Uncle Ed."

"Better come back to the house with me and ask your dad, first," suggested the sheriff. "He'll likely want to send one of the boys with you."

The thought of facing Cole Bannock appalled Kay. It was unthinkable, in her present state of mind. She wanted to get as far away as possible, and she had grasped eagerly at the opportunity offered by the call for help from the Stacys. She would have gone immediately, in any event. She was devoted to Nora and Jim and absurdly fond of their baby.

She grew conscious of the sheriff's puzzled, questioning look. She longed to tell him the amazing truth about herself. It seemed a poor time, and she was afraid she would break down. She didn't want Sheriff Harker to see her in tears.

"You tell him, Uncle Ed." She spoke quietly. "*Adios.*"

The sheriff craned his head, watched frowningly until a bend in the avenue hid mare and rider. His expression showed dissatisfaction, a hint of troubled perplexity. He was too sharp to be easily deceived. Kay was not herself. She had visibly paled at his suggestion that she should ask Cole Bannock's permission.

The worried sheriff spoke sharply to his team of long-legged bays, went rattling up the avenue. He had uneasy premonitions that Cole Bannock wasn't going to like it when he heard about Kay.

The big cattleman saw him drive into the yard.

"Hello, Ed." Bannock approached slowly from the ranch office. "What's the good word?"

Sheriff Harker edged himself between the buckboard wheels.

"Picked up some news about that feller Bert Nye," he said. "Thought you'd be some interested."

"He's a rascal," declared Bannock. "Just the same, I'll pay him hard cash for that Red Canyon land he claims he bought from Steve Starr. Is that your news, Ed—that the skunk wants to make a deal?"

Sheriff Harker eased his wiry frame out of his long dust-coat and tossed it into the buckboard seat.

"Ain't seen Nye and don't know what he figures to do about your offer, Cole." His smile was wintry. "I've had a feller watchin' him."

Cole Bannock gave him a sharp look, saw that his friend's expression was unusually grim.

"Nye knows the truth about Rengo," went on the sheriff. "He's one of the gang." He shook his head as the Triple R owner started to speak. "No—it don't mean Nye's told us what he knows about Rengo. We ain't caught up with Nye yet."

"How come you know Nye's in with Rengo?" queried Bannock. "Might as well we sit down while we talk," he added.

Sheriff Harker followed him into the office and made himself comfortable in a big arm-chair.

"Been suspicious of Nye ever since he showed up in Red Canyon," he drawled. "Nye's new to these parts and seemed to have too much money to spend for a poor homesteader. Used to be you'd find him most any night over in the Royal Flush. So I got to thinkin' about him a lot."

"He's not a homesteader exactly," pointed out Cole Bannock. "He claims he bought that Red Canyon land from Starr."

"Sure." The sheriff nodded. "Went about tellin' he figured to plant his forty to peaches. I was over to his place several times. Never could see signs he'd been doin' a lick of work. Only one answer, far as I could make it. Nye was in with the rustlers, or from where was he gettin' his money?"

The argument impressed Cole Bannock. "Looks like you made a good guess," he agreed.

The sheriff smiled. "It's more than guess-work now. Nye kind of messed things up for himself when he come to the office the other day with his yarn about the Pecos Kid."

"I was there," reminded the cattleman. "Sure, he said the Kid told him that Allan Rand was Rengo."

"Knew from the start Nye was lyin'," asserted Harker. "I know all about young Rand and why he's here in the Roaring River country."

"You never said nothin' to me about knowin' Rand," grumbled Bannock.

"A friend of mine, Sheriff Truman, wrote me about him. Truman didn't say much, 'cept to vouch for him, but Rand talked a lot, so I knew Nye was lyin' all the way down the line when he come in with his yarn about Rand bein' Rengo."

Cole Bannock stared at him resentfully. "Seems to me you might have told me what you knew about Rand. You was in the office when I hired him. Why didn't you let on you knew about him, Ed?"

"Wasn't my business to tell you," countered the sheriff. "You never asked me, and anyway you was hot enough to get him on the Triple R pay-roll. Wouldn't take no for an answer." Sheriff Harker's smile hinted of mystery. "I was some surprised young Rand took you up. From what he told me he wasn't in Roarin' River lookin' for a job."

"I'm beginning to savvy." The cattleman's good humour returned. He chuckled. "You mean Rand's an Association detective, huh?"

"Wasn't rustler business that brought him to Roarin' River," drawled the sheriff. Ignoring Bannock's sulky look, he went back to Nye. "Seemed like somethin' was smellin' high in the wood-pile," he went on. "Only one reason for him to get us thinkin' Rand was Rengo. It was Rengo put him up to it."

"Looks that way," agreed Bannock. He spoke grumpily.

"I got Billy Hall to put a man on Nye's trail, and it looks like we sure got the goods on him. This feller's an Indian and he's been on Nye's trail day and night." Sheriff Harker chuckled. "Guess Nye would be awful surprised."

"What did this Indian of yours find out?" queried the cattleman.

"For one thing he heard Nye talkin' with a feller named Rogan some place in the hills close to the Poison Sinks——"

"I know Rogan," interrupted Bannock. His face crimsoned

angrily. "Rogan's with the Double Star outfit." The cattleman's big fist smacked the desk. "Hell's bells, what does it mean, Ed? One of Steve Starr's punchers talkin' secret with this Nye feller?"

"Don't go off half-cock," counselled the sheriff. "From what the Indian told me this Rogan is mixed up with the Rengo gang, but that don't mean Steve Starr knows it."

"Wouldn't put it past Luce Henders," grumbled Cole Bannock.

Sheriff Harker was inclined to doubt that Henders was a cow-thief. "I've knowed Luce for years," he argued. "Luce is awful hard, and mean as the devil when he's crossed, but he hates a rustler the way you do."

"He's maybe got you fooled," snorted the Triple R man. "Luce Henders is smart. How do we know he ain't this Rengo feller that's makin' monkeys out of us."

The sheriff's expression was thoughtful, but for some reason he apparently chose to drop the discussion of the mysterious arch-rustler's identity.

"Met Wirt Gunnel up the road a-ways," he said abruptly.

"Wirt's gone over to Red Canyon——" Bannock frowned. "I told him to tear that fence down that Nye strung across his land. The summer's comin' on, and I ain't standin' for that damn' fence keeping my cows from the creek."

"He told me he was goin' to cut them wires," commented Harker.

"We'll keep 'em down if it means usin' guns," vowed the cattleman angrily. He straightened up in his chair, stared excitedly at the sheriff. "Hell's bells, Ed—comes to me we've got this Nye feller by the tail now you've the goods on him. You can clap him in gaol if you can prove he's runnin' with the Rengo gang."

"Got to catch him, first," grunted the sheriff.

"We'll nab him if he shows up in Red Canyon," gloated the rancher. He paused, stroked his heavy beard thoughtfully. "Did you tell Wirt what you've learned about Nye?"

"No," answered Sheriff Harker laconically. "No, I didn't tell him, Cole." He gave the other man a curiously sly look.

"Too bad," muttered Bannock disappointedly. "I'll send word to Wirt to leave Brazos and Gus Silver on the watch for him."

"Wirt was tellin' me about young Rand takin' old Limpy Gregg over to the Mesa camp," remarked the sheriff. "Wirt figures Rand's kind of simple. Took young Custer Boone and Stumpy Hill along with him. Wirt says he offered to let him have Brazos and Gus, but Rand turned 'em down."

"Those kids are good," declared Cole Bannock. He shook his head. "Kind of stumps me why he'd want old Limpy, though. Told him so myself."

"There's maybe a reason you don't savvy," murmured the sheriff softly. "You see, he told me about what he's in Roarin' River for."

"Don't savvy where Limpy Gregg comes in," grumbled the cattle-man.

"Limpy's an old-timer," pointed out the sheriff. "I'm thinkin' he wants to ask Limpy some questions."

"What you drivin' at, Ed?" Cole Bannock's voice showed irritation. He disliked mysteries.

"Rand told me he's lookin' for a feller used to be a friend of his dad's."

Cole Bannock seemed to stiffen in his chair, and when he spoke there was a hint of fear in his voice.

"What's the name of this feller Rand's lookin' for?"

"Tom Sherwood," answered the sheriff, "Tom Sherwood. Ever hear of him, Cole?"

There was a long silence, broken only by the buzzing of a big horsefly that rocketed in through the open door and out again. Sheriff Harker looked at his friend in some surprise, wondered at his strange pallor.

"No . . ." The rancher shook his head slowly. "No, I—I ain't rememberin' the name, Ed."

"Rand said this Sherwood maybe wasn't usin' his own name," Harker went on. "Some cow-poke used to work for Rand's dad had a yarn about his workin' for a feller down here in the Roarin' River country, claimed he'd seen a letter with Tom Sherwood written on it." The sheriff gestured. "Must have been more'n twenty years ago and before my time."

"Who in hell is Rand?" Cole Bannock asked the question harshly.

"He's got a ranch back in the Pecos country," Harker replied. "From what Truman wrote, Rand's well fixed." The sheriff laughed softly. "You can savvy why I was surprised when he took a job

with you. Ain't so surprisin', though," he added musingly.
"Reckon he figured to have chances to scout round with the old-
timers like Limpy Gregg—and then there's Kay. She kind of took
his fancy, I'm thinkin'."

Bannock glowered. It was obvious the sheriff's revelations dis-
pleased him.

"Wouldn't have hired him if I'd known what you've just told
me," he growled. "Don't like him snoopin' round. If he'd come
and asked me straight, I could have told him he's wastin' his time
looking for any Tom Sherwood in these parts. I ought to know.
Been here long before there was any town of Roaring River."

"Rand says this feller made some talk of a little baby girl," put
in Sheriff Harker. "He's awful anxious to find her, if she's still
alive."

"He's crazy!" shouted the cattleman.

"Don't see why you go on the prod about it," observed Harker
mildly.

"Won't stand for him snoopin' round," declared Bannock furiously. "If he wants information, why don't he come and ask me
man to man?" The rancher's big fist pounded the desk. "He don't
want me to know what he's up to—that's why."

"Rand didn't say for me not to tell you," protested Harker.
"What's eatin' you, Cole?"

"At that I'll bet he's lying," asserted Cole Bannock. He spoke
more quietly, was obviously struggling to keep control of his temper.
"He's up to mischief, maybe thinks he can make a play for Kay by
letting it out he owns a big ranch." Bannock seemed to find comfort in the thought. "Fills you up with a cock-an'-bull story about
owning a ranch . . . knows you'll tell Kay . . . get her interested
in him."

"You're loco." Harker was irate. "Guess I'll be on my way,"
he added as he got out of his chair. He came to a standstill, stared
back at the fuming rancher. "Forgot to tell you that Kay's gone
over to the S Bar."

"Huh!" Cole Bannock's face reddened. "Run away, huh?"

"Not that I know of." The sheriff stared at him. "She's gone
to nurse Nora Stacy's baby." He explained in terse words the situa-
tion at the Stacy ranch. "Met Kay as I come up the avenue,"

Harker concluded. "Soon as she heard the news, she said she'd go and help. Told me to tell you where she'd gone."

Cole Bannock's face was like a thunder-cloud. He got slowly to his feet and reached for the gun-belt that hung on a wall-peg.

Sheriff Harker watched him in silence for a moment, and then, worriedly, "Where're you goin', Cole?"

"I'm goin' after that fool girl." The rancher's voice was hoarse with rage. "I'm draggin' her back to where she belongs, and then I'm chasin' young Rand out of the country, if I don't kill him first."

"Don't go off half-cock, Cole," counselled the old sheriff. He was frankly worried. "Kay wasn't doin' wrong—ridin' over to the S Bar to help Nora out."

"I know my business better than you do," retorted Cole Bannock coldly. "Don't you butt in, Ed." He pushed past the bewildered sheriff. The latter hurried after him.

"Look here, Cole—you're in a killin' mood about something I don't savvy."

The rancher shook him off. "Don't you butt in," he repeated in the same rage-choked voice. "I know my business, and I don't need you to help me 'tend to it." He pushed on across the yard towards the barn.

Sheriff Harker turned to his buckboard. He was a puzzled and frankly worried man. Something was very wrong at the Triple R ranch, and young Rand seemed to be mixed up in it.

The old sheriff climbed stiffly into his buckboard, sat there for a moment, pondering deeply. It was up to him to warn young Rand that trouble was headed his way. Nothing he could do but get back to town and send Billy Hall high-tailing it to the Mesa camp. There'd be time enough for Billy to make it. Cole Bannock said he would be going to the S Bar first. Billy could easily make it to the Mesa camp before Bannock got there.

With a relieved grunt, Harker reached for his long whip, and in a moment was rattling out of the yard in a cloud of dust.

13

SOME twenty horsemen rode up the wide wash, vague, slow-moving shapes in the starlit night. They progressed with a dearth of sound, only the muffled beat of hoofs on sand, an occasional tinkle of spurs and creak of saddle leather.

A tall man on a silver-maned sorrel made the spear-point of the somewhat straggling, sinister procession. He wore a black flat-brimmed hat with dangling chin-strap, and short silver-embroidered jacket, and his trousers, snug at the thighs, belled over high-heeled boots.

The wash narrowed between low, barren cliffs, and presently trickles of water threw back silver gleams from the sand. The cliffs drew in closer, and the trickles of water became a flowing stream that tumbled down a boulder-strewn channel.

The stars grew less bright as the riders pushed slowly up the gorge.

"Moon's up," muttered one of the riders.

The gorge widened into a basin, and the moonlight showed the mouth of another canyon that broke down from the hills to the left. The same rider spoke again.

"'Most there," he said to his companion. "Less than a couple of miles to the S Bar from the fork yonder."

Shapes appeared in the mouth of the left fork, moved slowly to meet the riders streaming up from the lower gorge. The man on the silver-maned sorrel lifted a hand as the three horsemen approached.

"Hello, Wirt." He drew rein, grinned at the stocky Triple R foreman. "What's the latest from the boss?"

"He says to make the job look like it was Mex raiders from across the border." Wirt Gunnel's smile was full of sinister meaning. "The boss don't want nobody to get away."

"The Stacy woman too?" The Pecos Kid's tone was indifferent, his face an expressionless mask.

"You heard me," grunted Wirt Gunnel. "The buildings go too. You ain't leavin' a thing to show the S Bar was ever there."

"You ain't ridin' with us?" queried the Kid softly. "You and Gus and Brazos?"

The Triple R foreman shook his head. "We got other business to 'tend to. Down at the Mesa camp," he added, with another mirthless smile.

The Pecos Kid's eyes narrowed. "I'd rather have my job than yours," he muttered. "I'd rather play with forked lightnin'—than face Allan Rand."

"Hell!" Wirt Gunnel's thin lips twisted in a snarling grin. "You talk like this Rand feller was sudden death."

"You don't know him like I do." The young desperado's bold-featured face was oddly pale.

Wirt Gunnel grinned round at his two companions. "Reckon we ain't scared none of this Rand feller, huh, boys?"

"Only Custer Boone and Stumpy Hill with him," commented the beetle-browed Brazos. "If you can take care of Rand, guess we can handle those kids." He grinned. "Limpy don't count."

Gus Silver, plumpish and sandy-haired, said dubiously, "Stumpy's awful fast . . . mebbe a shade faster than any of us."

"You're a liar," scoffed Brazos.

Wirt Gunnel's confident nod showed that he agreed with Brazos. His keen glance ranged over the cluster of riders.

"Where's Bert? Thought he'd be ridin' with you."

"Nye headed back for town," answered the Pecos Kid. "Made out we wouldn't be needing him to finish the job."

The Triple R foreman swore wrathfully. "Bert's awful yeller," he fumed. "Wish he'd kept away from town. I've a notion Ed Harker's lookin' at him kind of fishy-eyed these days. If Harker grabs him, no tellin' but what the skunk'll squeal."

"If you'd told me sooner, I could have given him a dose of medicine." The Kid tapped holstered gun significantly. "It's sure good medicine for his kind."

The young outlaw's callousness drew an admiring chuckle from Wirt Gunnel. "They don't make 'em tougher than you, Kid. Well, so long. See you in town, when you get back from your little trip south."

"Won't be back this way." The Pecos Kid paused, gave the older man a sly, meaning look. "I mean, you won't be seein' me this side of the line again unless you do a good job down there at the Mesa camp."

"Reckon that settles it," grinned Wirt. "You can count on bein' back quick as you've shoved them S Bar cows across the line."

The moon lifted above the encircling saw-toothed peaks, touched the rugged slopes with silver lights and shadows. The Pecos Kid halted his horse and stared across the Mesa.

The S Bar ranch buildings loomed distinctly in the soft, revealing moonlight: the big barn, set back in the corrals, some out-houses, and the small ranch-house with its little garden and shading fruit-trees.

The glimmer of lamplight in one of the windows brought an annoyed oath from the Kid.

"Looks like they ain't gone to bed yet," he said to the others, staring with interest at the place they proposed to pillage.

"Don't see no cattle in the corral," grumbled one of the men. "Nye said there'd be all of five hundred head Stacy had rounded up for his drive to-morrow."

"Listen!" The Kid lifted a hand for silence. The sound that touched their ears was unmistakable. The distant, intermittent bellowing of cattle. "Got 'em somewhere in that gully across the Mesa," muttered the Kid.

"Means some of Stacy's outfit'll be down there with 'em," observed one of the desperadoes.

"Ain't more than four men in Stacy's outfit," the Kid said; "maybe a couple more for the round-up—say six fellers, and Stacy. Won't be more'n a couple of 'em ridin' night herd. That makes three or four in the bunk-house and Stacy in his own place." The Kid's gaze went back to the light glimmering in the window. "Looks like somebody's sick, or the woman's nursin' the baby."

"What are we waitin' for?" grumbled a voice from the rear. "Let's get this job done pronto."

"You can start the fireworks, Fargo," instructed the Kid. "One of you fellers go with him."

Fargo and another rider swung off towards the big barn.

"That straw-stack'll burn fast, too," the Kid called after them.

"We ain't needin' you to tell us," Fargo replied, with a hard laugh. "Won't be the first barn I've fired."

The Kid continued to give his orders. Several of the riders made for a thick growth of scrubby piñons to the left of the ranch-house.

"The fire'll bring Stacy and the fellers in the bunk-house on the run," the Kid said. "You can pick 'em off easy. The rest of us will head down that draw to the gully yonder. Soon as the fireworks begin, we start the cows runnin'. Savvy?"

"Slick work," grinned one of the outlaws. "Them cows is placed just right for stampedin' down to the Sinks."

"What about the woman an' the young 'un?" queried a voice.

"You heard Gunnel tell what the boss said." There was no hint of pity in the Pecos Kid's flat, colourless voice. "It's a clean sweep. Nobody left to do any talkin'."

There was a brief silence, broken by a low, lurid curse from the questioner. "I ain't killin' women an' kids," he declared.

They were his last words. At a covert signal from the pack's cold-eyed young leader, a man leaned from his saddle and drove a knife into the objector's heart. With a low groan the stricken desperado collapsed, fell heavily from his startled horse.

"We ain't takin' chances," the Pecos Kid said briefly in his deadly voice. "All right, fellers. Let's get busy."

They scattered to their appointed places, the main body vanishing into the draw, the others drifting like grey skulking wolves closer to the little ranch-house.

Fargo and his companion were at the straw-stack between the corral and the barn. The former struck a match, leaned from his saddle with the tiny flare. He twitched convulsively, sprawled head-long from his saddle. Fargo never even heard the sharp report of the rifle that shattered the silence of the night. He lay dead in the straw that suddenly ran streaks of red flame as the burning match took hold.

The dead outlaw's companion flung one horrified look and drove in spurs. All thoughts of firing the barn were gone. He wanted to get away from there. Again the rifle's report blasted the night. The fleeing desperado pitched from his saddle.

Imprecations frothed from the Pecos Kid as he swung away and made for the protection of the draw. Something had gone wrong. Just how he did not even attempt to puzzle out at that moment. No chance now to leave the S Bar ranch buildings in smoking ruins.

The ranch-house door flung open with a bang, revealing a man etched against the lamplight, a rifle in his hands. The Kid, roaring past, less than ten yards away, loosed a quick shot from the gun in his hand. He saw the man stagger, saw a slim girl suddenly framed in the lighted doorway. She seized the wounded man, started to drag him inside. The Kid's gun lifted again, only to slip from suddenly limp fingers as something struck him a violent blow across the shoulders. A second bullet smashed into him as he swayed and pitched from the saddle. The riderless sorrel galloped on a few yards, then slowed to a trot that carried him in a wide circle towards a group of horsemen racing in from the moon-misted hills lying to the north.

There had been no time to warn Jim Stacy. The raiders were already closing in when Allan and the two Triple R men rode from the coulee below the house. Stumpy Hill's deadly marksmanship was quick to account for two of the raiders. Allan was not sure whose bullet knocked the third man from his saddle. He would never forget the shock of that amazing moment when the lamplight revealed Kay Bannock as she pulled Jim Stacy back into the room.

He was off his horse, scrambling over the corral fence, racing frantically towards the house. From somewhere in the distance drifted a man's voice. He was singing. Allan was aware of an odd thrill as he caught the words of the song. *La Paloma!* The same tune, but Poco Gato's version. *La Conchita, La Conchita*—the signal that all was well! Poco Gato and his friends were coming in the nick of time.

Gunfire crackled through the night, spurts of flame made brief red streaks across the Mesa as the surprised rustlers scattered in confused flight.

Flames from the burning straw-stack shot skyward, threw a red glare over the yard. A bullet screamed viciously past Allan's head, and then suddenly the door flung open, revealing Kay Bannock framed in the lamplight, a smoking rifle in lowered hands.

"Allan!" Her voice was a faint scream above the roaring flames, the crash of guns, "*Allan——*"

The rifle fell with a clatter from her hands, and, with another little cry, she ran down the veranda steps and into his arms.

"I—I nearly killed you."

R.R.—6

The anguish in her voice hurt him. "You're not to blame." He spoke huskily.

His own anguish seemed to steady her. She drew away, said simply, "Jim's hurt."

He followed her up the steps, vaguely aware of men running from the bunkhouse. They were shouting excitedly and frantically filling water-buckets at the long horse-trough. Only fast work could save the barn from the flames of the burning straw-stack.

Jim Stacy looked at Allan with pain-blurred eyes as the latter hurriedly entered the room with the girl. She smiled reassuringly.

"It's all right, Jim. Don't worry. Allan Rand got here in time."

The wounded rancher managed a faint grin. "Been hearing mighty good things about you, Rand, ever since Kay got here. Reckon she wasn't telling any fairy-tales, either, from the way you show up johnny-on-the-spot."

Allan gave the girl an amused look, met her confused, shy smile.

"Didn't get here quite soon enough." He shook his head. "Did the best we could, Stacy."

"Sure played the fool, running out of the door like I did," grumbled the S Bar man.

"It's a clean wound," pronounced Allan, after a brief examination. "Won't be able to use your arm for two or three weeks."

"Knocked me silly for a moment," grinned Stacy. He gave the girl a grateful smile. "If it wasn't for Kay draggin' me away from the door, Mrs Stacy would be a widow by now."

"Poor Nora . . . I must tell her." Kay vanished into the bedroom.

"She's sick in bed," Jim Stacy explained. "Broke her arm—and the kid down with the measles. Kay come over to help us out . . . got in about sundown."

Allan said briefly, "Let's get at that arm of yours." He was aware of an odd constriction about the heart. The thing had been close, too dreadfully close. If he had not made that wild, desperate ride from the Poison Sinks to save Jim Stacy's S Bar he would not have saved Kay Bannock. He was not a praying man, but at this moment he inwardly gave fervent thanks for not disregarding the impulse that had brought him to the S Bar in time. Things had a way of working out to wonderful ends.

Kay brought hot water and bandages, watched with admiring eyes while Allan dressed the wounded arm.

"You're as good as a doctor," she praised.

"We learn about these things in the cow country," reminded Allan. "Jim here could do as well, or your own dad."

Kay gave him an odd look. She was wondering what he would say when she told him Cole Bannock's amazing story. Allan would be surprised to learn that Rob Hood was her father.

Jim Stacy voiced his approval of the bandaging job.

"Plenty good enough until I can get to Doc Gary," he declared.

Somebody clattered hurriedly up the veranda steps. Kay took one startled glance at the newcomer and hastily turned her head.

"Barn's all right, boss." The S Bar man stared interestedly at the bandaged arm. "Lucky the wind was blowin' from the north or we couldn't have saved her."

"Good work, Slim." Jim Stacy rolled amused eyes at Allan. "Better get your pants on," he added mirthfully.

The S Bar puncher looked hurriedly down at his legs, encased only in a long red woollen garment stuffed into his boots. With a horrified glance at the girl's visibly shaking shoulders he made a frantic dash for the door.

"Slim'll never get over it," chuckled Jim Stacy. "Slim's awful shy with ladies. He'll sure burn up with shame."

"You mustn't tease him," warned Kay. "I'll never forgive you, Jim Stacy." The laughter in her voice belied her attempt to be severe.

Allan turned to the door. He longed to have a talk with Kay, but there were things to be done. He wanted to have a look at the wearer of the gaudy Mexican jacket. Jim Stacy's voice held him back.

"Mighty obliged for what you've done," the rancher said. "Don't know yet just what's been going on, but looks like the shindig's over." His frank, likable face hardened. "Rengo's gang, I reckon."

"That's the way we got it." Allan's eyes narrowed thoughtfully. "Not so sure that Rengo is the answer, Stacy. Haven't all the facts yet."

"It's Rengo right enough," muttered the owner of the S Bar.

"I've my reasons for saying it's Rengo. Was telling Wirt Gunnel when he was round here the other day. Wirt gave me the big laugh, said I was loco." Jim Stacy scowled.

Allan stared at him with odd intentness. "What were the reasons you gave Wirt Gunnel?" His too-casual tone made Kay look at him sharply.

"I may be awful wrong." Stacy hesitated. "Reckon you'll think I'm loco too, but Steve Starr's got some jaspers on his pay-roll who'll bear watching."

"Meaning Luce Henders for one?" Allan asked the question softly.

"Meaning Luce Henders," admitted Stacy.

"Thanks for the tip." Allan's tone was non-committal. "See you later, Stacy." He hesitated, looked at Kay. "Some time to-morrow," he added, for her benefit.

She gave him back a faint smile.

"*Adios*, Señor Johnny-on-the-spot."

The low note of tenderness in her voice sent a sharp thrill through Allan as he stepped out to the moonlit night.

He found Stumpy Hill waiting for him near the corral gate. The poker-faced little man gave him a contented grin.

"Plenty fast action while she lasted," he observed laconically. "Stacy all right, boss?"

Allan reassured him. Stumpy looked relieved. "Jim's one square-shootin' hombre," he asserted. His voice hardened. "Gives me the shivers to think of what might have happened to him and Nora—and the kid."

"Kay Bannock's with them," Allan told him, "got in about sun-down."

The Triple R man gave him an aghast look. "My Gawd," he muttered. "Seen a girl drag Jim away from the door . . . wasn't dreamin' she was Kay." Stumpy swore softly. "I'd sure like to meet up with this Rengo skunk."

"Where's Custer Boone?" interrupted Allan.

"Custer's watchin' over that feller him and you knocked from his horse," replied the cowboy. "Custer claims he's the Pecos Kid. Never saw the Kid myself and cain't back up Custer's say-so."

"I'll take a look." Allan's oddly hushed voice drew a wondering glance from Stumpy.

"The feller ain't dead," he drawled. "Won't last long, the way he's losin' blood."

They made their way across the yard, touched with the reek of smoke from the smouldering, water-drenched straw-stack. Vague shapes suddenly lifted out of the draw beyond the fence, approached swiftly across the Mesa.

"Poco Gato," guessed the Triple R puncher. "Reckon things is all right with the herd or he wouldn't be back so quick." Stumpy gave his tall companion a puzzled glance. "Was you knowin' Poco was due to show up with those Mex hombres like he did?"

"Poco said something about sending for help," admitted Allan. "Wasn't sure they'd get here in time."

"Mighty lucky they come when they did." Stumpy spoke soberly. "We wouldn't have lasted long against that bunch of wolves." The cowboy grinned. "Listen, boss—it's the password song they're singing."

Louder and louder lifted the voices of the nearing horsemen.

"Conchita, Conchita—'tis thee I adore . . ."

Jubilation throbbed in Poco Gato's great voice as he led the roaring chorus of the charging riders.

Stumpy Hill said softly, "I'm sure always goin' to like that song."

"Me too." Custer Boone, standing near the dying outlaw, spoke feelingly. "Believe me, feller, that song was sure good news."

Allan only half heard the words. He was staring with troubled eyes at the motionless form of the man lying at his feet.

The Pecos Kid's eyes fluttered open. Allan bent down to him.

"Listen, Seely—can you hear me?"

The Kid's lips moved in a faint whisper. "Sure," he said. Something like sardonic mirth flickered in the glazing eyes. "Looks like the end of the—the trail, Al——"

"You're going fast," Allan told him bluntly. "I want to know about that escape from gaol, Seely. Didn't Steve Starr frame that escape?"

"Sure he did," whispered the dying man.

"Quick," begged Allan, "who is Rengo?"

The question seemed to cause the Pecos Kid diabolic amusement, brought a dreadful grin to his pain-contorted features.

"You'd be surprised, Al . . ." He was suddenly silent.

Allan straightened up, stared with dismayed eyes at the dead out-law. Another moment and he would have had the name of the mysterious man known only as Rengo. Death had cheated him.

"You acted like you knew him, boss," remarked Custer Boone. "You called him Seely."

"He's from the Pecos country." Allan's tone was curt. "I'm from down there too." He offered no further explanation. There was no need for him to tell them the notorious Pecos Kid was his cousin.

"There'll be a lot of folks wantin' to shake hands with the feller that finished him off," commented Stumpy Hill. "The Pecos Kid was one bad hombre."

Allan wondered dully whose bullet had brought Billy Seely, alias the Pecos Kid, to the end of his blood-stained trail. He would never know. His—or Custer Boone's.

The red-headed cowboy was staring at him curiously.

"Funny, how much you look like him, boss," Custer said. "Now that the Kid took off his dinky moustache you could pass for brothers."

Stumpy Hill glared at him indignantly. "Where's your manners?"

"Reckon I was just talkin'," muttered the suddenly abashed Custer Boone.

Allan stared down at the dead outlaw. Luce Henders had made the same comment about the unfortunate resemblance. Perhaps—perhaps there was an idea there.

He gave the embarrassed cowboys a thin smile. "Thanks, Custer. There's a chance you've started something. Maybe we can fool somebody—if we work fast."

14

THE casual observer would not have noticed anything out of the ordinary as he rode into Roaring River's wide, dusty main street. The usual dogs, hunting shade from the baking midday sun, the usual number of horses drooping at their hitch-rails, dusty buck-boards, and high-wheeled wagons. Dad Meeker's four-horse stage in front of Rankin's General Merchandise Store, crotchety old Dad enjoying his customary heated and never-ending discussion on political affairs with Postmaster Rankin. The veteran stage-driver's voice possessed the penetrating, ear-splitting rasp of a buzz-saw in conflict with a particularly stubborn knot, and at these moments, when he irately expressed his views on the Postmaster-General's shortcomings, there would be a pause in the musical clink of hammer on anvil over at the blacksmith's shop. Pat Riley too loved his politics, and there were occasions when Dad Meeker's railings irked him mightily. At such times he would loudly voice his disapproval from the doorway of his blacksmith's shop.

There was nothing in this usual midday scene to account for the unwonted gleam of excitement in old Shawnee Jones' eyes as he sat in his big rocker on the porch of the Cattleman's Hotel opposite Rankin's. He was accustomed to old Dad's political fireworks, made a point of listening in from his big porch chair and on occasions shrilly expressing his own views.

It was plain that Shawnee's excitement was in no way connected with the political wrangle across the street. He was not even listening, which proved his complete absorption in other affairs. Only a very deaf man could be oblivious to the stage-driver's buzz-saw rhetoric.

Any possible doubts about Shawnee's ears were quickly banished when the sound of footsteps from somewhere in the hotel brought him spryly to his feet. Seizing his stout manzanita stick, he hobbled into the lobby.

A stoutish, elderly man with grizzled sideburns and wide-brimmed Stetson was descending the stairs. Behind him loomed the burly owner of the Triple R ranch. There was dark gloom on the latter's face, a hint of fear in his eyes.

Shawnee Jones watched them with narrowed gaze. The signs were not good. Doc Gary's ruddy face wore a grave look, and there was no mistaking that grisly fear in Cole Bannock's eyes.

The doctor shook his head in response to the old hotel man's questioning stare.

"No." He placed his long bag on the desk and fished a cigar from a pocket. "Rod's a sick boy, Shawnee. We can only do what we can and hope for the best."

"Ain't got the straight of it," Shawnee said, staring at Bannock. "How come Rod got beat up and poisoned?" Shawnee's tone was a mixture of resentment and curiosity. "Limpy Gregg good as told me to mind my own bus'ness when him and you brought Rod in before sun-up this mornin'."

"Doc Gary knows as much as I do." Cole Bannock spoke wearily. "Ask the doc about it, Shawnee. I've got business with Harker that won't wait." The screen-door banged behind him.

"Cole's about crazy," murmured Doc Gary.

"He said you'd tell me about Rod," reminded Shawnee.

"Cole was on the way over to his Mesa camp and ran into Limpy and Rod headed for town," the doctor explained. "Limpy had Rod tied to his saddle to keep him from falling off his horse. Seems that Limpy and some other men found Rod in a shack some place in the Poison Sinks. Couple of jaspers had him prisoner there. There was a fight and these jaspers got killed." Doc Gary frowned. "Been too busy with Rod to get all of Limpy's story. The boy's suffering from a brain concussion and he seems to have some of that damn' Poison Sinks water in him. His mind's all haywire . . . got something on his mind and can't get it out."

The story left Shawnee dissatisfied. He shook his head. "Wasn't Limpy saying nothin' about young Rand?"

"I told you I was too busy to hear all of Limpy's talk," grumbled the medico. He squinted over his cigar at the dining-room door. "I could do with some of Mrs Riley's food, Shawnee. Haven't had a bit of food to-day, and here it is past noon."

Shawnee grinned. "Mrs Riley figured you'd eat here at the hotel," he said. "She set to work and made you a fresh apple-pie,

Doc." He chuckled. "Shouldn't be surprised but what she's made ice-cream to go with the pie. Heard the freezer racketin' away like mad back on the kitchen porch."

"Bless the woman's heart!" Doc Gary beamed. He had a weakness for apple-pie *à la mode*.

The rattle of buckboard wheels drawing up in front of the hotel swung them round towards the front door. The doctor muttered an exclamation.

"Jim Stacy!" he said in a resigned voice. "Got his arm tied up, and that means some more work before I can get any food into me."

The two men hurried out to the big porch. The gleam in Shawnee Jones' eyes grew more pronounced. The girl in the driver's seat was Kay Bannock. Jim's wife was in the back seat with the baby. Nora's arm was still in a sling. The girl's red mare trailed behind on a lead-rope.

"Looks like an ambulance," chuckled Doc Gary.

The S Bar man's face lighted at the sight of the doctor.

"Wasn't sure you'd be in town," he said as he followed the women up the porch steps. "Got a bullet in my shoulder."

"You're keeping me busy," complained Doc Gary. "First it's Nora breaking her arm, then the baby down with the measles—and now you getting shot up." He pretended a ferocious scowl. "Too much for one family to inflict on a hard-working country doctor."

Mrs Riley hurriedly appeared, gathered her daughter and grand-child to her ample bosom with a delighted cry.

"I'm that glad!" And then, startled gaze on her son-in-law, "Why, Jim—what's happened?"

"Nothing to worry about, Ma. Guess the doc can fix me up in no time."

Mrs Riley took the baby, and they trooped up the stairs, Doc Gary following with his bag. Kay met Shawnee's inquisitive look. She gave him a faint smile, sank down on a chair.

"We've had an awful time, Shawnee," she confided. "Jim's place was raided last night. There were men killed."

"Didn't know you was over to Stacy's," Shawnee said in a vexed tone.

"I guess Uncle Ed forgot to tell you," smiled the girl. "I went over rather suddenly. Uncle Ed came out to the ranch and told me about Nora."

"Your dad's in town," Shawnee told her. "He's over with Ed Harker this minute." He shook his head. "You won't be knowin' that Rod's upstairs, awful sick."

Kay looked at him doubtfully. "You mean Rod's drunk?" There was no sympathy in her voice.

"Not this time," grunted the hotel man. "He's been beat up and poisoned. Your dad and Limpy Gregg come in with him before daylight this morning."

Kay gazed at him with startled eyes. She was remembering that Limpy Gregg had gone to the Mesa camp with Allan Rand. Disturbing thoughts assailed her. Rod had gone to the Mesa camp looking for Allan. Something dreadful had happened. It was all very confusing. She only knew that Allan could not have been at the Mesa camp. He was at the S Bar, and Stumpy Hill and Custer Boone were with him.

"How do you mean, he's poisoned?" she asked Shawnee. "I don't understand."

Shawnee gave her the facts as he knew them. "Ain't knowin' myself why these jaspers was holding Rod prisoner in the Poison Sinks," he finished.

"Poor Rod!" exclaimed the girl. In spite of Cole Bannock's dreadful plans concerning Rod and herself, she was suddenly all sympathy for the youth she had so long imagined was her brother. "I'll go up to him," she said.

Shawnee shook his head. "Doc Gary won't want you to see him," he declared. "Rod's out of his head, ravin' something fierce. Limpy's with him," he added. "Limpy says he's staying with him close until he's either dead or comes to his senses. Rod can tell things the sheriff should know, Limpy claims."

Kay was silent for a long moment. She looked tired, worried. She dreaded meeting Cole Bannock. She grew panicky. No need for her to stay in town. There was nothing she could do for Rod.

"I don't know, Shawnee——" Her tone was irresolute. "I think I'll go on home. No use my staying if I can't do anything to help."

"You look awful wore out," Shawnee said. He studied her with shrewd eyes. "You're worried a lot about something, but it ain't Rod."

"Yes," she told him simply. "I'm dreadfully worried, Shawnee. Of course, I'm upset about Rod, but I won't lie about it. I'm in a lot of trouble." Her lips quivered.

Shawnee said slowly, "I've knowed you a long time, Kay. You can count on me—if there's trouble huntin' you."

She lifted her head, looked at him searchingly. Her face was very pale, he saw with growing concern.

"Shawnee—you knew my father?" The words came from her painfully. "You—you were here before I was born."

He made no pretence of misunderstanding her.

"Yes," he answered slowly, "I knew your dad, Kay." His tone was suddenly harsh. "Who's been talkin' to you?"

"Cole Bannock." Kay shivered. "I don't know what to do, Shawnee. I'm frightened."

The old ex-cowman stared at her incredulously.

"I'm knocked all of a heap," he muttered. "Don't seem possible Cole would go and tell you about Rob Hood." He shook his head. "Don't make sense. Cole never wanted folks to know you weren't really his own daughter."

"It's got to do with—with Rod. . . ." The girl faltered, forced herself to continue. "He—he wants me to marry Rod. That's why he told me, Shawnee."

"I—I'll be——" Shawnee checked himself with an effort. Kay smiled faintly.

"I could swear too," she said. "I'm sick about it. . . . I would rather die—than marry Rod Bannock." She got up from the chair. "You can understand why I don't want to stay in town if Dad—Cole Bannock—is here."

"Cole's awful set in his ways," muttered Shawnee. He was deeply distressed. "It's sure an awful mess," he mourned. "Don't blame you for feelin' all broke up." He hobbled with her to the door. "Don't you act rash, Kay. No tellin' what'll happen. One thing certain, Cole won't be pullin' off any weddin' while Rod's laid up crazy in the head."

Kay drew a sharp breath. "I'm sorry for Rod," she said earnestly. "I don't wish him any harm." She paused, asked timidly, almost shyly, "Shawnee, have you seen anything of—of Allan Rand to-day?"

"Ain't been in town so far as I know," answered the old man. "Guess I'd have seen him if he was this way." He gave her a shrewd look. "Was you wantin' to see him?"

"He—he's wonderful, Shawnee. You ask Jim Stacy about last night."

She was a bit puzzled by the quick relief in the hotel man's eyes.

"Reckon that explains how come Cole run into Limpy bringing Rod into town by his lonesome." He nodded, gave her a wise look. "Rand got word that Jim was to be raided, huh?"

"I really don't know much about it," Kay confessed. "Allan—Mr Rand—was in the house only a few minutes. I didn't see him again." Kay gave the old man a troubled look. She was recalling Allan's parting words. He would see her again soon, "perhaps to-morrow." "Custer Boone and Stumpy Hill were with him," she told Shawnee. "I suppose they went back to the Mesa camp."

"Guess that's the answer," agreed Shawnee. "Looks like Steve Starr ridin' up the street," he added. "Luce Henders with him." Shawnee scowled. "Don't let on to him that Rod's here. Cole don't want folks to know."

"Oh!" The girl took one startled look at the approaching riders. "I'm getting away from here. I can't bear that man." She ran down the porch steps, snatched the red mare's tie-rope loose.

"Won't tell Cole you was here," Shawnee called down to her guardedly.

She nodded, scrambled into the saddle, and rode across the street into the alley that paralleled Rankin's store. From there she could take the short-cut behind Agee Hand's livery stable.

The owner of the Double Star gave no sign that he noticed the girl. He swung from his horse and vanished into the Royal Flush saloon. His foreman continued up the street, drew rein in front of the hotel, and gave the glowering Shawnee his wintry smile.

"Choctaw and Rogan stoppin' here?" he queried.

"I run a hotel for *decent* folks," tartly rejoined the old man.

Luce Henders let the insult pass. "Some puzzled where those two fellers have holed up," he grumbled. "Was thinkin' they'd maybe gone on a bender and was sleeping it off in your place."

"Not in the Cattleman's Hotel," spluttered the indignant Shawnee. "I don't rent rooms to crawlin' sidewinders."

"If you wasn't so old and crippled I'd take you apart," growled the Double Star man. "You can go to hell, mister." He rode on up the street and dismounted in front of the sheriff's office.

"Figures Ed's maybe got his damn' cow-pokes locked up in gaol," grumpily reflected Shawnee.

The old man would have been startled could he have seen Luce Henders' suddenly shocked face as he opened the sheriff's office door and stepped inside.

15

Business was dull in the Royal Flush. The craggy-faced barman yawned, ruminatively fondling his heavy handle-bar moustache.

"Ain't seen young Bannock last day or two," he remarked to the lone patron sitting in gloomy meditation at one of the small tables. "Bert Nye ain't been round either," he added. "Was you wanting to see 'em, Mr Starr?"

"No." The cattleman's tone was surly.

"Bert Nye most always drops in 'bout this time," the barman said hopefully.

"You won't be seeing Nye to-day, nor any time." Starr's lips curled.

"No savvy," grunted the puzzled barman. His eyes bulged a bit.

"Been watching Nye for weeks," Starr went on. "You know how things have had us cattlemen about crazy, Klondike?"

The barman nodded. "You mean this Rengo feller?"

"He's too smart for old Harker," grumbled Starr. "He's one hell of a sheriff, so I got myself elected sheriff in my own county. Got sick of leaving things to Ed Harker."

Klondike stroked his huge moustache. "You ain't in your own county now," he observed uneasily. "Don't quite savvy how you can butt into Sheriff Harker's bailiwick."

"Harker's too slow to catch a man with Rengo's brains," sneered the sheriff from across the river. "I worked the thing out, Klondike, come over here time and time again, got friendly with Bert Nye—found out plenty."

"Hell!" The barman's tone was admiring. "Wasn't dreamin' your game, Mr Starr." His beefy face darkened. "Sure would have jumped Nye myself if I'd known he was Rengo."

"I didn't say Nye is Rengo," grimaced Starr.

Klondike looked disappointed. "You've got me guessin'," he admitted ruefully.

"I learned enough to know that Nye could spill the beans on Rengo," Starr continued. "Had it all fixed to nab him on my side of the county line." He scowled. "Was waiting for him near the ford when Harker's deputy, Billy Hall, grabbed him. Hall didn't know I was watching."

Klondike let out a low oath. "Kind of complicated things, huh?"

Starr grinned. "You'd have laughed to see Billy Hall's face when I stepped out and took his prisoner away from him. Nothing he could do to stop me. Billy was out of his bailiwick."

"I'll say he was," grunted the hugely interested bar-tender. He selected a bottle from the array on the shelf and pushed it through the wicket-gate. "Have one on the house, Mister Sheriff." He placed the bottle on the table. Starr poured liberally.

"Best stuff in the house," recommended Klondike with a grin. "Bert Nye's private bottle. Bert won't be callin' for it ag'in."

A curious pallor spread over Starr's flushed face, gave his skin a sickly, blotchy look. With a quick sweep of his hand he sent the brimming glass spinning from the table. It landed with a splintering crash against the bar front.

"Damn you!" His snarling-lipped fury made the startled barman take a backward step. "I'm not drinking a dead man's whisky!"

The frightened Klondike stared at him, a hand mechanically brushing the spilled liquor from shirt-front.

"Wasn't meanin' nothing," he stuttered.

Starr's rage was gone as quickly as it came. He relaxed in his chair, regarded the stammering Klondike with a furtive smile of mingled apology and fear.

"Guess I'm jumpy," he said. "Kind of gave me the creeps—you telling me it was Nye's private bottle."

Klondike's ruddy face paled. "Wasn't knowin' Nye's dead," he muttered. "Was thinkin' you'd only gaoled him."

Starr's smile was wicked. "Nye made a break," he told the shocked bar-tender. "His own fault he got killed."

"He'd have swung anyhow," commented Klondike philosophically. He pushed back behind his bar. "I'll get you another bottle, Mr Starr."

"You needn't." Starr shook his head. "Kind of off the notion."

Luce Henders slammed in through the swing doors and with a curt nod at the barman took a chair opposite his boss. The foreman seemed ill at ease, his sardonic face had a greyish, drawn look.

"Gimme a double shot of rye, Klondike." He spoke hoarsely, and then, aware of Starr's sharply questioning gaze, he gave the latter a mirthless grin. "Cain't locate Rogan and Choctaw nowheres, Steve."

Starr continued to stare at him suspiciously. "You've got a funny look in your eyes, Luce," he observed. "If I didn't know you wasn't a drinkin' man, I'd say you were drunk or that you'd seen a ghost."

"Not a ghost," muttered the foreman. He forced a smile in which there was no mirth. "I just now seen the Pecos Kid, over there in Ed Harker's gaol."

"You're a liar." Starr's voice lacked conviction. "The Kid's too smart to be back this way. He's in Mexico."

Luce Henders filled a glass from the bottle Klondike placed on the table.

"Reckon I know the Kid when I see him." He put the glass to his lips, stared intently at the man opposite as he gulped the liquor. Starr's eyes took on a glassy look. He muttered an oath, pushed up from his chair. His foreman put the empty glass down.

"Where you goin'?"

"Over to the gaol," answered Starr in a curiously strangled voice that was scarcely more than a hoarse whisper. He was breathing heavily.

"Harker won't let you see the Kid," sneered Henders. "Not after what happened last time you went there to see him."

"The Kid belongs in the Puma County gaol," asserted Starr with another curse. "The Kid's my meat, Luce. He can tell me about Rengo. I can make him talk, and that's more than old Harker can do." He stamped away, pushed violently through the swing doors.

For a long moment the tall Double Star foreman sat there, staring morosely into space; then, with a sudden angry gesture, he sprang from his chair and hurried into the street.

The paunchy bar-tender rubbed his head thoughtfully. He was deeply puzzled. He had never seen the cool, laconic Luce Henders act so queerly. The perplexed Klondike's mystified gaze fastened on the fragments of glass that littered the floor. He reached for broom and dustpan.

Cole Bannock was mounting the hotel porch steps as Starr hurried past on his way to the sheriff's office. The big cattleman seemed about to halt as he saw Starr; then with an obvious effort he continued up the steps. Shawnee Jones was standing in the doorway of the lobby.

"The doc says for you to hurry." Shawnee's voice was shrill with excitement. "Rod's got his senses back . . . he's got things to tell you, Cole."

Bannock went pounding up the stairs. There was a bleak and terrible look in his deep-set eyes.

Sheriff Ed Harker gave the owner of the Double Star a mildly inquiring stare as the latter banged into the office.

"You look some heated, Steve. What's on your mind?"

"Plenty." Starr's tone was vicious. "Luce says you've got the Kid in your gaol."

The veteran sheriff's grizzled moustache twitched. "He won't get a chance to escape this time, Steve," he said with good-natured sarcasm.

Starr ignored the gentle reminder of his recent mishap. "Where'd you catch the Kid?" he asked sourly.

"Allan Rand nabbed him over at Stacy's S Bar," readily informed Harker. "The Kid tried to pull off a raid."

The news plainly affected Starr. He lost colour, gave the sheriff a furtive, speculative glance.

"I want him, Ed," he said blusteringly. "The Kid belongs in the Puma County gaol. I want him bad."

"He's my prisoner," reminded Sheriff Harker dryly. "Guess I'll hold him for trial, Steve." The old sheriff stared reflectively at the 'wanted' poster on the wall opposite. "I've a notion the Kid will talk some if he thinks he can save his neck," he drawled, "tell me plenty about Rengo." His glance flickered briefly at the other man.

"We've the same notions about him." Starr's grin had something of a snarl in it. "I'm gunnin' for Rengo myself. That's why I want the Kid."

"You went and took Bert Nye away from Billy Hall," the sheriff of Roaring River curtly rejoined. "Nye would have told me what I wanted to know about Rengo, but you snatched him from us." Harker's brows drew down in a frown at the rival sheriff. "Why don't you ask Nye some questions, Starr?"

"Didn't have the chance." Starr shrugged lean-muscled shoulders. "Nye made a bolt for it . . . we had to shoot him."

Sheriff Harker gave him a long, searching look.

"Too bad you done that," he finally said disappointedly. "Nye could have told plenty." The sheriff paused, bent a slightly puzzled look on the other man. "Always thought you and him was good friends. Nye was tellin' me you'd sold him that Red Canyon land he was ranching." '

"I was stringing him along." Starr grinned. "You weren't the only one doing some wondering about that hombre." His tone was suddenly impatient. "Well—what about the Kid?"

Sheriff Harker shook his head. "You don't get him," he said laconically.

"Save your county a wad of money," urged Starr. "Cole Bannock'll say you're loco. Trials cost money, and he's the biggest taxpayer in Roaring River County. Cole don't care how a rustler gets hung, so long as he's hung."

Harker was not impressed by the argument. "No use your talkin'," he said in a bored voice.

Something like panic momentarily flickered in Starr's eyes. He got to his feet with a muttered imprecation, stood staring into the sunlit street for a long minute. The sheriff's face took on an extraordinarily grim look as he watched him. Starr turned his head and stared sullenly at the old law officer.

"No harm letting me have a talk with the Kid, huh, Harker?"

The sheriff shook his head dubiously. "I'm remembering what happened the other time you come to the gaol for a talk with the Kid," he said dryly.

Starr had the grace to show embarrassment. "How was I to know he'd grab my gun?" he muttered, and then, briskly, "Won't give him the chance, this time." He jerked his gun from holster and dropped it on a chair near the door. "How's that suit you, Harker?"

The sheriff made a gesture of grudging assent, rose from his creaky swivel chair. "I'll mosey over to the gaol with you," he said. "Billy will want to know I said for him to let you see the Kid."

The two men crossed the dusty street and proceeded up the board sidewalk towards the low, adobe building standing alone in the square beyond Agee Hand's livery barn. Steve Starr failed to notice his foreman lounging near his horse at the hitch-rail below the sheriff's office. Henders' hard features wore an oddly grim look. He reached out a hand to the tie-rope, drew it back irresolutely, and fumbled for cigarette-papers and tobacco instead. He stood there, making a cigarette with fingers that shook perceptibly. Three horsemen appeared at the far end of the street, came on slowly, dust drifting lazily in their wake. A man suddenly appeared on the hotel porch—Jim Stacy, bandaged arm in a sling. Old Shawnee Jones limped spryly at the S Bar man's heels. The pair stood for a moment in earnest conversation, and suddenly Jim Stacy was clattering down the steps and coming up the street on the run.

The sheriff and Starr saw none of these things. They were in the tiny gaol office. Billy Hall looked briefly at his superior officer. The deputy's face entirely lacked his usual cherubic smile.

"I want to see him alone," Steve Starr said, with a sour smile at the two unfriendly faces.

"It's all right, Billy," murmured Harker. He gave the visibly uneasy Double Star man a tired smile. "Steve left his gun back in my office. No chance for the Kid to grab a gun like he done the other time."

The deputy glanced at the visitor's gunless belt, took another look at the sheriff's poker face, and slowly unlocked the door leading into the corridor.

"Third cell on the left," he said brusquely. "Make it short, Steve."

"You bet," grimaced the Double Star owner. The door swung shut behind him.

It was dark in the corridor. Starr paused, blinked his eyes, waited to accustom himself to the gloom, also to make certain he was not followed. His head turned in a long look at the door behind him.

A few quick steps brought him to the third cell on the left. A man lay on a pile of straw in the corner, chin low on his chest, apparently dozing. Starr stared at him. The prisoner's face was only a vague blur in the uncertain light. He wore a flat-brimmed black hat with a dangling chin-strap, and a short Mexican jacket. Starr's eyes took on a venomous gleam as he gazed. He pressed close to the bars.

"Seely," he whispered, "Seely——"

The prisoner stirred, raised his head slightly in a sideways look.

"How'd you get in here, Steve?" The prisoner spoke in a husky, guarded voice, scarcely above a whisper. "Hell, Steve—get me out of here."

"You sure messed things up at the S Bar," grumbled Starr.

"Wirt told me you had things all set for us," muttered the man in the cell. "Rand was waitin' for us. We didn't have a chance."

Starr showed surprise. "Sent Wirt to get hold of Nye," he said in his hoarse whisper. "Harker's had a feller trailin' Nye. We got scared Nye'd squeal if Harker got hold of him."

"Nye's yellow," agreed the prisoner. "If Harker gets him it'll sure be tough for me, mister." There was a threat in his sullen whisper.

"Nye won't squeal," assured Starr, with his ugly grimace. "I've seen to that."

"You've killed him?"

"Sure. Took him away from Billy Hall . . . made out he tried to escape and got shot."

"You're a devil, Steve." The prisoner's voice changed to a snarl. "Get me out of here damn' quick—if you don't want Harker to know you're Rengo."

Starr stared at him silently for a long moment.

"So that's your game," he said very softly.

"I'm going to save my neck if I can," mumbled the man behind the bars.

Starr's right hand crept up to his shirt-front, slipped inside.

"You won't have the chance to tell him anything, Seely," he said in the same deadly, purring whisper. "I'll tell 'em you came at me with this hidden gun . . . that I got it away . . . killed you." Starr's hand came away from his shirt, fingers curled around the butt of a stubby Derringer.

There was a sudden movement of the man lying on the straw, a stream of flame, a deafening explosion. Starr reeled back from the bars with a scream of pain, stood staring stupidly at his shattered hand still clinging weakly to the little Derringer. Blood sprouted from the torn knuckles like little red flowers. He made an effort to lift the weapon. It dropped from his nerveless grasp. The corridor door banged open. Starr heard the sound of booted feet. He made no attempt to look. He was staring with horrified eyes at the man in the cell. The latter was on his feet, smoking gun in lowered hand.

"*Rand!*" Starr's voice was a despairing groan.

Allan reached out a hand, pushed the cell door open. "No, Starr," he said grimly; "the Pecos Kid won't do any talking. The Pecos Kid's dead, but we don't need him to tell us about Rengo. You've told us yourself what we want to know about Rengo."

The dazed owner of the Double Star ranch suddenly felt the grasp of hard hands, heard Sheriff Harker's dry voice.

"You had us fooled a long time, Steve."

Starr gave him a wild look. There were others there in the gloomy corridor. Billy Hall, Custer Boone, and Stumpy Hill, and, framed in the doorway, the giant form of Poco Gato, and on all their faces he read no doubts, only grim certainty.

"It's a lie," he said dully.

"You've been mighty smart," Harker went on; "you covered your tracks awful well, got yourself elected sheriff over in Puma, made out to be a law-abiding citizen." The old sheriff's voice had a rasp in it. "Was awful tough to prove it on you, but Rand done it. He's smart, Starr—smarter than you."

Voices clamoured loudly in the outer office. Jim Stacy pushed past Poco Gato. He was breathing hard from his run up the street.

"Rod Bannock's got his senses back," Jim said excitedly. "He was over at Starr's place the other night, he says—went there drunk. Starr didn't know Rod was sleeping it off in the bedroom. Rod heard him talking with the Kid and Wirt Gunnel——" Jim broke off, stared at the haggard-faced rancher, widened his eyes at the dangling, bleeding hand. "Guess you ain't needing Rod's story," he finished grimly.

"No, Jim," Allan spoke quietly, "we don't need Rod's story—but it explains a lot."

Starr's face twisted in a dreadful grimace.

"I should have killed you, Rand." His voice lifted to a maniacal scream. "Should have killed you—that night in Conchita's." He went suddenly limp in Billy Hall's iron grasp, hung like a bag of meal in the deputy's arms.

Sheriff Harker's voice broke the hush.

"Rengo won't be troubling us none any more," he said solemnly. Something like pity crept into his stern gaze at the dead man. "Maybe it's the best way.   Guess Steve Starr must have been crazy, and we didn't know it."

16

In Shawnee Jones' opinion the signs portended an event always of vast interest to dwellers in the cow country. He uttered the prophecy with the laconic assurance of the old-timer who knows his weather.

"Rain comin'," he said to Agee Hand as the latter mounted the hotel porch steps.

"Wind's right," agreed the livery-man. He expertly directed a dark brown stream over the porch railing.

"South-west," Shawnee said, "clouds toppin' Vicente. Never seen it fail when old Vicente smokes up and the wind south-west."

"Sure need a spell of rain," observed Agee.

"She'll come," confidently asserted the hotel man.

It was an interesting topic, but there was more than the promise of rain on their minds. Shawnee leaned forward in his big porch rocker and gazed intently up the street.

"Ed Harker's just gone over to the gaol with Cole," he told his friend. "Reckon Cole's mighty upset about Wirt Gunnel being mixed up with this Rengo bus'ness."

"His own foreman." Agee Hand shook his head soberly. "Must have hit Cole awful hard, his own foreman a cow-thief. Cole trusted Wirt."

"Wirt'll dance on air," prophesied Shawnee with some relish. "Gus Silver too."

"Lucky thing Luce Henders jumped 'em when they rode into town," commented the livery man. His eyes gleamed. "Never seen faster shootin'."

"Wirt got wise soon as he seen Rand comin' out of the gaol," Shawnee said. "I seen the whole play too, right here from the porch. Wirt went for his gun, started shootin'. Rand's bullet knocked him out of his saddle. Brazos started smokin' his gun, and Henders sure cut loose with that Colt of his. Got Brazos smack between the eyes."

"Guess Gus Silver figured he'd rather go to gaol," commented

Agee. "He'll swing, though, and Wirt too, if he lives long enough to stand trial."

"Doc Gary says Rand's bullet didn't more'n nick the polecat's spine—paralysed him temporary," reassured Shawnee. "Wirt'll live to dangle at the end of a rope." The old hotel man nodded grimly. "Sure would like to pull on it."

"Luce Henders is awful sore," mused Agee Hand. "Luce hates a cow-thief—and him all the time working for Rengo."

"Don't blame him for being red-eyed," chuckled Shawnee. "Steve Starr played a dirty trick on him."

"Played hell with *all* of us," grunted his friend.

Allan appeared in the lobby entrance. Shawnee gave him an inquiring look.

"Leaving us, son?" He waved aside the gold piece in Allan's hand. "Your money ain't good here at the Cattleman's, son. Not after what you've done for us Roaring River folks."

Allan saw that Shawnee meant his words. He dropped the coin back in his pocket.

"Thanks, Shawnee."

The old man appeared to be pondering some weighty matter. He tugged worriedly at his drooping moustache.

"Headin' for the Triple R?" he asked abruptly.

"Well—guess so. . . ." Allan hesitated. "Not so sure but what I'll quit my job. Thought I'd have a talk with Mr Bannock."

"Cole told me he was staying in town for a few days—until Rod's strong enough to be moved out to the ranch," Shawnee informed him. "Rod says he's done for keeps with actin' the fool. Cole's awful tickled."

"Glad to hear it," murmured Allan. He was thinking of Kay Bannock. He longed desperately to see her. He knew now she was the only reason keeping him in the Roaring River country. Any faint hopes of finding some trace of Tom Sherwood had dwindled completely. There was a chance that Shawnee Jones or Agee Hand might have heard of Tom Sherwood. They were old-timers, according to Sheriff Harker.

"Sure I remember Tom Sherwood," Shawnee reluctantly admitted in response to Allan's question. He was suddenly silent, stared at him uneasily.

"Don't recall him by that name," put in Agee Hand cautiously. "It's a long time back, Rand."

The two old men exchanged troubled looks, and Shawnee asked slowly, "You ain't wantin' to know for some bad reason, son?"

"Tom Sherwood was my father's best friend," Allan replied simply.

Shawnee and the livery-man exchanged relieved looks.

"Tom was a square-shooter," the latter asserted; and then, at Shawnee's nod, "you could ask Cole Bannock about a feller who used to call hisself Robin Hood."

Allan gave them a thunderstruck look. Robin Hood of Sherwood Forest! The picture of the little graveyard out at the Triple R ranch leaped to his eyes. Rob Hood's grave!

Realization of the truth made his head swim. He'd been dumb, plain stupid, not to have guessed the amazing truth. *Rob Hood was Tom Sherwood.*

The two old men, watching him intently, saw the understanding light in his eyes. They grinned uncertainly.

"Cole can't claim we told you," muttered Shawnee. "Guess you'd a clue so close you couldn't see it."

Allan nodded soberly. "There was talk of a girl-baby," he said questioningly.

Shawnee Jones gave him a long, searching look. It was obvious the old man's excitement was at fever pitch.

"You've seen her, son—only she ain't a baby now."

"Kay?" Allan's tone showed no surprise.

"Guessed it, huh?"

"She doesn't look like a Bannock," Allan said.

"Rod's mother was an Indian woman," Agee Hand informed him dryly.

Allan nodded, recalled his earlier suspicions of young Bannock's Indian blood. The revelation that Kay was not his sister in no way surprised him. He was more dazed than astonished to learn the girl was Tom Sherwood's daughter.

Cole Bannock was coming out of the gaol office. Allan watched him for a moment; then, with a curt nod at the two old men, he started down the steps.

Perhaps something in the manner of his approach warned Cole

Bannock. The cattleman came to an abrupt standstill, stared at him searchingly.

"Harker's been telling me your business in Roaring River," he said heavily.

Allan looked at him, waited for him to continue.

"I can see it in your face that you know," Bannock went on. "Shawnee's been talking."

"Not much." Allan shook his head. "I knew the answer the moment Agee Hand told me to ask you about Rob Hood."

The big cattleman winced.

"I should have guessed the truth when I saw Rob Hood's grave," Allan said.

"I was going to kill you, Rand." Bannock spoke hoarsely. "Wasn't going to stand for you blockin' my plans." He paused, added more quietly, "Kay is Tom Sherwood's daughter."

"I know she is, Bannock."

"The Triple R was Tom's," the cattleman went on with an effort. His bearded face looked suddenly old. "The ranch belongs to Kay, every acre of it, Rand."

Allan stared at him in grim silence.

"I was Tom's foreman when he was killed. I took hold, worked my head off to make something of the place. Seems like it always was mine, and like Kay was mine. Wasn't meanin' any harm."

"I'm sure of that." Allan's tone was sympathetic.

"Was in my mind for Rod to have the ranch after I was gone, but lately I got to thinking, worrying, about Kay. Didn't seem right for her not to have what was Tom's." Bannock paused, gulped painfully. "I told her she wasn't really my daughter, told her I wanted her and Rod to marry. Seemed a good way to fix things for her."

Allan paled, looked steadily at the big man. "She was willing, Bannock?"

The quick panic in his voice brought a wry grin from the rancher. He shook his head.

"Kay wasn't willing, Rand. Maybe you can guess why she wasn't wantin' to marry Rod."

"I hope I do," Allan answered simply. His eyes glowed, and then, in a harder tone, "Why aren't you killing me, Bannock?"

"You saved my boy," the cattleman replied in a quiet voice. "He's all I have. I owe you his life."

"Rod's had his lesson." Allan spoke with conviction. "He'll make a good cowman now that he's got wise to himself."

Rod's father nodded, said thoughtfully, "We'll head up to Montana, make a fresh start." His tone took on a dogged note. "I ain't so old."

Allan shook his head. "Don't be in a hurry to quit the Triple R, Bannock. You've put your sweat and blood into that ranch. Kay will want you to stay with the Triple R as long as you've a mind to, and Tom Sherwood would say she's right."

Bannock stared at him. It was plain he was too moved for words. Allan held out his hand.

"I'm on my way," he said simply. "Any objections, Bannock?"

For a long moment the two men gazed at each other, and slowly a wide smile crept over the cowman's face. He drew himself up like a man from whose shoulders had fallen a wearisome load. His eyes sparkled, danced with a sudden rush of mirthful understanding.

"No," he roared, "no objections, young feller." His booming laugh reached the straining ears of the two old men watching from the hotel porch, made them exchange delighted grins. "Tell Kay I sent you, son," Cole Bannock said in his big, hearty voice.

The buckskin horse moved along at his easy running-walk, slowed to a halt in the dusty road, opposite the *cantina* of Conchita Mendota, set back under the shading chinaberry-trees. Poco Gato stood there in the low, wide entrance. His voice lifted in a loud shout that brought Conchita running out to his side. Allan waved to them.

"What's the good word, Poco?"

"Beeg news, señor." The Mexican's face split in a wide smile. "Soon we have the grand wedding, Conchita and I——" His arm went round the comely innkeeper's lissome waist. "You come— no, señor?"

"You must come, señor," added the pretty Mexican in her soft Spanish, "you are our good friend."

"I will come," promised the man on the buckskin horse. He went on his way.

Kay saw him as he rode out of the willow brakes and started up the long slope. Her heart turned over, began to pound.

She sat there on the red mare, watched with starry eyes. She was so sure he would come to her, so sure nothing could keep him from her.

Words were not needed between them, and as the buckskin horse drew alongside Allan leaned over and gathered the girl up from her saddle, drew her into his arms.

The sunset was purpling the hills across the valley behind them as they rode up the rugged slope, but before them reached an indescribably beautiful dawn that left them both breathless and filled their eyes with the glory of its promise.

Moon Quan took one brief look at them as they rode into the ranch yard. The old cook turned quickly into his kitchen, smiled blandly at the housekeeper.

"Me cookum foh chicken foh dinnah," he said to Rosaria, with a finality that forbade any argument.

Arthur Henry Gooden recalled that "I was still a babe in arms when my parents took me from Manchester, England, to South Africa for a four-year stay in Port Elizabeth, then back to England for a brief time, and finally the journey that made me a Californian. Reaching the San Joaquin Valley in those days meant work from sunup to sundown. Always plenty for a boy to do. But there were compensations—my rifle, my shotgun, my horse. By the time I was ten I was master of all three and the hunting was good." Gooden began his career as a Western writer working in Hollywood beginning in 1919. *The Fox* (Universal, 1921) was the first feature film based on one of his screenplays and starred Harry Carey. For what remained of the decade, Gooden worked in the writing department at Universal, turning out scenarios for two-reelers and feature films as well as serials like *The Lawless Men* (Universal, 1927) based on Frank Spearman's popular character, railroad detective Whispering Smith. In the early 1930s Gooden left Hollywood to live in a stone cabin in the foothills of the San Jacinto, overlooking the sand dunes of the Colorado Desert. The life he led there was primitive: no electricity, no gasoline, no telephones, but he had his typewriter and began writing Western novels, beginning with *Cross Knife Ranch*, first published by Harrap in London in 1933. In fact, although he would eventually have various American publishers, the British editions of his novels continued to be published by Harrap until 1951. *Smoke Tree Range* (Kinsey, 1936), one of his finest stories, was brought to the screen by cowboy star Buck Jones in 1937, Gooden's only screen credit during that decade. Gooden had a distinguished prose style and was always able to evoke the Western terrain and animal life vividly as well as authentically address the psychology of many of his complex characters with the sophistication of a master storyteller.